They'd counted six brief time they'd had to observe from the road. Flanagan, Tackett, Wade, and Brannigan were currently much closer to that road than Burgess and his element, for a couple of reasons. Not the least being that they couldn't be sure there weren't more soldiers in the tent, and so they would need to rush in and make sure the entire checkpoint was clear, once the six who were lounging around the swing arm, smoking and talking, were eliminated.

Fortunately, neither of the machineguns, more of the old M1919s from the looks of them, were quite what Flanagan would call "manned." Their crews were standing near the emplacements, but neither were behind them, and one of the old Brownings had its muzzle pointed at the sky, the T&E not attached to the tripod. The checkpoint unit was in no way, shape, or form ready for what was about to happen.

He settled his front sight on the rightmost soldier and whispered, "On target."

Brannigan was behind him, his radio to his lips. That took a gun out of the fight, but somebody had to coordinate this shot.

"Execute, execute, execute."

Flanagan's trigger broke about halfway through the second "execute." The Galil bucked in his shoulder and barked, the unsuppressed muzzle flash bright in the night, but he was in the prone and in a good shooting position, and his target was barely thirty yards away.

BRANNIGAN'S BLACKHEARTS

LEGACY OF TERROR

TERROR

PETER NEALEN

CHAPTER 1

Forty Years Ago

Carlos Hierro looked up at the brassy sky, squinting against the scorching sun. They had run out of water hours before, and he was sure the soldiers down below knew it. That was why there had been only sporadic exchanges of gunfire over the last hour or so.

They know they only have to wait us out.

He shook his head as he looked around at his comrades. Adalberto was no longer moving. He had bled out from his wounds sometime in the last few minutes. They simply no longer had the medical supplies to save him.

The others, all ten of them, were ragged, sunburned, their lips cracked from lack of water, most of them down to their last couple of magazines. Nilo and Omar weren't going to be able to go far even if they ever had a chance of breaking out, Nilo with a broken leg from a soldier's bullet as they'd reached this little refuge in the rocks, and Omar nursing a gut wound that would be his death.

Carlos knew they were all dead men. He glanced up at the sky again. Here, in the last moments, he found he was grateful that

Palmira was safe, in hiding with their son. These brutes wouldn't get their hands on either of them.

He knew what would happen if they were found. Palmira had protested bitterly when he'd made the decision, insisted that her place was at his side, but he had held firm, and now, as death closed in, he was ever more glad that he had.

Keeping his head down, he moved to the gap in the rocks overlooking the government positions below, and the sea beyond. The heat beat on him, reflected off the rocks, and he struggled to swallow against the dryness in his throat.

The soldiers weren't being all that careful. He could see them down there, moving from rock to rock, barely bothering to take cover. They didn't need to, not really. He and his comrades didn't have enough ammunition left to risk wasting it on chancy shots, and the soldiers had to realize it.

He lifted his Kalashnikov, nevertheless. It was beginning to sink in that there was no getting out of this outcropping of rocks alive. The city of Santa Paz, green and lush in the middle of the coastal desert, seemed to taunt him, the knowledge that these animals still held firm control eating at him.

Someone below must have seen the sun glint off the gunmetal. Muzzle flashes flickered in the rocks below, and he ducked just before a burst of machinegun fire splashed fragments of shattered stone and dust over him, the crackle and slam of the impacts echoing across the hillside.

Gritting his teeth, he leaned against the scorching rock as dust continued to sift down out of the air as the machinegunner punished him for daring to show himself.

Not like this. The thought was a sudden intrusion, but it was as clear as if it were a bolt from the cloudless sky above. He didn't believe in divine inspiration, but if he was going to die, he wasn't going to die of thirst while his enemies gloated down below, fed and watered and comfortable.

He rolled to put his back to the rock. "Nilo, Omar. Can you get into position to start shooting at them down there?"

2

Nilo nodded, though it looked like Omar might be too far gone. He was still moving, still breathing, but he hardly seemed aware of where he was anymore.

The wounded man dragged his shattered leg behind him as he crawled to the rock where Carlos waited, though he paused to take Adalberto's one remaining magazine. He was obviously in a lot of pain as he hiked himself up to where he could lay his battered Galil in the crack in the rocks to start to shoot down into the government positions below.

While Nilo got into position, Carlos crawled back into the rocks, looking up and around for a good way out. Their final redoubt was near the crest of a hill overlooking the capital city, and there wasn't a lot of cover they could use. But he was determined to get down out of that outcropping and deal some death to the monsters who fought for the government before he died.

"Come with me." His voice was a hoarse rasp through his cracked lips. His tongue felt thick and rough in his mouth.

Without waiting for a response from the dead-eyed men who'd come with him on this ill-fated final raid, he looked to the only opening in the rocks off on the flank, heaved himself to his feet, and dashed through it.

It was more of a lumbering lunge than a dash, but he got out and threw himself flat as a bullet smacked into the rock nearby. They were watching all sides of the rebels' last covered position.

He kept crawling, the desert growth and the rocks tearing at his hands, his knees, and his already dusty and tattered clothes. His rifle burned his hand where he gripped it, and banged and knocked against the ground and the rocks. He ignored the noise and any damage that might be done. None of it mattered. So long as the rifle fired, and the Kalashnikov *always* fired.

More gunfire was starting to snap toward their position, and he heard a sudden burst of meaty impacts behind him, barely audible over the crackle of bullets going by overhead. Alonzo was dead.

He didn't look back. He just kept crawling. He wasn't even looking that far ahead, knowing only that there were soldiers in every direction, and that he needed to lash out, to take some revenge before he died.

It was pure good fortune—not that he believed in such a thing—that brought him to a small arroyo running down from the top of the hill. He fell into it, just as another burst of machinegun fire spat grit and dust over him, the bullets sending up geysers of dirt and shattered rocks right where he had just been.

Tomas appeared above him, having scrambled to his feet to try to race to cover. More bullets slammed into him, blood erupting from his chest, and he collapsed at the lip of the arroyo, his eyes open and staring fixedly at nothing, red running from under him into the dust.

Carlos had no idea how many of them were left now. He didn't know if he cared. A strange detachment had come over him, and everything seemed to be muted but clear.

Rising up out of cover, even as the gunfire kicked up dust and grit all around him, he leveled his AK-74 and opened fire.

The Kalashnikov bucked and rattled in his hands, bullets skipping off rocks and kicking up dirt, though he was pretty sure that some of them struck home, green-clad soldiers dropping out of sight in the dust.

Then he felt a fiery impact in his side, and then one leg went out from under him.

He pivoted as he fell, seeing three more of the men in green looming above the arroyo, where they'd come up on his flank. He swung the rifle toward them, sending off one last stuttering burst that caught the soldier on the left, the bullets slamming into his ribs and then tearing out his throat, sending him spinning to the desert ground with a spray of gore.

Then the weapon *click*ed on an empty magazine.

Both of the soldiers who were still standing had ducked for cover as he'd shot at them, evading the burst of fire that had killed their comrade. One of them rose up onto a knee as Carlos stared at his empty weapon, realizing at the last that it was over.

4

The soldier's rifle barked, and Carlos felt another blow. It didn't even hurt that much, though he was sure the pain was coming. Another blow and another slammed him back against the rocks at the bottom of the arroyo. He felt something wet around his mouth, and he realized it was getting hard to breathe.

As the two soldiers scrambled down into the arroyo above him, and proceeded to empty their magazines into him, one last thought floated through his mind, just before the pain made everything turn black.

Ernesto. Keep the Cause alive.

CHAPTER 2

Present Day

John Brannigan was not a happy man.

It wasn't that life was bad. Nor was it the company. His relationship with the man behind the wheel of the SUV currently rolling through Alexandria, Virginia, wasn't nearly as adversarial as it once had been. Mark Van Zandt, formerly *General* Van Zandt, USMC, had overseen Brannigan's precipitous and unwilling retirement from the Marine Corps, many years before. Since entering the private sector himself, however, Van Zandt had worked with Brannigan and his small team of mercenaries, the men who called themselves "Brannigan's Blackhearts," enough that he'd changed.

No, the discomfort wasn't about sharing a ride with Van Zandt, or even the business casual that was pretty far from his usual attire these days. No, it was entirely about where they were.

He'd bent over backwards, in uniform and out, to avoid Northern Virginia, the Beltway, and DC itself. Now here he was, right in the belly of the beast, and he couldn't do a thing about it.

Of course, he *could* just go home. But there hadn't been a lot of action for the Blackhearts since Prague, and he knew that the other boys would be disappointed if he turned down a job just because it meant going into the swamp.

"Here we are." Van Zandt took a turn onto a long, winding driveway flanked by a pair of massive oak trees. "I don't need to brief you on proper etiquette here, do I?"

It was a dig, and Brannigan knew it, but he didn't rise to the bait. "I've briefed the Joint Chiefs and even the President in my day, Mark."

Van Zandt had the good grace to look a little abashed. He was still more clean-cut than Brannigan, who had let his hair grow longer—though it still wasn't exactly *long*—and had added a massive handlebar mustache. There hadn't been much about Van Zandt's grooming that had changed since the Marine Corps. "I know. You can just be a little…"

"Blunt?"

"That's… better than what I was going to say."

"Abrasive? Belligerent?"

Van Zandt sighed. "Just take the diplomacy for what it is, John."

Brannigan subsided, though not without cracking a faint smile. They really had come a long way, him and Van Zandt. Such an exchange only a few years ago would have ended in a fight.

They rolled up to the front of the house, an enormous mansion that looked like it dated back to colonial days, though that might well have been the object when it had been built. Brannigan knew who they were meeting, but he hadn't researched the house. He had other concerns.

Van Zandt parked out front of the massive stone steps leading up to the front door. "You didn't come strapped, did you?"

Brannigan sighed and pulled the commander-sized 1911 out of his waistband, still in its holster, pushing it into the center console. "You didn't think I wouldn't, did you?"

Van Zandt just shook his head and got out.

There were two men in plainclothes, with the unmistakable air of security about them, waiting at the door. They didn't search the two former Marine officers, which was a rare courtesy, but ushered them inside. "The Senator is waiting for you, gentlemen."

8

With one in the lead and the other trailing, they moved into the house. The entryway looked like a set from *Gone with the Wind*, with the grand staircase leading to the second floor and a massive chandelier overhead. Brannigan did know enough to know that the Senator came from old money, so this wasn't *all* from government graft.

The Senator's home office was on the second floor of one wing. Paneled in what looked like mahogany—and Brannigan didn't doubt that it was the real thing—it looked like a classical study, and he was sure that it was maintained that way for appearances alone.

Senator Braxton was sitting behind an enormous wooden desk, thoroughly absorbed in writing something. Brannigan's eyes narrowed as he studied the balding, white-haired man. He knew enough about Braxton to be sure it was an act. The man was the epitome of the lowest common denominator rising to the top by sheer artifice and bombast.

"Have a seat. Just be a moment." The "elder statesman" voice sounded just as phony as the writing to Brannigan's ears. *Hell. Is he using a fountain pen?*

There wasn't anything they could do, though, and Van Zandt just shrugged and sank into one of the overstuffed armchairs facing the desk. Brannigan stifled the urge to shake his head and did the same, noting with disgust that he sank deeper into the chair than normal, which would put him below Braxton's line of sight from the desk. It was a cheap power play, and one he'd seen before, but it was probably to be expected from someone of Braxton's caliber.

Finally, the Senator put the notepad and the pen aside and looked up at the two of them, leaning his elbows on the desk and clasping his hands. "Well. General Van Zandt. Colonel Brannigan. Thank you for meeting me. I'm afraid we need to have this meeting here in my home because certain forces within the US government have precluded anything more official."

"We're listening." Brannigan kept his face impassive, though he thought he could sense Van Zandt very nearly wince next to him.

His bluntness made Braxton hesitate and drew an irritated glance from the older man. However, he apparently decided that whatever he'd brought them here for was more important than his senatorial ego.

"I don't know if you've been following the news in the Caribbean?" Braxton raised an eyebrow as he asked the question.

Van Zandt nodded, while Brannigan only shrugged.

Braxton nodded, though with just enough of an air of exasperation that it hardened Brannigan's already low opinion of the man. The entire meeting already felt forced and scripted, scripted in such a way to make Braxton feel like he was in total control.

He hated it, but if this was how to get the work...

"Well, there's been an uptick in piracy, particularly in the southern waters, south of Jamaica and north of Colombia." Braxton leaned back in his chair and folded his arms. "The most recent attack was on the MV *Traveling Family*." He said that as if the name should mean something, but it was just another cargo ship to Brannigan. When neither Brannigan nor Van Zandt responded, Braxton sighed again. "The *Traveling Family* is not only a US-flag ship, but she belongs to the Dorian Family corporation." Once again, that was probably supposed to mean something, and Brannigan assumed it was a major donor or something. He just nodded, as if he understood. He didn't want another patronizing explanation that wasn't necessarily relevant to the mission.

"This was the first US flagged ship to be taken, and it has to be responded to. Unfortunately, we know who is behind these attacks, and that makes things a little difficult."

The senator pointed to a map of the Americas on the wall. "The pirates are coming from a small country on the north coast of Colombia, right next to the Venezuelan border. Costa de las Joyas. It's ruled by a small and brutal military junta, that's been

10

in power since the late seventies. Now, nobody would miss them if they went away, but the reality on the ground makes direct US intervention next to impossible. That close to Venezuela, no one wants to send the Marines or even the SEALs. Especially after that circus of a coup attempt in Venezuela only a few years ago."

Brannigan wasn't sure he bought that. Venezuela was an enemy of the US, a generally communist country, but it wasn't so much of a threat that the US he had grown up in would hesitate to teach them a lesson, even if by proxy. And the description of the military junta that ran Costa de las Joyas didn't make them sound like they were exactly Venezuelan allies. Or Colombian allies, for that matter.

No, there was something else going on here.

Am I getting paranoid in my old age?

"A certain committee that I am a part of has worked with the State Department to come up with a solution. A full-scale military intervention—which would be the only real way to put a stop to the junta's active support of piracy—is off the table, but we believe that we have found a better way to accomplish regime change. Which is where you and your little group of contractors comes in."

He pushed a folder across the desk. Brannigan took it, aware that it was an affectation itself, as much as he might personally prefer paper to electronics. Inside was a photo of a man in his late thirties or early forties. Clean shaven, with a flyaway shock of black hair, there was a burning intensity in his eyes that Brannigan wasn't sure he liked.

"That is Ernesto Hierro," Braxton explained. "He has been at the forefront of the reform movement in Costa de las Joyas for a couple of decades now. His father was killed by the junta, back in the eighties. He was captured a few months ago and is currently being held in the prison wing of the Fortaleza Generalissimo Marto, right outside Santa Paz, the capital city and the single major city in the entire country."

Braxton leaned back in his chair again and eyed Brannigan, as if he were uncertain about whether or not to

11

continue, uncertain that Brannigan was the right man for the job. Brannigan just leaned back in his own chair, putting the file on the arm next to him, and returned the senator's stare levelly.

Finally, with a nod that was every bit as theatrical as the rest of this meeting, Braxton seemed to make up his mind. "We need you to get Hierro out and back to his fellow reformers. There are plans in motion to get them more support, and the Agency believes that they have extensive grassroots support among the populace. The military junta is brutal and corrupt, and the people have just about had enough. It's time for a reform, and it would be better, in that part of the world, if it came from their own people, not from the US military."

Brannigan suspected that that last statement had far more to do with the desire to avoid an overt US military intervention than the aforementioned worry about Venezuela. He wasn't *entirely* against the idea, either, but there was still something about this that seemed a little off.

"If they're corrupt, would it be possible to simply bribe someone to let him out?" It wasn't that he was worried about the Blackhearts' ability to run a jailbreak, but if they could do it quietly, without gunfire, so much the better.

"It's possible." Braxton didn't seem to like the idea. As if killing a bunch of people to noisily break a dissident out of a military prison was a much preferable concept than bribing a corrupt officer. "We will provide you with some operational funds, but duffel bags full of cash might not be available."

Brannigan just nodded. It seemed as if the senator and whoever else was backing this operation had a preconceived idea of how it should go. He'd deal with that as it came. "Well, I suppose stopping piracy against American shipping is a noble cause, even if this seems to be an awfully roundabout way to do it. We're going to need a pretty thorough breakdown of the country, its history, terrain, known factions, etc. Is there any kind of timeline we need to be aware of? Is he slated for execution or anything?"

"Not that we know of, but this does need to be done quickly. We don't want any more American ships getting seized." Braxton seemed satisfied that the Blackhearts were going to take the job, and he sat up, shuffling papers on his desk. "My secretary will have a packet for you with more information."

Clearly, the meeting was over. Brannigan glanced at Van Zandt, who was already getting up, and followed suit. "Thank you for your time, Senator."

Braxton waved, already apparently absorbed with the papers in front of him. Brannigan and Van Zandt turned and left the room.

Braxton's secretary—unsurprisingly a young brunette—was waiting with a sealed manila envelope, which she handed over as they came out, barely looking at the two retired officers before going into Braxton's office and closing the door behind her.

"Looks like the brief's been given and the job is set." Van Zandt looked a little uncomfortable, though he was also apparently relieved that Brannigan hadn't pushed in there. "Let's get out of here and start planning."

Brannigan tucked the envelope under his arm and followed Van Zandt toward the car. He would run this past the team, and they'd see.

It wasn't as if the Blackhearts hadn't done some sketchy jobs before. Hell, they'd been ostensibly working for a transnational criminal syndicate in Prague, but the target had been the Humanity Front, so that had, at least on some level, been justified.

There was something about this that told him they'd have to move very carefully.

Very carefully, indeed.

CHAPTER 3

"Contact left!"

Carlo Santelli's bellow was cut off a moment later by a crackle of gunfire that echoed off the forested hills, as the lead element turned and poured bullets into the targets arranged along the hillside.

After the first burst, Joe Flanagan, lean and black bearded, rose, turned, and dashed for the opposite hill, sprinting almost exactly three seconds before he turned, dropped to the prone, and picked up the fire again.

The rest of the element, consisting of Kevin Curtis, John Wade, Tom Burgess, and Ignatius Kirk, followed somewhat more raggedly. In Curtis's and Wade's case, they'd simply held and kept up the fire a little bit longer, while Kirk was moving a little slower these days. The retired Special Forces soldier had been through the wars, and while he'd mostly recovered from wounds taken on an earlier job with the Blackhearts, he still didn't have quite the speed or the endurance of his younger days.

Tom Burgess, his salt-and-pepper ponytail waving behind him, was almost right behind Flanagan.

Outside of the kill zone, the second element, with Miguel Gomez taking charge, had immediately taken cover and then started to maneuver around to the flank. Vincent Bianco, as massive as ever, moved the shortest distance, though it wasn't

15

because he was slow. While they only had rifles at the moment, he and Curtis were usually the team's machinegunners, and so Bianco was simply setting up a base of fire.

As Bianco opened up, his bullets tearing through the targets, Doc Puller, Hank Brannigan, and Dan Tackett fell in behind Gomez, finding cover and getting down before adding their own bullets to his, as the lead element fell back toward the trees.

Santelli, short, stout, and balding, watched from the tower over the range until he was satisfied. "End-Ex!" He had to roar louder than usual to be heard over the gunfire, but the shooting died down after a moment.

Flanagan and Wade were picking themselves up. Wade looked around the range with his icy stare, evaluating how they'd performed.

This entire little kinetic get-together had been Wade's idea, after all. It had been a little while since the Blackhearts had been out on a job, and the big, intense former Ranger had decided that they needed to knock some rust off. Santelli suspected that Wade had mainly been bored, especially with running this range—it had once belonged to a fallen Blackheart named Don Hart, who had left it to the team when he'd been killed in action—and had just wanted to do something more high-speed than teaching basic pistol and carbine classes to civilians.

Knowing Wade's temper, Santelli often wondered just how well some of those classes really went.

He could already hear Curtis bitching. "I *know* some of us have belt-feds. Why didn't we bring a couple of them out? Completely destroys the training value."

"Ammo costs money, Kevin, and I wasn't going to pay for your machinegun budget out of *my* pocket." Wade didn't look at the short, fireplug of a man as he spoke.

Of course, Curtis being Curtis, that only got him more spun up. "This was *your* idea, John. I *thought* that, since you put so much value on a training exercise, that you'd at least make the extra effort."

16

Wade did start to turn to glare at him then, only to pivot back toward Flanagan as the quiet man started to chuckle. "What?"

Flanagan just shook his head. "I just think it's funny that somebody else has to put up with him for a change."

Curtis looked at his old friend with an exaggerated pout. "That is *hurtful*, Joseph. How boring would your life be without me? 'Put up with him,' indeed."

"It would involve fewer fistfights with gangbangers at midnight in Vegas, that's for sure." Flanagan let his rifle hang on its sling, brushing dried grass off his gear and his trousers. "Not sure that would be a bad thing."

"Pfft." Curtis turned toward the shelter where the ammunition was staged. "Never thought you'd turn into an old woman, Joe."

"Well, I never thought you'd grow up, Kev, and it looks like I was right."

Curtis just sputtered, as Wade pushed past him, unable to keep a faint grin off his face.

Santelli mirrored that grin as he climbed down from the tower. It was good to have the band back together again.

Doc Puller stepped up beside Kirk, who looked like he might be limping slightly as they all got back to the overhang. "You okay, Kirk?" There was a slight hesitation before he said it, which was somewhat understandable, given Puller's history. The Blackhearts had recruited him out of necessity and a little desperation, but Flanagan had found him drunk and despondent after being fired from an ambulance job. He'd been on tenterhooks ever since, trying desperately to prove himself and fit in. Unfortunately, it tended to just make things awkward.

Fortunately, Kirk just waved him off. "Just stiff. I'm getting old. This shit is still fun, but damn, I ain't moving as well as I used to."

The team gathered around, empty magazines coming out to get refilled, while Santelli looked over his notes. He really didn't have much. They might have come together to knock the

17

rust off their skillsets, but they'd all been in the profession long enough that there wasn't actually that much rust to knock off.

That didn't mean there was no need to train, nor was there no room for improvement.

His debrief points would have to wait, however. As he looked up from the notebook, he heard the rumble of a pickup pulling into the parking lot on the other side of the tire barrier that separated the range itself from the rest of the property. He thought he knew who it was; there weren't usually many visitors to the old Hart farm who weren't previously scheduled.

"Keep topping off mags." He started toward the gate. "I'll be right back."

The gate itself creaked open before he could reach it, and Brannigan loomed in the entryway. "Who all's here?"

"Everybody." Santelli fell in beside the colonel as they moved toward the shelter.

An eyebrow went up. "Everybody?" Brannigan's eyes went toward the group gathered around the wire spool tables, jamming mags. Specifically to the brown-haired man who still kept to himself a little, though he had integrated with the rest of the team seamlessly during the drills they'd been running for the last two days.

"Tackett made his decision. Seems that getting a taste of the action again finally got to him."

Brannigan nodded. Dan Tackett had contacted the Blackhearts a while back, looking for help to get one of his old comrades from a job with Mitchell Price—former SEAL and PMC magnate—against a group of Chinese pirates near the Straits of Malacca. He'd been hesitant to get back into the game. Santelli still didn't know all the details of what had happened in the Anambas Islands, but it had clearly left some deep scars.

Still, Tackett had insisted that he be called if a job involving the Humanity Front—which had kidnapped his friends and Price, as well—came up. The Prague job had, indeed involved the Front, a shadowy terrorist organization hiding behind the

18

façade of the biggest and most respected humanitarian NGO on the planet.

Now, it seemed, Tackett had decided to throw in with the Blackhearts all the way.

"Good. He's an asset, and I'm glad to have him along." Brannigan nodded as they came up to the pair of cable spools that the mercs were using as ammo tables.

"So, we've got a job?" Hank had seen his father coming and moved around to meet them. He'd missed the Prague job, and he was eager to get back in the action.

"We've got a job." Brannigan set the packet of papers under his arm on the table as Burgess and Gomez moved some of the ammo cans out of the way. "There are some reservations, though."

"What else is new?" Wade snorted, shoving his last magazine back into his battle belt and folding his arms. "We live in Sketchy World."

Brannigan laid out the events of the meeting with Senator Braxton and opened the file folder to bring out the collection of photos and dossiers. Leaning on the edge of the spool, he looked around at the now-familiar faces. "There's a lot that's *not* here. A lot. I'll be honest; I hadn't even heard of this flyspeck of a country until yesterday. This packet includes almost nothing on Costa de las Joyas itself. There's some—mostly reports of the military junta's brutality—but not much that's going to help us plan."

"A military junta in South America is a brutal dictatorship?" Bianco put his hand on his chest. "Color me shocked."

Brannigan ignored the interjection. "We have a list of the six generals who are a part of the junta, but aside from names and a couple of very pixelated photos, we don't have much more than that. Supposedly the junta came to power back in the eighties, shortly after Costa de las Joyas achieved its independence, and they killed the package's father. Other than that, there's nothing."

He glared down at the dossier for a moment before turning his eyes back up to his boys. "I don't like that. We're in the dark, and it looks like Braxton and whoever else is working with him on this wants it to stay that way.

"We don't have a hard and fast timeline on this, but there is definitely going to be pressure if we dawdle too long. However, travel arrangements will take some time, and I want us all to do some digging during that time. There has to be *something* out there about this little country and its military government. Furthermore, there should be something about Hierro and this reform movement." He looked pointedly at Bianco, who winced slightly. "Yeah, Vinnie, I'm afraid you're getting tapped for this one." He smiled evilly. "You're good at putting the pieces together. Put that to use in some intel collection."

Bianco still looked pained. "Worldbuilding for a role playing game is different from doing an actual area study, particularly remotely, Colonel. I can make most of that stuff up."

"I know. You're still the team intel guy." Bianco looked a little crestfallen, but he knew better than to argue. "Now, right at the moment, logistics are limited to getting into the country. We have a contact over the border in Colombia who is supposed to be able to get us weapons, ammo, and gear." When he looked around at the reactions, he nodded. "Yeah, I'm a little sketched out about that, myself, since it seems that this guy is a local, not an American. Unfortunately, unless we can work out a way to smuggle what we need into the country, we may be stuck there." He turned to Santelli. "Carlo, I'll leave it up to you to do your magic with transportation." Another glance around the team. "Who's going to volunteer for advance recon?"

CHAPTER 4

Most of the Blackhearts had dispersed to go pack for the operation. Few of them would pack heavy; it just wasn't a good idea on these sorts of trips. Especially since they had all been more than one job where they'd needed to leave everything behind and run at the end.

Brannigan stayed on at Hart's place, since he was about as packed as he was going to get. Besides, Wade and Bianco were also staying there, while Bianco commenced his open-source deep dive into Costa de las Joyas.

For his part, Brannigan was looking into the pirate attacks that had triggered this job. There wasn't a whole lot to be found, and he had sources that went beyond a mere internet search. Most of what he could find were short, minor reports about small cargo ships going missing near the north coast of Colombia, though the newest had seen the crews put afloat on lifeboats while the ship was ransacked and then scuttled.

There was no such report on the MV *Traveling Family*. All that was known was that it had gone missing. He would have expected a bit more information, especially if the company that owned the freighter was as well connected as Braxton had implied, but there was little more than a paragraph on the whole incident.

That suggested to him that most of the targets were being manned by third country nationals, and that, until the pirates had

21

hit a ship that *had* been connected, then nobody had really cared. At least, nobody in the western press. Or the Latin American press, for that matter. The handful of mentions he found, mostly using translation programs since his Spanish wasn't the greatest, were all somewhat dismissive.

It was interesting that even the dismissive reports still said that it was the National Army of Costa de las Joyas that was responsible. The locals didn't seem to hold them in very high regard, but there seemed to be an undercurrent of sentiment that the targeted ships maybe had had it coming.

That was interesting. There was a deep-seated resentment of the US endemic throughout Latin America. He wondered if that was all there was to it.

He had just leaned back from the screen with a sigh, rubbing his eyes, when Bianco came back out into the living room and dropped onto the couch with an equally tired sigh.

"Find anything, Vinnie?"

Bianco ran both hands over his face as he leaned back in his seat. "Not much, Colonel. In fact, there's damned near nothing. It's like absolutely nobody cares enough about this little flyspeck country to pay any attention to it at all. The Wikipedia article is a stub. The only news article I could really find dates back to 1958, when the country gained its independence, a year before the military junta apparently took over. It all seems to have gotten lost in the end of La Violencia in Colombia, but as near as I've been able to tell, the same generals have been ruling the country ever since."

Brannigan frowned. "Since 1958?"

"Okay, maybe there's been *some* turnover, but I couldn't even find a list of who the generals in the junta are." Bianco dropped his hands to his lap. "I think I see why they want the local dissidents to handle the whole 'regime change' thing. There's not much information to be found, and I don't need to tell you that trying to overthrow a government with next to no intel is probably not going to go well."

Brannigan looked out the window at the sunset over the forested hills to the west. "Maybe. I've seen those sorts of ideas fall flat, too." He turned back to Bianco. "Any information on this Hierro? Or his father?"

Bianco grimaced. "Nothing. I mean a flat *nada*. There's one sentence in the Wiki article about dissidents and some massacres to put them down, but that's about it. No names, no personalities, nothing." He rubbed a thumb along his jaw. "There is one thing, though, that stood out to me."

"What?"

The big, younger man hesitated, looking down at the floor. The carpet was getting kind of ratty over time; without Hart living here anymore, there was less energy to be put into keeping the place up. "The name 'Hierro.' I wondered about it, since it doesn't sound like most Hispanic names I'm used to. Turns out, it's Spanish for 'Iron.'"

Brannigan leaned back, lacing his fingers behind his head. "Now, that is interesting."

"Sounds pretty 'revolutionary nom de guerre' to me," Bianco said. "You getting the same vibe?"

"It sounds that way." Brannigan stared at the ceiling, thinking through the implications. "How realistic did you think those accusations of massacre were? Were they real, or did somebody get caught in a crossfire and it got blown out of proportion for propaganda purposes?"

Bianco spread his hands. "I can't say, Colonel. There's just not enough. If the junta really is behind the piracy, though…"

"Hmm." Brannigan thought it over. It certainly wouldn't be the first time that the US backed the wrong set of "plucky rebels," though military juntas in Latin America didn't tend to have a great track record, either. It wasn't entirely outside the realm of possibility that the junta was, indeed, deserving of being taken down.

Unfortunately, the paucity of information was a real problem.

Tires crunched in the gravel outside, and headlights swung across the front of the house. A moment later, Santelli's stumping footsteps echoed on the porch, and he pushed his way through the door.

The former sergeant major looked at the two men on the couches, his eyes moving from one to the other as he shut the door behind him. "That doesn't look like the research has gone well."

"It hasn't." Brannigan sat up, putting his elbows on his knees. Santelli stepped around to join Bianco on the couch, pulling a beer out of the bag in his hand and offering it to Brannigan, who waved it off. "This job appears to be in a backwater that nobody has cared about for decades, and the amount of intel we can find is negligible."

Santelli popped open a beer as Bianco accepted the one Brannigan had refused. "So, are we going through with it? I mean, we've done some sketchy stuff, I'm not gonna lie, but going in blind?"

Brannigan shook his head with a faint, ironic smile. "Oh, we won't be going in blind, no matter how much the client might want us to. I'm taking Joe and running some advance recon, while the rest of the team stages in Colombia and links up with this arms dealer contact."

"Only two?" Santelli frowned. "That doesn't sound like a great idea, boss. Two gringos in a place like that are going to stand out."

"I suppose I could take Mario."

"Mario's not Colombian." Bianco scratched his head. "He's going to stand out, too." He squinted at the wall, thinking. "What if we sent four guys? There's a little bit of a tourism industry in Costa de las Joyas. Not much, but a little, and the government keeps trying to prop it up, despite the fact that it's not a very nice place to visit." Santelli snorted at that characterization. "There's a resort right on the beach, not actually that far from the main military base. What if two were the Ugly Americans, drawing all the attention and heat, while the other two kept mostly out of sight and did the sneaky stuff?"

24

Santelli tilted his head a little as he thought it over. Brannigan was starting to nod, though he had reservations.

"What if those two get rolled up? Playing the Ugly American in this part of the world is a dangerous game."

Bianco shrugged. "On the other hand, if there were just two, the others would still be on the loose to break them out. Isn't this supposed to be a jailbreak mission in the first place?"

Brannigan shared a look with Santelli. "I appreciate the enthusiasm, Vinnie, but that's one hell of a chance to take. Latin American prisons are no joke, and one run by a Latin American military that already has some indicators of being not only the usual level of brutal, but also pirates who have targeted Americans, is probably going to really suck."

Bianco grimaced. "You're probably right. But how else are we going to get in there, without sneaking across the border, which is going to take more time? With this plan, we can get eyes on faster. What's more, look at how little ground-level info we have about this country. We *need* to have somebody on the street, even for just a little while."

"He's got a point, John." Santelli took another sip of his beer. "For what it's worth, I'll be one of the Ugly Americans. I might not have *been* in prison, but I'm still reasonably sure I could hold my own, if it comes to that, at least for a couple of days."

"This isn't going to be like spending a couple days in the drunk tank, Carlo."

"I know." Santelli glanced at Bianco, who nodded. It had been his idea, and he was going to roll with it. "Just make sure we don't have to wait in there for long, *if* it happens. I'm going to do what I can to make sure that it doesn't."

Brannigan thought it over for a long moment. He didn't particularly like the idea, but both men made a good point. It would be possible to sneak over the border from Colombia, go full greenside recon, but there was a drawback to that, and Bianco had hit the nail on the head. They knew next to nothing about this country, and their suspicions about the entire job could go

25

unanswered without that sort of on-the-ground analysis of the population and its atmospherics.

He'd seen it before, especially as a Marine officer. The intel at headquarters rarely matched up with the reality on the ground, but being separated by either camouflage or simply the distance between combat troops in a war zone and the populace that both feared and hated them could keep that difference from being apparent until it was too late. Talking to the locals almost always turned up vital information that could change everything.

"Okay, we'll roll with it. Comms are going to be sketchy, so Carlo, see if you can get some satphones for us. How are the flights coming?"

"Slowly. It's not an easy part of the world to get to. It's going to take a couple of days to get down there, best case."

"Well, the sooner we can get going, the better." Brannigan sighed. "We might have to rally on the ground in Colombia, but the recon team should get to Santa Paz together."

"Already on it, sir." Santelli finished off the last of his beer. "I should probably get back to it, though."

Brannigan nodded, already lost in thought again, trying to figure out how to plan an operation where there were so many unknowns.

CHAPTER 5

The Santa Paz airport wasn't the worst airport Brannigan had ever flown into, but it was also far from the best. It was a tiny, one-strip airfield with a control tower that was only two stories tall and a terminal that would have been a glorified ranch house in some places.

The gates were only doors that opened onto the tarmac. Instead of the telescoping gateway that was common in the First World, a stairwell was rolled up to the side of the plane and the passengers had to walk to the terminal.

The heat was oppressive, and despite the fact that most of Costa de las Joyas was desert, the humidity was worse, thanks to the proximity of the Caribbean Sea. The city had been striking from the air. The close packed, mostly whitewashed buildings weren't anything out of the ordinary, but the sheer amount of greenery stuck out in the brown of its surroundings. A great deal of effort and water had been expended to make the city look tropical, which was interesting when he considered the nature of the local government.

Of course, there were plenty of examples throughout history of tyrannies that had poured resources into beautifying their surroundings, if only to pump up their own egos, usually at the expense of their people.

The first thing he noticed as he descended the steps, besides the heat and the generally run down look of the airport, was the pair of gun trucks parked on either corner of the terminal, facing the tarmac. They were ancient Willys Jeeps, with what looked like old M1919 Browning machineguns mounted on pedestals in the back. Each vehicle had half a dozen men hanging around, all dressed in green fatigues and battle belts, with their ancient-looking FALs either slung or leaning against the tires. Most of those rifles appeared to have most of their bluing worn off.

The soldiers looked bored and uncomfortable, for the most part. One of them was sitting in the passenger seat of his Jeep, clearly asleep. There weren't any officers around, or if there were, they were every bit as lazy and complacent as their troops.

A moment later, however, as Brannigan shouldered his travel bag and started across the short stretch of tarmac toward the terminal, a man in a much crisper uniform, with yellow shoulder boards, came out of the terminal, and one of the soldiers said something, nudging the sleeping man. With a scramble of movement, all of them got to their feet and straightened, a few quickly snatching up their weapons as the young man with spit-shined boots marched toward them, though he was watching the passengers disembarking the plane more than he was the soldiers who had just been caught napping.

Brannigan felt the young officer's eyes on him as he walked past. The officer had stopped a few paces from the door, and stood there, staring at the handful of passengers that had gotten of the small plane, his attention seemingly riveted on the four Americans. Joe Flanagan was lean and tough, but he was average sized enough that he *could* blend into a crowd. Even Santelli, as stout and bowlegged as he was, didn't tend to attract too much attention. Brannigan and Bianco, however, were both well over six feet, and probably stood close to a head above most of the locals.

They needed to get through Customs, to the resort, and get out of sight. But they needed to run this gauntlet of local soldiers first.

None of the guards moved to stop them as they walked into the terminal. They just watched, and Brannigan thought he could sense a mix of curiosity and hostility in those stares. It really didn't seem that Americans—*Yanquis*—were all that popular here in Costa de las Joyas. At least, not among the military.

Inside, it was still muggy and hot. If there was an air conditioning system in the building, it didn't feel like it was working. The locals didn't seem too bothered, though. There were plenty of soldiers standing around inside, easily as many as were out on the tarmac, all still armed and wearing their war belts. They were still being lazy, leaning against walls and putting their weapons down, those who weren't sitting, and there didn't seem to be a single one that wasn't sporting considerable sweat stains, but they were still there, and in force.

None of the four Blackhearts commented on it. They just took it in and moved toward the gate faced by a desk with "*Control de Pasaportes*" in large gold letters on the front.

The Customs desk was flanked by two more soldiers with Uzis, who were standing a little straighter than their compadres near the exterior doors, watching the oncoming Americans like hawks. They might genuinely hold the hostility they were showing as they stared, unblinking, at Brannigan and Bianco, but Brannigan suspected that the much more clean-cut young man in uniform standing behind the fat, sweating Customs official, a pistol in a patent leather holster at his hip, probably had more to do with it than anything.

The jowly, balding Customs official looked up as the four Americans got in line. They appeared to be the only foreigners in the airport, the handful of other passengers from the plane going to a different line. They were still having their baggage thoroughly searched, Brannigan noticed.

"*Pasaporte?*" The Customs official looked bored, though there might have been a bit of a glint of curiosity in his eyes. Or was it something else?

Brannigan handed his passport over, and the Customs official pointed to a table nearby. "*Equipaje.*"

Setting his bag on the table, Brannigan watched as the Customs official scrutinized his passport, as if looking for any sign that it might be a forgery. It was all very theatrical and Brannigan had no doubt that it was being done for show, to make the *Yanqui*s sweat.

He was sweating all right, but it was because it was so damned muggy in the terminal. Sure, the locals could cause them some trouble, especially the armed soldiers who were everywhere, but he'd been in the Third World enough to recognize the difference between a shakedown and a grab, and this felt like the former.

No one was coming over to inspect his bag, which was a little suspicious, but the fat man behind the desk finally put the passport down—out of reach—and reached for the bag. Instead of getting up, he hauled it over to the desk, opened it, and started to go through it.

To Brannigan's complete lack of surprise, several relatively valuable items were "confiscated" with the Customs official mumbling something that sounded like, "*No permitido.*" Of course, none of them were anything that might be considered contraband, but they'd honestly been expecting something like this when they'd packed, which was really the whole reason that watch, cigars, and small bottle of liquor were in there.

There's more than one way to pay a bribe, and while it burned him to watch the play go forward, Brannigan knew that the bribe was simply an expected part of life down here.

Especially when there were this many guns around.

Finally, though he took several more minutes to paw through Brannigan's luggage, the Customs official put the still-open bag back on the table, stamped the passport with studied reluctance, and handed it across, along with a mumbled admonition that might have been a warning to stay out of trouble, if the man hadn't talked like he had a speech impediment.

The man held up a pudgy hand to forestall Bianco until after Brannigan had packed up his bag and moved out of the way. This was apparently going to take a long time. Just to show the foreigners their place.

Each of the others took just as long, though it did seem by the time Flanagan stepped up to the desk that the fat official was starting to get bored. After all, the Blackhearts hadn't reacted to the shakedown, thus robbing the official of some of his self-important satisfaction.

They might have been in the terminal for a little over an hour before they were finally free to go. Only once they got to the parking lot outside, looking around for a taxi that might take them to the resort on the coast that any of them dared to shake his head in disgust.

"Boy, I haven't missed that part of the Third World." Santelli spat into the dirt near the lot.

"Is it really that much different from some of the asshole bureaucrats back home?" Bianco asked. "They get pretty much the same thing."

"Yeah, it is different." Santelli beat Brannigan to the punch. "Those bureaucrats might be a pain in the ass, and the very concept of most of them might be essentially protection money, but they're at least going to follow *some* rules, and won't call in some bully boys with Uzis to beat you down or maybe shoot you if you object. There's a difference."

Bianco had frowned through the little speech, but Brannigan understood, perhaps better, what Santelli was getting at. "Nobody's saying the bureaucracy back home is a *good* thing, Vinnie. We just have to understand that there are varying levels of bad, and this kind of thing isn't the same."

An ancient Renault was parked on the curb nearby, in yellow taxi livery. "Come on. Let's get the hell away from here."

CHAPTER 6

Uribia wasn't a large or a fancy town, but it sure was colorful, Wade had to admit that. Most of the buildings were built of plastered brick and painted in blues, pinks, oranges, and yellows. The trucks, cars, and tuk-tuks that crammed the streets were a similar mélange of colors, and the whole place seemed to be in a celebratory mood, at least the small part they'd seen so far.

It had been a long trip already, first flying into Riohacha and then taking a bus almost six hours to Uribia. Wade was tired, hungry, and cranky, and he was pretty sure that he was going to strangle Curtis in the next few minutes if they didn't meet with their contact soon.

"I don't see anybody who looks like our guy." Curtis stood with his hands on his hips, his baggage over his shoulder, surveying the Plaza Colombia, a round, paved square surrounding a white obelisk, with several sets of platforms and sheltered overhangs where people could sit or watch a show on the plaza itself. At least, that was what Wade assumed they were for. There were people walking, biking, and driving all the way around the plaza. It was a happening place, from the looks of it.

"You think you were just going to pick him out of the crowd right away?" Hank Brannigan had been a Marine officer, much like his father, getting out after his stint as a company commander. He was no greenhorn, though he was still the youngest and least experienced member of the group. He was also nearing the end of his patience with Curtis, much like Wade. "Maybe wearing one of those sandwich board signs, 'Covert Arms Dealer Looking for Americans?'"

"Keep your voice down." Kirk might be just as weary with Curtis's wisecracks as any of the rest of them, but he was a professional and an old hand at the private warfare business. His time in Special Forces, a lot of years ago, had prepared him for his walk on the grayer side of the tracks. He knew better than any of the rest what they were dealing with here, even if he'd never been to Uribia—and Wade suspected that he probably had. He was old enough to have been running around Colombia back in the days when Latin America had been *the* AO for special operations.

Wade tried to ignore the byplay. The seven of them were grouped together, which kind of bothered him, since there wasn't a lot of disguising the fact that they weren't locals. They tried to play tourist a little, but none of them were really that good at it, and most of the other obvious tourists in the city were families, with women and kids along. Not seven grown men, all of them with a certain aura of competence and leashed violence about them.

Still, aside from a few looks, they hadn't drawn any serious attention yet, and he was taking some solace in that. They still had to be careful, but there were no indicators that the Colombians were looking for American paramilitaries or intelligence people. Not so far, anyway.

That still wasn't going to make finding their contact any easier. He knew a few things about gun laws in Colombia, especially after another job near the Venezuelan border a while back, and if the local authorities *did* get wind of an arms deal going on in their territory, things were probably going to get a little interesting.

They did have a sign and countersign, that was supposed to identify them to each other, but so far, he hadn't seen anything that looked like the identifier he'd been briefed to look for.

Then Tackett nudged him. When he looked over, the quiet man jerked his head to point his chin at a dumpy looking man leaning against the nearest overhang. The man was balding and pot-bellied, dressed in a blue shirt and gray pants, and if not for the black bag over one shoulder, he would have been completely unremarkable among the rest of the people milling around the plaza.

That particular combination of clothing and the bag was exactly what they were looking for.

Wade motioned for the others to wait, then moved up toward the pudgy man. As he did so, he pulled a hat out of his pack and put it on. He'd initially expected an American ball cap to look out of place in Colombia, but there were plenty of other people on the street wearing them, too.

The man glanced over as Wade stepped up next to him, looking toward the obelisk. "There you are, my friend." His English was impeccable. "I've been waiting for you." He looked over his shoulder. "Are the rest here?"

Well, this wasn't the sort of tradecraft Wade had necessarily expected, but there also didn't appear to be any Colombian police or soldiers springing out of the woodwork to arrest them, either. "Yes. Do you have a vehicle?"

"I have a van. Come." Clearly, this guy wasn't worried about much. That could be a good sign, or a very bad one, and in Wade's experience, he tended to lean toward expecting the bad. Still, with a slight hand signal to the rest, he turned and followed.

The man led the way to the edge of the plaza, where there was, indeed, a fifteen-passenger van waiting. It wasn't even nearly as ancient as Wade had expected; it looked like it was almost brand new.

Wade wasn't the only one feeling a little paranoid as they closed in on the van. He saw Kirk, Burgess, and Tackett fall back, spreading out and watching the nearby vehicles, while Curtis, Hank, and Puller moved in on the van. They looked like they were just going to get in, but while Curtis might be a clown, and Puller was shaky, they were all Blackhearts, and quite capable of handling themselves if things got sporty.

For his part, Wade scanned the vehicles, the storefronts, and the crowds as he walked after the pudgy little man toward the van. Nothing stood out. No one moved quickly, and no one seemed to be paying much of any attention to them. He kept walking, staying fairly close to the man, while Curtis got in the passenger seat, and the rest started to climb into the back.

"Come, we will go get to know each other." The guy was obviously trying hard to jovial, to put them at ease. "I know a good place where we can share some *aguardiente*. Good stuff."

Wade wanted to push the issue, since he didn't know how much time the team up north in Costa de las Joyas really had. He wanted the gear and weapons as soon as possible, in case the rescue mission that Brannigan had hinted might be necessary popped up. If any of the team on recon got arrested, they might have to move fast.

At the same time, while Wade had a reputation as a very angry, impatient man, sort of the epitome of the "RANGER SMASH" mentality, he hadn't stuck around because he was dumb. He recognized that there might be some intel value to gain from drinking with this guy, not to mention that he was getting an idea about how to conduct a little bit of psychological preparation, themselves.

As the little man pulled away from the curb, Wade turned to Curtis. "Feels like old times, huh, Kev? Like Dubai?"

Curtis turned halfway around with a frown. Wade silently cursed. That had been clumsy as hell. He hadn't been with the team in Dubai, way back before the Khadarkh mission that had been the Blackhearts' first, but Curtis had, and he wasn't sure why Wade was bringing it up.

Come on, Kev, don't make me spell it out.

Then the light came on. "I don't know. Maybe a little bit." He turned to the man behind the wheel. "I know, I know. Uribia looks *nothing* like Dubai. Less desert. But get this; we were there to meet up with some people to get some supplies, just like here."

He chuckled and twisted around in his seat. "Did you ever meet Roger Hancock, Hank? I know he used to work for your dad."

"I met him. Long time ago." The younger Brannigan was clearly as confused about this conversation as Curtis had been.

"Well, he was kind of running point on this little meet up. Only wouldn't you know, the guys we were trying to do business with decided they were going to jump us instead." Curtis still wasn't looking at the driver, though it was clear enough that the man was listening. "I still don't know what they thought they were going to do with us, except maybe take the funds we'd brought, but they thought they had us boxed in real good. Until Roger hit one of them in the head with a rock, and all hell broke loose." Curtis laughed. "It was *mayhem*! Rebar, rocks, whatever we could get our hands on, at first. Just busting heads right and left!"

Don't lay it on too *thick, Kevin.* But Wade was watching the driver, and it was pretty obvious that the warning was getting through. The guy looked nervous, though it might have just been the nervousness of being in the same vehicle as just over half a dozen guys who found such a story entertaining.

"Well, it is a good thing this place is nothing like Dubai, yes?" The man met Wade's gaze in the rear view mirror, and there was something almost like pleading in his eyes. Wade watched him for a moment, trying to gauge whether or not this was just fear at the implicit threats of violence, or if it was fear because his plan had just been blown.

Curtis was undeterred. "Anyway, once we cracked a couple of skulls, we took the guns they were going to use on us and then the tables were really turned." He turned back to the driver. "So, yeah, a little different from here, I'm sure."

"That is a crazy story." The man they'd been set to meet seemed to have regained his equilibrium. "We will have some *aguardiente* and maybe tell some other crazy stories, hey?"

Curtis glanced back at Wade and shrugged, faintly. The warning had been issued, as best he could. If there was treachery in the works, then they might have headed it off, because

37

sometimes all it took to dissuade an ambush is to reveal that the quarry knew it was there.

Time would tell.

***

"So, we are twenty miles into the hills, chasing these FARC bastards." Javier lifted his glass, peering through the clear *aguardiente* at a time long past and some distance away. "Carlos was wounded, and Emilio had twisted an ankle, but the captain is determined. We were going to kill those sons of bitches. The jungle was *thick*—I think we had lost the trail—but we were close enough that we could hear them."

The Blackhearts were all nursing their own drinks carefully, just in case this was still a setup, but Javier, their contact, was thoroughly absorbed in his story, the third about fighting FARC in the jungles between Colombia and Venezuela. The man might be corrupt, and he might have gone to seed, but if half the stories he was telling were at all rooted in fact, he'd seen some shit.

"So, we spread out as best we can, and I suddenly find that I've got so much brush right in front of me that I have to get down and crawl to get through it. I start to move, and I suddenly find myself staring *right* at this FARC bastard's ass." He laughed. "He must have either thought we were much too far behind them, or he just couldn't hold it anymore. He'd copped a squat right there in the bushes, and I shot him, right through the spine."

The Blackhearts listened, mostly impassively. It was plain that Javier was more experienced and probably more dangerous than the corrupt supply bureaucrat they'd initially taken him for, but none of them were too eager to take him entirely at his word, either. This felt to Wade like bluster, an attempt to regain face after Curtis's story about Dubai.

Still, it was preferable to the ambush that they had been somewhat prepared for. Yet the bloviating was getting tiresome.

"It's getting late." Kirk had either picked up on Wade's impatience, or he was getting tired of Javier's stories, too. "Are we going to do this deal tonight?" The odds that something like this was going to be put off until the morning without a double-cross felt pretty long.

Javier put his glass down, seemingly a little deflated that his attempt at camaraderie hadn't gone as far as he'd hoped. "Yes, yes. Of course." He heaved himself to his feet, a little unsteadily. The Blackhearts had been careful with their drinks, but he hadn't.

There was, of course, the possibility that his tipsiness was an act, but there wasn't a man in that room who wasn't ready to take him apart if that was the case.

He led the way toward the back of the little farmhouse outside of Uribia where he'd taken them. Tackett ended up closest to the back door as Javier went out, and he and Wade shared a quick glance and a nod, Tackett's hand going to the knife in his pocket as he went right, turning to check the corner as he cleared the door. Wade went left, doing the same.

The back was nothing but dust and scrub, with a rough sort of fence set up around the little compound. A ramshackle shed stood against that fence, backed by more of the short, scrubby trees.

Wade was struck once again by the resemblance to parts of Africa and the Middle East. There was a commonality to the poor parts of the Third World that was striking to those who'd worked all over the world.

Javier led the way to the shed, where he fumbled with the padlock on the door. The rest of the Blackhearts spread out quietly and nonchalantly, Curtis and Puller easing toward the back, where they could see into the scrub beyond the fence, just in case. Puller might have crouched to pick up a rock once he was out of sight of Javier. Wade suppressed a smirk. The doc had been listening to Curtis's story.

The door opened with a rasping creak, and Javier turned on a flashlight, playing it around the inside of the shed. Wade stepped forward, while Burgess positioned himself behind Javier, where he could take the man down quickly if he got treacherous.

Wade had his own light, and it outshone Javier's old incandescent as he examined the inside of the shed. Several crates were stacked against each wall, and while he couldn't see anything that looked like a pressure plate or a wire trigger, that didn't mean there wasn't a trap in there. Still, Javier wasn't trying to make himself scarce, so there was that.

The closest crate was open, the top slightly ajar. Very carefully, Wade slid the top aside.

Stacked inside were several old IMI Galils. They gleamed dully in the glow of his flashlight, though even at first glance, it looked like they'd probably need some work. He could already see some rust.

The next crates produced a couple of Daewoo K3 machineguns, several Colombian Cordova 9mm pistols, camouflage uniforms, load bearing gear, magazines, and ammunition. He looked over at Javier, who still hadn't tried to retreat, so he relaxed a little bit. If there had been an IED under the floorboards, he didn't think their contact would have stuck around. "There were supposed to be radios and medical supplies, too."

Javier eased past him into the shed, going to the stack in the back. The boxes back there held several ancient Motorolas and some loose first aid supplies. "Doc!" Wade called Puller in.

Their medic, recruited to replace the fallen Erekle "Herc" Javakhishvili, still hadn't quite found his groove. Flanagan had known him back in the day, but he'd fallen into some alcohol abuse and other problems, and while he hadn't failed the Blackhearts yet, he'd always been shaky enough that Wade suspected he wasn't alone in just waiting for it to happen.

Puller dug into the boxes of medical supplies and came up with a grimace. "It'll work, but we're going to have to go old school if anybody springs a leak. A few tourniquets, but not enough, and they look like cheap knockoffs. No combat gauze. Hell, this looks like it's mostly just cravats and gauze."

"It'll have to do." Wade turned back to Javier. "It looks like it's all there." He didn't mention that it all looked like it had come straight from a National Army of Colombia warehouse, but he supposed that was expected, given Javier's implied background. "Transport?"

The Colombian pointed just down the road. "There are trucks waiting at another farm. I can take you there. You should probably know, though, that the Venezuelans keep a very close eye on their border. You will not get too close without being observed."

He thinks we're here to run ops into Venezuela. Not an entirely unreasonable idea, given current relations with the regime over there. Wade wasn't going to disabuse Javier of the idea. He was their contact to get the weapons and gear they needed to spring this Hierro guy from the Costa de las Joyas jail, and that was it.

Getting chatty with local contacts was never a good idea.

"How about you take me down to get the trucks, while these guys sort out the weapons and the gear?" He pulled up his shirt just far enough to show the money belt at his waist. He saw the greed glint in Javier's eyes, but it was somewhat tempered when Kirk handed him one of the 9mm Cordovas and three magazines. He loaded the pistol and put it in his waistband, the two reloads going into a cargo pocket. "Then we'll settle everything and be out of your hair."

Javier looked a little reluctant, but as the guns were already getting passed out, he suddenly seemed to realize that he had put himself into something of a compromised position. He couldn't exactly object if they decided to force the issue.

"You'll get your money." It was getting late, they hadn't had any word from Brannigan and the rest of the advance team yet, and Wade was getting impatient, too impatient to be especially diplomatic. He got a look from Kirk and shrugged. Kirk was the Special Forces guy. In retrospect, he probably should have led the way on this part of the operation, but it was a little late now. "Let's go."

Javier clearly wasn't happy about it, but he turned and led the way toward the van. He carried himself like a man who'd just

41

realized he'd miscalculated. He was probably expecting that Wade was lying, and he wasn't going to get his money, now.

Wade wasn't lying. He valued his own integrity more than that. Oh, he was certainly tempted by the amount of money he was carrying, but in the long run, he knew he wouldn't take it. Not with this crew. Maybe another time, if the Blackhearts ever fell apart and he found himself working a job like this with a different bunch.

Getting into the van with Javier, he settled in for the ride to the trucks, Tackett getting into the back without a word. Both men were armed, now, and Wade felt considerably better for it. He still split his attention between the night outside and Javier behind the wheel, as they pulled out of the fenced compound and headed for the trucks.

A part of Wade hoped this went smoothly. Another part would be just as happy if it didn't.

CHAPTER 7

Flanagan led the way as he and Brannigan moved along the beach toward the Fortaleza Generalissimo Marto. They hadn't gotten close enough from the city to get eyes on any signs that would have identified it as anything but "the Santa Paz military base," but they hadn't done much moving around since getting into town, either. Once they'd reached the resort, it had been time for the two of them to disappear, while Bianco and Santelli played tourist.

They were both dressed in nondescript, dark clothes, that would blend into their surroundings while not looking overly military. Brannigan had expected the shakedown at the airport, so camouflage would have been completely out of the question. That would have probably gotten them rolled up with a quickness.

Brannigan had gone pretty much straight from the Marine Corps into work as the leader of the Blackhearts, but Flanagan had done a couple of trips overseas as a contractor since he'd gotten out. He'd been in a couple of countries where his fellow contractors had been pulled aside by local security forces because they were carrying stuff that could be *considered* paramilitary gear.

With a military government running this little country, Brannigan had expected that any such reaction would be highly amplified.

43

The beach wasn't the easiest approach, especially as they tried to stay out of the lights that studded the fence that surrounded the base. There were places where it was a nice, sandy beach, but those spots were narrow, few, and far between. Most of the coast was rocky and steep, and they'd already had to clamber up and down a couple of nearly sheer cliffs to get as far as they had.

Brannigan was puffing, despite the fitness forced by his mountain lifestyle back in the States, his clothing soaked in sweat. It felt like grit and sand was getting pushed into every joint. Flanagan, up ahead, seemed like he was taking it easy, but then, it was too dark to see that clearly without NVGs—another useful piece of gear that they'd been forced by circumstances to leave behind—so the younger man was really only a slightly darker shape against the sand, rock, and water.

The Blackhearts' best scout—though Gomez might dispute that from time to time—had paused in the shadow of a short finger that nearly divided a couple of short sections of beach, and Brannigan had to duck behind another rock as a spotlight swept over the sand. The locals were being a little paranoid, but then, Brannigan had yet to see a military government anywhere in the world that wasn't. It was the nature of the beast.

Still, it was a remarkable amount of alertness for a Third World military that, despite themselves, hadn't faced an armed response to their own acts of piracy and terrorism, at least so far.

He waited until the light swept past, then moved up to join Flanagan, since the other man hadn't started to move on once they were back in the shadows.

"What have you got?" Brannigan was glad enough for the break, but he knew Flanagan too well to expect that the backwoodsman would hold up just to rest, this close to the objective.

Flanagan pointed. "They've got patrols out."

Squinting through the dimness, some of his night adaptation shot by the close pass of the spotlight—though if he were to be honest, he'd have to admit that at his age, his night eyes just weren't as good as they had once been—he could just make

44

out movement. Flanagan could probably see them better than he could. "How many?" He hated to ask, not only because it meant talking, even though the rush of the waves nearby should drown out their voices, but also because it meant admitting that he couldn't see as well as he once had. He'd need cheaters to read before too long.

"Only about four, I think." That could still be a hell of a threat, considering neither of them were armed. "They're moving this way, but they don't look like they're very alert.

"You can see that?" Brannigan peered into the gloom beneath the fence.

"Barely." Flanagan's own eyes were fixed over the top of the rock, though he was keeping as low as possible. "I've got to sort of look off to one side, and even then, it's more a vague impression of their body language." A light flashed, suddenly silhouetting two of them. "And the fact that they're sloppy as hell."

"That could be standard for any Third World military, too." Even in the dark, Brannigan could almost see Flanagan's shrug of agreement. They'd both been there. Their indig counterparts in places like Iraq, Afghanistan, and half a dozen other places had almost always been lazy and sloppy.

"Maybe." Flanagan moved aside as Brannigan got deeper into cover, and the patrol got closer. The soldiers were talking, loudly so that they could hear each other over the surf, and while Brannigan's Spanish wasn't that great, it definitely sounded more like complaining than tactical coordination. The one with a flashlight was still shining it at rocks and the water, but they were acting like they had been ordered to patrol the beach, so they were going to go out and head back just so they didn't get yelled at. Or beaten, if this was that sort of army.

The four of them got closer to the rock, that flashlight still waving lazily back and forth. All it would take would be for light and eyes to be turned to the wrong place at the wrong moment...

But they stopped, the man in the rear shifting his rifle on its sling on his shoulder, complaining even more loudly. The point man turned away from the two Blackhearts' hiding place, saying something that sounded exasperated, before the four of them turned back toward the base up on the low bluff beyond and started back the way they'd come.

The two Blackhearts stayed where they were, motionless, as the patrol retreated back up the beach. The sound of the surf was probably enough to keep them from being detected if they moved quickly, but experience and training had conditioned them to be careful. Their lack of weapons was another reason to be extremely cautious.

Finally, Flanagan started moving, though he didn't follow the patrol. He moved around the rock and headed for a narrow draw eroded in the rocky bluff above the beach. It provided some cover, and soon both of them were crawling up the crack in the rocks, freezing whenever the lights swept over their position, even when they were far enough away and the spots diffused enough that it was unlikely that they'd be spotted, even if the bad guys had good optics, which they probably didn't.

It took nearly half an hour to get up to a small hill just outside the perimeter. Brannigan didn't know why it hadn't been kept inside the fence, but he'd seen some equally boneheaded security decisions made in the US military, up to and including putting a FOB at the bottom of a narrow valley. This wasn't nearly that bad, and he suspected that the base personnel thought they had good enough eyes on the hill—plus they were sending patrols out—that they didn't think they needed to expend the materials or the effort to extend the fenceline out.

The two of them, gritty and sweaty in the humidity right on the seashore, crawled through the rocks to the crest of the hill. Almost the entire base was spread out beneath them, giving them a good view.

The outer perimeter was surrounded by a chain link fence topped with razor wire. The base itself covered nearly an entire square mile, and most of that was packed with barracks, motor pools, logistics warehouses, and a tank farm right up on the coast to the north.

While there was a sizeable bay on the north of the peninsula, the locals hadn't put their naval base there, for whatever reason. Two long jetties extended out from the cliffs into the Caribbean, and several docks had been built between them. The boats at those docks were not what Brannigan would have characterized as much of a navy, but they were apparently enough to prey on civilian shipping.

The prison was their target, and therefore the primary focus of this reconnaissance. It was easy enough to pick out, being surrounded by an additional barbed wire fence, set at the northwestern corner of the base, and built like a bunker, a windowless block of concrete. It might even have been a bunker, if Brannigan hadn't already identified the fuel and ammunition bunkers built into another hill on the other side of the base.

He widened his scan to take in the perimeter defenses. They had already picked some of them out at a distance from the spotlights, but from here, it was easier to see the full layout of the towers' arrangement. They studded the exterior fence at almost even intervals of a couple of hundred yards. They weren't the hardened sort of guard towers that Brannigan had seen in a few places in the Middle East; these people hadn't had American backing when they'd built this place, and from looking down at the base, Brannigan could have imagined that to these people, the last fifty years may as well not even have happened.

That could make the mission somewhat easier, but assuming that could very well lead to its failure. Years of experience with poorly equipped insurgents in the Middle East and Central Asia had made it clear that a barely trained kid with an AK can kill you just as dead as a high-speed, motivated death machine.

Reaching into a pocket, he pulled out the hardened case that had protected the small digital camera they'd brought as "tourists." Settling down on his elbows, he started to photograph every yard of the base below them.

CHAPTER 8

"Boy, you'd think this place was about to be overrun by the horde any minute." Bianco looked around as they walked toward the central plaza of Santa Paz, sunglasses hiding his eyes from most of the crowds. More importantly, they hid his eyes from the soldiers in green on just about every street corner.

"The junta must be a little nervous." Santelli looked around in turn. "I'm sure they talk a big game about external threats, either the Venezuelans, the FARC, or the Americans, but my guess is, judging by what I'm seeing, that they're more worried about domestic unrest." He squinted, not nearly as concerned as Bianco about who saw where he was looking. "Have you seen a single regular cop since we got here?"

Bianco paused under a palm tree. There seemed to be more greenery in the city than the entire rest of the peninsula. It was as if the regime had tried to transplant a part of the much more lush jungle Colombia onto the northern coast, even as they had broken away decades before, and were no longer a part of that country.

"No, now that you mention it. It's been all Army uniforms."

Santelli nodded, trying to stay casual even as they worked their way toward the small stores that lined the plaza. None of them were particularly impressive; Costa de las Joyas was desperately poor, despite the name and the pretentions of the military junta running it. They simply didn't have that much to sell, or much to buy it with.

That was probably why the junta had turned to piracy.

Thrusting his hands into his pockets, he wandered toward a street kiosk, where one of the locals was selling vegetables. None of them looked that great, but Santelli had been in enough souks in the Middle East to recognize that that was the norm in most of the world. They grew what they could, sold what little surplus they grew to try to pay for other stuff, and got along from day to day. It was just the way life was.

Santelli was playing it cool precisely to avoid attracting any more attention than was absolutely unavoidable. They were already going to stand out, just by virtue of being *Yanquis*. Sure, Costa de las Joyas might have a resort that they tried to advertise as a tourist mecca on the south shore of the Caribbean, but that didn't mean it really was much of a tourist destination. A tiny, hidebound country, run by a paranoid junta of generals who'd been holding power since the 1980s, carved out of a small desert peninsula in the middle of nowhere, was not going to be a big draw to the Instagram set.

Unfortunately, playing it cool required that he be careful just where he looked. He was trying not to be as overtly cautious as Bianco, but it meant he had to watch the soldiers out of the corner of his eye. The impression he was getting was that none of them were going to take a direct stare very well.

The locals sure as hell weren't looking right at any of them. Which was a tell, as well.

I wonder just how much the locals are going to back the junta if all hell breaks loose? From what I can see, there's a lot of fear here, but that usually means there's a lot of resentment that they don't dare display. Especially in a Latin American culture. The young guys who aren't in the army have to be fuming.

That assumed, of course, that all the hot-headed young men with an urge to violence hadn't already joined the army.

There seemed to be enough men in uniform that he had to figure the army was the biggest employer in the country.

"We're getting some looks." Bianco kept his voice low, almost a whisper, as they passed another intersection, heading toward the massive statue of heroic soldiers in bronze that dominated the center of the plaza. "The soldiers are watching us, but I think we've got somebody following us, too."

That wasn't good. Santelli didn't react, but just kept walking, trying to get a look in one of the dusty windows to see behind them. He found a likely-looking shop, selling local baskets—though there were also eggs and other produce for the locals who weren't interested in such things—and stopped to peruse their wares, taking the chance to scan the reflection of their surroundings.

Unfortunately, the angles weren't right. He could see people on the other side of the street, but the kiosks set outside the building weren't facing the right way to see back the way they'd come. He'd have to take Bianco's word for it.

Waving off the proprietor, who seemed to think that because he'd stopped, he'd committed to buying something, Santelli started on his way again. As he did so, though, he glanced up and looked right at the pair of soldiers on the corner the next street up.

They were watching the two gringos, all right. And just before Santelli let his eyes slide off the pair of them, so as to avoid the impression that he was staring at them, he saw one of them look just over his shoulder. The kid wasn't that good at disguising his reactions, and he nodded.

That was about all the confirmation that Santelli needed. While he'd never been a high-speed, special operations soldier/spy, he'd grown up in some pretty rough parts of Boston. He knew what a mugging looked like, and so he knew pretty well what a follow looked like, especially when the shadower was signaling compatriots to head off the quarry.

The two soldiers started to step out into the street. While his face was blank, Santelli was raging inside, watching every

51

corner and door for any other threats—or a way out. *We haven't even been on the ground a day.*

He started to drift across the street, away from the two soldiers and toward another shop. It didn't work, as the two men in uniform continued across the street, angling to cut him off.

Shit. And with no weapons or even a good escape route. Maybe they're just going to harass us. Ask for papers, that sort of thing. Maybe. I hope. Just show the gringos who's in charge, boys, that's it.

"*Parar.*" The heavier soldier held up a hand to order him to halt. Santelli considered just playing dumb, going all in on the Ugly American stereotype, and pretending he didn't understand Spanish. That could easily backfire, though, and while he didn't want to engage with these guys at all, he also didn't want to antagonize them to the point that it turned into a beatdown in the street. Then they'd *definitely* be heading for the maximum security jail, where they'd get to meet their objective a little earlier, and under far less ideal circumstances, than they'd like.

"What's the problem?" He wasn't going to pretend he couldn't understand the context, but at the same time, Santelli's Spanish wasn't *nearly* good enough to try to put them at ease by carrying on a conversation. Especially since their dialect was probably pretty different from anything he might have learned up north, and if he knew Third World soldiers, he was pretty sure that trying to ingratiate himself with them could very well only piss them off. Security forces in places like this could smell when you were trying to get away from them, and it was like running from an aggressive dog.

"*Pasaporte.*" The man's voice was businesslike, but there was something in his eyes, though his face was blank, that Santelli didn't like. The smaller man, sporting a larger mustache than the pencil-stache that the first man was wearing, was standing back a couple yards and off to one side, in the street.

He'd unslung his rifle, and while he wasn't pointing it at either of the Blackhearts, he was holding it ready. It wouldn't take much to drop the muzzle and open fire, and at that range, he could hardly miss.

And neither of them could do anything about it.

Santelli carefully pulled his passport out of his back pocket, aware that the two soldiers were pretty wound up. He wanted desperately to look over his shoulder, to see what shadowy secret policeman had put the two of them on him and Bianco, but he didn't dare. "Is there some kind of problem?" He handed the document over. "We've been through Customs, got stamped, and everything. Everything should be in order."

The soldier snatched the passport out of his hand and looked at it. If he understood what Santelli had just said, or even what was written on the passport, he gave no sign, and Santelli suspected that this guy and his partner knew about as much English as he knew Spanish.

"What is your business here in Santa Paz?" The voice from behind them was heavily accented, but the English was clear enough. Santelli took the appearance of the new actor as a reason to turn and look behind him.

The man wasn't in uniform, but there was something about him that suggested he usually was. That was a bad sign already. If the Army had gone to the trouble of sending a plainclothes officer out after them then it meant that their cover might have been blown from the get-go.

"We're just here on a trip." He gestured toward the city around them. "My son and I wanted to see the Caribbean, but we don't have a lot of money, and when we heard about how you built this city as an oasis in the desert, well. We had to see it."

He was talking too much, and he knew it. He cursed himself faintly, but he was committed now, and he had to hope that Bianco played along convincingly.

The man who had stepped up behind them was thin and wiry, his face lean and hawkish, with the same pencil mustache that the heavier soldier was wearing. The two soldiers had stiffened as he'd approached, suggesting that he was, indeed, an officer, presuming the junta didn't have a separate secret police.

He was dressed in a polo shirt and slacks, his hands clasped behind his back.

From the look on his face, he didn't buy Santelli's explanation. "This is not usually a tourist destination for *Yanquis*." He nodded to the heavyset soldier, who handed the passport back. Santelli shoved it back in his pocket, hoping against hope that maybe this was about to deescalate. If this really was just a way to make sure the Americans knew they were being watched, then maybe it was almost over.

It was not to be, however. "You will need to come with us."

While he knew it was probably futile, Santelli tried to argue the point. "What for? We haven't done anything. We're just walking the streets."

"We must be assured of your intentions. If you are innocent, then you may resume your tour. Your presence here at this time seems like an unlikely coincidence, however." The man gestured, and the two soldiers stepped up to flank the two Blackhearts, their rifles in their hands. Unarmed, there was nothing the two men could do.

While the crowds on the street watched impassively, apparently unwilling to show any reaction that might be used against them later, the two Americans were marched away from the plaza and toward whatever fate awaited them.

CHAPTER 9

The hotel room in the resort was far from the worst Flanagan had ever seen, but it was no five-star, either. In fact, it reminded him of a few hotels he'd seen in the Middle East, though even for some of those places, it was subpar. There was a fine coating of dust on everything, and the tile work on the floor was all slightly off, none of it laid in straight. The furniture was mostly plastic, except for the beds, which still felt like they were going to collapse at any moment—particularly under Brannigan's weight—and creaked with every move they made.

Still, after the reconnaissance mission on the coast, they were both tired enough that they went almost instantly to sleep, though not before wedging a chair under the door handle, just in case. Santelli and Bianco had been planning to go out in the morning, sometime after the two of them had returned from surveying the military base, but they'd knock if they needed to come in.

It wasn't the planned knock that woke him up.

At least, he was pretty sure it wasn't, not when the heavy banging continued, accompanied by a voice speaking Spanish. It was next to impossible to make out the words over the hammering on the door, but Flanagan thought he could figure it out easily enough.

Brannigan was up in an instant, as Flanagan rolled off the bed, shoved his feet in his boots—he'd cleaned up as best he could after crawling around in the sand and rocks, but they were both sleeping fully clothed—and grabbed his pack. There wasn't much in it that might have drawn attention, but like the rest of the Blackhearts, he'd managed to hide a decent E&E kit in the seams.

Neither man said a word. They'd briefly talked this over before they'd gone to sleep. The locals had moved faster than either of them had expected, but they'd already been in combat mode since they'd hit the ground.

Brannigan was already at the window. They'd had their choice of rooms, and they'd picked this one for a reason. Backed up against the bluffs, there was no good way for anyone from the city side of the resort to come at them, and while it was going to be a dangerous descent, they had come equipped for it.

The window, unfortunately, wasn't particularly large. There hadn't been a lot of money going into the construction here, and it was old, four-pane, wooden-framed, and only about two and a half feet wide. It was going to be a tight squeeze, and that plastic lawn chair, plus the lock, wasn't going to hold for long.

Brannigan pointed, signaling Flanagan to go first. For a moment, he felt like arguing. He'd be able to get through that window a lot more easily than the colonel, and it made sense to him that the guy who could move the fastest should probably go last. But the door shuddered under what had to have been a kick, and the look on Brannigan's face brooked no argument.

Letting his pack hang out of the window, though he kept the carry handle looped around his wrist, he crawled through. It was still awkward, given the narrow opening. He might be shorter and skinnier than Brannigan, but he was still pretty lanky, and it took some doing to get his legs out. He almost lost his grip on the windowsill and fell, but fortunately, while there wasn't a *lot* of room at ground level, there was just enough that he wasn't going to go tumbling down the bluffs if he lost his grip.

Getting his feet under him, he quickly moved out of the way, as Brannigan's go bag came through the opening. Flanagan caught it and pulled it out of the way, as the colonel grabbed the frame at the top of the window, levered his legs through, and slid out, more gracefully than Flanagan had, though he had to shift and twist his body to get his shoulders through the opening. He dropped to the ground just as a splintering crash announced that the door, the doorjamb, and the chair had just failed.

Flanagan handed the colonel his go bag, and then they were moving, quickly clambering down the rocky bluff toward the ocean below. They got only a couple of yards before Brannigan halted, and Flanagan followed suit, clinging to the cliff and trying to go absolutely still.

Voices were raised in the room above them, though the wind was coming in off the Caribbean strongly enough that he couldn't hear much more than that. They sounded angry, though, probably because they had expected their quarry to be in the room.

The seconds stretched by, Flanagan's arms and hands starting to burn as he clung to the rocks, hoping that they didn't come around to look outside. When he craned his neck to look up, he couldn't see the window from his hiding place, which meant that the soldiers in their room would have to come out onto the narrow ledge outside to see where the two Blackhearts were hanging.

The voices retreated, and with a faint sigh, Brannigan started climbing down again. Flanagan followed. There was no going back to the room, not now.

Just how screwed the mission was still remained to be seen.

**

They found a small, sheltered spot on the shoreline, several miles away, and hunkered down, wedged into the rocks and soaked with spray. It hadn't been the worst movement along the shore, though they had both been soaked to the bone in short order. There were beaches on the northeastern shore, but they were narrow and few. Most of the time they'd been picking their way through the rocks and the surf.

57

"Well, I think we can safely assume that Carlo and Vinnie were arrested." Brannigan had been thinking it through as he and Flanagan had made their escape. "They wouldn't have hit the hotel if they weren't sure they were going to get all four of us."

"Question is, where will they take them?" Flanagan unsuccessfully tried to wring some of the salt water out of his shirt. At least it wasn't cold. "Straight to the target?"

"Maybe." Brannigan hoped not, despite all the talk before they'd left about the possibility of getting infiltrators into the prison to link up with Hierro in the event this reconnaissance went south. Without any way of communicating with Santelli and Bianco, if they *were* in the max security prison on the military base, that infiltration would be of limited utility. "We did pinpoint a couple of security bases within the city. I suspect that they'd be taken there first."

"Unless they figure they're CIA, in which case they'll probably take them straight to the base." Flanagan wasn't going to be too optimistic about it. A moment later, though, he was digging in his pack.

"What?" Brannigan knew what the dawning of an idea looked like.

"I brought a scanner. Little one." Flanagan pulled a small waterproof case out of the bag and popped it open, revealing a small radio. "No guarantees that they're on an uncovered channel, but given what I've seen so far, I wouldn't bet against it, either." He frowned. "My Spanish ain't great, but I've been working on it since we've done a few jobs in Latin America."

Brannigan nodded. It was good thinking. If the local army thought they'd captured a couple of spies, then there would probably be a lot of radio chatter about it. While the local military had the city as locked down as any he'd ever seen, they still didn't act like the most professional force in the world. They were bullies in uniforms and carrying guns, for the most part.

Flanagan pulled out a small earpiece, plugged it into the scanner, and started to listen. After only a few moments, he looked up with a cocked eyebrow. "Jackpot." He frowned. "Yeah, they're all talking about it, all right. Seems like Vinnie and Carlo are *the* subject on the net right now." Brannigan scanned the waves as Flanagan listened. This would be a hell of a time to have a patrol boat—or one of the pirate boats, for that matter—come drifting by. The timing had not been to their advantage. Sunset wasn't for hours yet.

"Boy, these guys are like high school girls." Flanagan shook his head. "They've even got a few of their superiors telling them to shut up and get off the net, but they're still chattering away."

"Anything useful?"

He shook his head again. "Not yet." Flanagan raised a finger. "Wait a second."

Brannigan held his peace as the other man continued to listen, pulling out a waterproof notebook and starting to scribble notes. It couldn't be an easy task, trying to not only pick out useful information from the chatter, but translating it as well.

It was a long wait, Flanagan no longer commenting as he became absorbed in his work. Brannigan set to watching and listening, holding security as best he could by himself, without a weapon besides the rocks he could pick up and the non-metallic knife on his belt. They all had some of those, and he winced a little as he thought about the consequences Bianco and Santelli were likely facing for being caught with them. He didn't doubt they'd been searched thoroughly, and that would have produced the satellite phones and the knives.

Finally, after probably a couple of hours, Flanagan powered down the scanner and re-stowed it. "Okay, I *think* I've got it figured out. There's some guesswork involved, but from what I can gather, it sounds like they've taken them to the Hector Ospina Station. I think it's named after one of the founders of the junta, or something." Again, the lack of available information was telling on them.

Fortunately, while it wasn't terribly informative at the best of times, they did have a tourist map of the city, provided by the resort. It didn't cover the military base—in fact, that was a completely blank spot on the map—but it did highlight the three "*Estaciónes de Seguridad de la Policía Militar*," including the Hector Ospina station.

"Anything about whether they think they'll move them anytime soon?" Brannigan was preparing to move. They didn't want to stay in one place very long, considering he was sure the locals had a dragnet out for them, and they needed to get to the border quickly to link up with the rest of the team if they were going to have any chance of getting the other two out before the hit on the maximum security prison became a much more major rescue operation.

"Nothing that I can pick out." Flanagan shouldered his pack again. "The gist seems to be that they're in for it, though. Something about a Commandant Espino. Sounds like he's a hardass and sort of the go-to guy for big-time 'enemies of the state.'"

"Great." Time really was wasting. "So, we need to get those guys out as quickly as possible."

"Absolutely." Flanagan looked out to sea. "Thing is, that means we've got to get around to the other side of the city to get to the border and make rendezvous. How do you want to do it? Carjack, or boat hijack?"

Brannigan rubbed his chin, the salt adding to the sandpaper feel of two days' worth of stubble. "A carjack is going to attract more attention, and I wouldn't put it past the locals to be on the alert for it. They know we're on foot, so they've got to suspect that we're going to make a break for it." He looked toward the water. "There should be a fishing village somewhere farther along the coast. We'll leave some cash for the fisherman, but we've probably got a better chance of evading them at sea than on land."

Flanagan nodded, then turned to start up the little cleft in the rocks toward higher ground where they could move faster. Brannigan followed, hoping that Bianco and Santelli could hold out.

CHAPTER 10

Vincent Bianco sat in the windowless, darkened room, trying to keep his heart rate from skyrocketing so much that it pounded out of his chest.

He knew he was in trouble. That had been obvious as soon as those soldiers had cut them off on the street, but as soon as they'd found the satellite phone and, worse, the polymer knife, things had really gotten serious.

Now he was sitting handcuffed to a steel chair, facing a blank concrete wall with a single, naked light bulb above his head, his back to the steel door. It was cold in that room, especially since he'd been stripped to his shorts. It seemed weird to be that cold, given the heat outside, but he honestly wasn't sure if he was even above ground anymore.

The place smelled like cigarette smoke, sweat, and fear.

For that matter, he wasn't sure what time it was, either. He hadn't seen the outside since he'd been hauled in here, and they hadn't ever turned the lights out. He'd been moved from cell to cell over what felt like hours, but probably wasn't nearly as long as it was supposed to seem.

Bianco hadn't been a special operator like some of his companions. He'd been an infantry machinegunner with a talent for some other skills beyond that, and he'd done some time as a contractor after getting out. That meant he hadn't ever been to

SERE school, never had the formal training in resisting interrogation.

That had him scared. He couldn't expect any sort of humane treatment from these people. He knew enough about Latin American military governments to know that. And while he knew there was some common sense involved in resistance, that plenty of men had stood up to torture before without breaking, he really wished he'd had some more training at that point, and what's more, that he had some way to ask for help.

He hadn't seen Santelli since they'd been arrested. He knew that was deliberate, but he couldn't help the despair that threatened to overwhelm him. He'd spent a lot of time by himself, working on role playing game design, but that was entirely different to being entirely, desperately alone, locked in with men who would probably kill him out of hand if they found a reason to do so.

Not only that, but he also had no way to know if Brannigan and Flanagan had gotten away. If they'd been sleeping, there was a good chance that they'd been caught by surprise. The longer his captivity had gone on, the more convinced he became that they'd been compromised from the beginning, and that they'd only managed to get as far as they had because the local army had been setting them up, waiting until they had everything in position to capture the entire team in one fell swoop.

A small, distant voice in his mind told him that he was making leaps of despair based on incomplete information, but he was tired, he was hungry, he was cold, and most importantly, he was scared, and his conscious mind didn't want to listen.

So, he was not in the best frame of mind when the door finally opened behind him.

Footsteps rang on the concrete, though they were drowned out a moment later by the screech of metal chair legs on the cement floor.

Bianco kept his eyes on the floor as the brightly polished boots stepped around in front of him, and the chair was picked up and set down with a *bang*. He didn't want to look at the man. He

62

knew it was wishful thinking, but somehow it felt like if he just didn't look up, maybe this wouldn't start right away.

A vicious jab hit him in the ribs. It felt like a pipe or a truncheon, and it hurt like hell. He jerked, though the cuffs holding him to the chair kept him from going very far. The chair was also bolted to the floor, so it was unyielding.

"Look at me, Señor Bianco." The voice was calm and almost gentle. That was something of a surprise, but it only made Bianco's guts knot up even more. This was *not* going to be good. "You are not going to delay the inevitable by simply trying to act as if it has not come to your door."

Slowly, reluctantly, Bianco lifted his head until he was looking at the man. Rail thin, hawk-faced, with his hair slicked back and a thick, Saddam Hussein mustache, the man's uniform was impeccable, starched and creased, with gold shoulder boards. He was leaning back in his chair, a cigarette between his fingers as he studied Bianco.

Not only was he scared, but he felt exposed and disheveled sitting in front of this well-groomed interrogator. While he knew, deep down, that he wasn't the bad guy here, he couldn't help but feel like a kid called on the carpet, feel that he was in trouble for doing something very bad.

A part of him recognized that most of this was in his head, and that the treatment he'd received so far had been calculated to isolate him, break him down, and get him too far into his own thoughts. Even recognizing that, though, he wasn't in much shape to do anything about it.

The man took a drag off the cigarette. "You are not in a good position, Señor Bianco. The weapon found in your possession is a very serious matter in the first place." He tilted his head as he watched Bianco with heavy-lidded eyes. "This is not the United States. You do not have the right to ignore our laws simply because you come from a wealthy country that flaunts its power all over the globe. This is *our* country, no matter how poor and tiny it may seem to you. *Our* laws preserve order here. And we do not allow just anyone to walk around our nation with weapons. You would be in a great deal of trouble because of that, alone."

He nodded to someone behind Bianco, and a small table was brought around and placed forcefully on the floor next to the two of them. The satellite phone was placed on the table and the soldier who'd brought it in stepped back out of sight. Bianco felt his shoulders hunch as he began to expect another blow, knowing already what that phone probably meant to them.

"That is not all, however." The man blew a small cloud of cigarette smoke toward Bianco, then pointed the cancer stick at the phone on the table. "What kind of regular American carries a satellite phone, hmm?" He leaned forward. "You are a CIA spy."

Despite the desperation of his position, Bianco suddenly felt the urge to relax, even to laugh. "That's ridiculous." He hadn't ever worked for the CIA. Even if some of the intel that had led to a few of their jobs might have originally come from the Agency, as far as he knew, even General Van Zandt and General Abernathy had no direct ties to the CIA.

Under the circumstances, he was being more professional about the situation than he might have otherwise expected. He had found the loophole, however technical, to deny their accusations.

The blow to the back of his head shattered his brief moment of self-congratulation. It wasn't all that hard, but it was hard enough to knock him forward a few inches and rattle his teeth, since he hadn't been ready for it. He suddenly felt sick, knowing that there wasn't any game or evasion he could use that these guys would accept.

His interrogator simply looked bored as Bianco looked up at him again. "Did you really think we would not expect such a denial? Not only your equipment but your very presence here, at this time, condemns you."

"What time is that?" He wondered if maybe he could get a little intel. It was useless, he knew, since no one knew where he was, and he had no way to communicate, but he clung to the possibility out of the need for some way to fight back, something that was otherwise denied him by the handcuffs and the chair.

It only earned him two more blows, one to the ear. "We ask the questions here, Señor Bianco. Not you. What did the CIA send you here to do?" The man stood, his cigarette still in his hand, and loomed over Bianco. "We know that your government seeks our destruction, simply because we do not bow to their whims."

"I told you, I don't work for the CIA, and I never have."

The interrogator only looked disappointed, then stepped back and motioned to someone behind Bianco.

Then the beating really began.

CHAPTER 11

Santelli was more comfortable than Bianco, at least physically, but that somehow made this worse.

He was still fully clothed, though he was handcuffed, and his own knife and satellite phone were sitting on the table in front of him, just out of reach. The interrogator stood against the wall to his right, smoking while he was forced to watch the scene on the TV in front of him.

The feed was grainy and the sound tinny, but that was to be expected of a CCTV feed that was still using a TV that had to be close to fifty years old. In some ways, it was a blessing, because it allowed him to distance himself somewhat from what he was being forced to watch.

Vinnie Bianco was slumped in the chair now, while the two guards continued to go at him with batons. They were being careful, more careful than Santelli would have expected in a Third World military government like this. They hadn't hit Bianco in the head more than a couple of times, venting most of their fury on his arms, torso, and legs.

The kid was tough. The last two times they'd let up with the beating for the interrogator to ask him questions, he'd stuck with his story, that he'd never worked for the CIA and that he had no idea what they were asking about. The knife was because he was worried about crime. The satellite phone was because he and his dad had some money and wanted to stay in touch back home.

It was only a matter of time before he cracked. Everybody cracked eventually, under enough pressure. Santelli didn't think that Bianco would anytime soon, but if they didn't get out of this hellhole in a timely manner, he might give into despair. He'd already looked pretty rough when they'd first turned on the feed, giving Santelli a good view of his fellow Blackheart before the interrogator had even showed up.

The pressure on Santelli himself was a little different from what they were applying to Bianco, and that was why he refused to look at his own interrogator while the man stood there and smoked.

There was a reason why they were beating Bianco and making Santelli watch. These guys were a little more sophisticated than their initial intelligence had suggested, though that was a sophistication that Santelli refused to respect. It was the sophistication of the Gestapo or the KGB. They had learned, through a couple of generations of rule by iron fist, how to break people.

They were counting on Santelli's loyalty to Bianco to break him. They could beat Bianco half to death, and he might or might not crack. Pain had varying effects on people. In fact, if they really believed that Bianco was CIA, they might also believe that he had special training to enable him to withstand this sort of interrogation.

In Santelli's experience, that was only in the movies, but these savages didn't know that.

So, torture might or might not work on Bianco, but they might have much better luck leveraging his suffering against Santelli.

And, Heaven help him, it was working.

The interrogator on the screen signaled again, and the two soldiers stepped back from Bianco, their chests heaving. They'd been putting in some work. Vinnie's head hung nearly to his chest, though from what little Santelli could see, he was more huddled against the blows than he was close to unconsciousness. They really had been careful about hitting him in the head. They didn't want him that damaged. Not yet.

Santelli's own interrogator shoved away from the wall, walked over to the TV, and shut it off. He crushed the butt of his cigarette out in an ashtray on the metal table in front of Santelli, then lit a second. There was already a faint haze of cheap tobacco smoke in the air.

This close to Cuba and they can't even get the good stuff.

"This can all end, Señor Santelli. Your young friend—or son, if we are to believe your story—need not suffer much more. All you need to do is confess your role in this plot, tell me where your CIA's contacts in Costa de las Joyas are, and tell me where your other two companions have gone. The beatings will end."

"And then what?" Santelli looked up at the fat, jowly man in the sweaty uniform. He'd drawn a much more slovenly interrogator than Bianco, from the looks of things. "You'll shoot us in the back of the head rather than torture us to death?"

The man didn't look like the words had fazed him in the slightest. He just took another drag on the cigarette. "You should have known the penalty for spying before you came here. Have you Americans gotten so arrogant in your wealth and detachment that you think you are somehow exempt from the way the world works?"

It wasn't so much that Santelli thought there was anything else in store for them if this proceeded to its logical conclusion. He hated to think of it, hated to think of Melissa and the kids wondering what had happened to him, or worse, seeing his execution posted on the internet. So far, there didn't seem to be a *lot* of high tech in this speck of a country, but there were still cell phones, which meant there was still internet, and he didn't doubt that the junta had access. At the very least, it would be on national television, and it would make its way back to the States.

No, it wasn't that he was shocked or even that he was especially scared. He was worried for his wife and kids, but that was a distant worry. In fact, he found that he was remarkably

69

detached, the only real emotion remaining being a fear that he was going to let Vinnie Bianco down.

In a way, he felt like he already had, since he was in here watching while Vinnie was in a cell somewhere else in the building getting the snot beaten out of him.

"You're barking up the wrong tree, man." He didn't know if the man would understand the colloquialism, and he was actually pretty sure he wasn't going to believe it, but he had to play the role. It felt wrong, somehow. He knew that they were going to keep beating on Bianco as long as he maintained their innocence, possibly even bring out the heavier stuff, the car batteries and whatever else, but if he admitted that they were there to spy, let alone break out Ernesto Hierro to overthrow the military government, then it wouldn't lighten things up for his friend at all. It would only get worse from there.

He had to keep things on an even keel as long as possible. He hadn't been able to get word to the rest of the team where they'd been taken, but he had to trust that Brannigan and Flanagan would find a way to get to them. The fact that they hadn't been included in this little interrogation drama told him that they must have gotten clear. He was pretty sure that if they had been rolled up, the interrogators wouldn't have missed mentioning it.

A part of that was just hopeful thinking, but in this position, he needed to hold onto every thread of hope he could find.

"We're just tourists."

The fat man in the sweaty uniform didn't look impressed at his denial. "So you say. And I am sure that you were carefully coached to say that, and that you will say it for some time. But we will get to the truth, eventually. We already know who sent you. Once you can no longer stand what we are going to do to your friend, then you will speak to me, and we will uncover all of this plot."

Santelli fought desperately to keep his expression blank as the two bully boys on the screen started to work Bianco over again.

70

Keep the faith, Vinnie. Hang in there.
Hurry up, boys, we can't hold out forever.

CHAPTER 12

Dan Tackett was getting a bad feeling about this job.

It wasn't that he regretted signing on with the Blackhearts on a more regular basis. These guys were pros, and he felt at home with them in a way that he hadn't in a very long time. He'd had a long conversation with Cassie about it. More than one, actually. She'd urged him to go out on the mission to rescue Vernon, Max, and Mitchell Price, and she'd been the one who had finally gotten him to see that he needed to still keep his hand in, especially as they'd found out about the Humanity Front's role in not only that mission, but a whole lot of nefarious plots around the world.

It went deeper than that, though, and she'd recognized it before he had. He hated, on some level, to think that he was closer to Cassie than he had ever been to Julie. It felt like a betrayal of his late wife. But he and Cassie had been through hell together in the Anambas, and she knew things that Julie had only ever guessed at.

No, he couldn't just walk away from the work. He couldn't walk away from this team, not after what they'd been through together in Kyrgyzstan and Prague. He needed to stick with this. And Cassie had told him as much. As much as they loved each other, as much as she worried when he was gone, she knew that, despite the hell that those jungles had been, he'd been the most alive he'd been in years while he had fought his way through pirates and Chinese commandos to get them out.

No, it wasn't the Blackhearts that had him worried. It was the job itself.

He could tell that Brannigan and most of the others had the same misgivings. There were too many unknowns, especially about their objective. Tackett had mostly worked the Middle East and Central Asia, prior to the Anambas contract, but he'd grown up reading everything he could find on the Cold War and narco war special operations in Latin America. Back then, South America was *the* place where the action was. So, he knew a thing or two about the atmospherics down here.

And he knew that the opposition to a military dictatorship in Latin America was usually either narcos, Communists, or both. That there was no information on this Hierro's affiliations was worrisome.

But he knew he wasn't alone in that, and he'd seen enough to trust Brannigan's judgement. The colonel was keeping his cards close to the vest, but Tackett figured that he was already planning how to turn this around if it turned out to be a bait and switch.

Unfortunately, things had already gone south, and that was adding to the sense of disquiet weighing on Tackett's mind.

He was currently sitting underneath a wind-twisted tree on the beach, watching the water, waiting on the boat that was bringing Brannigan and Flanagan from Costa de las Joyas into Colombia. The two men had managed to get a call through via satphone while they'd steered well out into the Caribbean to avoid the Costas' patrol boats and pirate vessels. The beach was too soft for the trucks they'd gotten from Javier, so Tackett had gone down to make contact and bring the two of them up to the rendezvous.

He squinted into the dark, wishing—not for the first or last time—that Javier's cache had included some night vision. Even a set of ancient PVS-7Bs, as much as he hated them, would have been helpful, even if only for a brief scan every now and then. Instead, he was stuck watching the night with only as much night adaptation as he could naturally develop.

There. He could hear the putter of an outboard, and after a moment a faint wake showed in the dark, the white water around the boat almost glowing in the starlight. He lifted a small red lens light and blinked it once. When he got a double blink in response from out on the water, he followed up with three, then got on his radio. "This is Shy." He hated the callsign, but Curtis had insisted on it since he'd been a little reluctant to go all the way with the Blackhearts initially, and Tackett had been around long enough that he knew better than to fight it. That would only make it far worse. "I have eyes on. Five minutes."

He got two clicks in response. Wade was still running the team in Colombia, and he was a stickler for a few things. Now that they were geared up and in mission mode, he wasn't going to do a lot of talking. Tackett could appreciate that, just like he appreciated Flanagan's sparing use of words. He'd never been much for talking, even when he'd been in charge following the complete collapse of the op in the Anambas.

The boat came hissing into shore, scraping on the beach. It would have fit in among any number of Third World fishing fleets. A simple wooden boat with a rattling old outboard, it had been painted at some point, but the paint was peeling off where it wasn't completely gone.

Flanagan was in the bow and quickly jumped out before the boat was all the way on the sand, dragging it higher up the beach as Tackett came down to help, the duffel he'd brought to the shore over one shoulder. Brannigan stayed at the outboard for a moment before he, too, jumped into the water and waded ashore.

"Don't pull it too high. Let the tide float it off." He moved up next to Tackett and shook his hand. "Good to see you, Dan. Things were getting dicey. You got some gear for us in that bag?"

Tackett nodded as he started back toward the tree. "Yeah. Guns and chest rigs, anyway. The rest of the stuff is at the trucks."

"Good thinking. Let's go."

They made their way up the strand toward the dark shapes of the vehicles. Wade had the rest of the Blackhearts, except for

Kirk and Burgess, who were driving, on security in a perimeter around them.

Wade came out to meet them and there was another brief exchange of handshakes before Brannigan got down to business. "Let's get geared up, then I want everybody in the back of one of those trucks." He looked up at the canvas-covered five-ton. "We've got a brief to give and some planning to do, and then we've got to move fast. I don't want to leave those boys to get worked over any longer than absolutely necessary."

CHAPTER 13

Getting across the border wasn't as simple as just hiking in through the desert. The military junta that ran Costa de las Joyas was paranoid as hell, and the border with Colombia was heavily lined with razor wire and minefields, with two checkpoints heavily manned by armed Costa de las Joyas soldiers being the only way in without a lot of mine clearing and wire cutting. There were also gun trucks that patrolled the line regularly.

Despite the fact that Colombia apparently couldn't have cared less about Costa de las Joyas, since they had made no more than one attempt to retake the small portion of the peninsula since independence, the junta was determined to be ready for an attack at any time.

Tyranny not only leads to suffering for those subject to it, it leads to paranoia for the tyrants.

Running the checkpoint was probably not going to work out well and would almost immediately result in a warning being transmitted to Santa Paz. Brannigan's and Flanagan's reconnaissance of the Fortaleza Generalissimo Marto had confirmed that the locals did, indeed, use the same old Ford five ton trucks, but they had no identification, not enough of them spoke Spanish—and Gomez didn't speak Colombian Spanish—and they weren't in National Army uniforms. There might have still been a chance to bluff their way through if they'd had the uniforms and the language, but not as it was, not wearing old-school woodland camouflage when the locals wore plain green.

So, they parked the trucks just over a low hill covered in scrubby woods, and now they were moving in on the checkpoint.

Burgess prided himself somewhat on being one of those mercs who could make do with just about anything. He'd been a SEAL, back in the day, with access to the best and the most high-speed gear, but those days were long behind him, with a lot of contracting on the wrong side of the tracks between then and now. He'd worked on a shoestring in Africa too many times to count, and he'd developed the bushcraft skills to compensate for the lack of technological edge.

That didn't mean he wasn't currently wishing for some NVGs, at the very least.

It was just after one in the morning, and he was slipping through the scrub as quietly as he could, keeping to the shadows and careful not to look directly at the lights that the Costas had shining on the narrow road that was one of two land approaches from Colombia. His Galil was held in his hands at about waist level, and he'd carefully bound up every loose end and piece of gear in the load bearing vest he was wearing to avoid rattles or even to keep any of the straps from catching on the underbrush.

While this wasn't the first time they'd had to make do with less than perfect gear, it was the first time they'd had to deal with a minefield.

He knew—they all knew—that time was short for Vinnie and Carlo. Burgess remembered a few situations very much like this, including a hunt through suburbia for where the Humanity Front's particularly ruthless contractors had taken a paraplegic Sam Childress. The difference here was, they couldn't rush. This had to be done right.

There were right and wrong ways to clear a minefield. The right way involved metal detectors, probes, and, ideally, a robot, at least for the more methodical methods. For speed, the M58 MICLIC, basically a rocket-launched explosive rope, also did a good job, though it was considerably louder.

The Blackhearts had none of those options. So, Gomez was leading this element toward the checkpoint, his rifle slung across his back as he crawled forward on hands and knees, a knife in his hand that he thrust into the ground ever few feet, probing for mines.

He'd found several already, and they'd been exposed enough that Burgess had started to hope that the locals had been sloppy, which would allow them to get up to the wire that much faster. Approaching the checkpoint along the road would not be a good idea, especially as those floodlights covered almost a hundred yards, and there were no curves to hide behind until they were right on top of it. Even if they'd come in guns blazing, the sandbagged machineguns would have torn at least the lead vehicle apart.

There was no way to be sure, though, and getting careless in a minefield was a good way to get everybody dead.

Burgess turned toward the checkpoint, still keeping it in the corner of his eye, taking in the movement of the guards through his peripheral vision, trying to keep his dark adaptation as intact as he could. They were moving about, but there was nothing in their manner that suggested they'd heard or seen anything to alert them. They were still good.

They just had to get through in time to get to Santa Paz and the Hector Ospina police station before things really went south, and the Costas decided to move Santelli and Bianco.

Gomez froze, and if Burgess hadn't been paused on the balls of his feet, he might not have heard the faint *clink* of the other Blackheart's knife point finding another mine. Burgess took stock as Gomez very carefully started to uncover the explosive device, preparatory to moving it out of the way. They didn't have the tools to disarm the mines, but fortunately so far, they appeared to have been simply armed and partially buried. The National Army's soldiers weren't particularly cunning or resourceful about keeping their minefields tamper-proof.

From what Burgess could remember, though it was a little hazy in the dark thanks to the lack of night vision and therefore

79

the corresponding lack of visible detail, they'd already cleared through almost half a dozen mines in the last hundred yards. The mines weren't actually all that close together. In some ways, that was smart, as it made it less likely that they'd chain-fire if one of them went off. It also left some significant gaps, and they'd already penetrated much closer to the wire, which he could just make out glinting in the starlight ahead of him, than he suspected the junta had intended.

Maybe they'd counted on the first mine making an invader think twice. Maybe they just didn't have enough mines—it wasn't as if this flyspeck of a country could afford to buy that much in the way of munitions—and so they'd spread them out as best they could.

He hoped so. That would lessen the chance that Gomez might miss one, or worse, he'd find them all and then either Burgess, Kirk, or Puller strayed a little too far to the right or the left and hit one that he *hadn't* found.

Gomez, having uncovered the mine, very gingerly felt around it, just to make sure *this* one wasn't the one that had a tripwire attached to it or a grenade buried underneath it. That was an old, old trick, to pull the pin on a grenade then place it in a hole underneath a mine or other explosive, so that the weight of the mine was holding the spoon in place.

Burgess doubted the locals would have bothered with that on a minefield that stretched for miles along their border with Colombia, but it paid to be cautious.

Slowly, cautiously, Gomez lifted the mine out of the hole, placing it off to one side, off their path. The mines might be scattered widely enough that they could have gone around it, but they didn't know that, and rolling the dice on it right now wouldn't be a good idea.

With that one cleared, Gomez resumed his advance, crawling ahead inch by inch, probing with his knife, while the other three Blackhearts behind him followed, staying low, either crawling or duck walking to avoid showing too much of a silhouette against the light-colored, sandy earth.

They were almost across the cleared minefield. The wire glinted just ahead in the starlight and the splash of reflected light from the checkpoint. They were almost to the decision point.

Burgess wanted to check his watch, but there was no way the Indiglo wasn't going to be spotted, even if the soldiers on the checkpoint had completely destroyed their night vision with the spotlights, and didn't think there was anyone coming, anyway. They were still relaxed, and Burgess could faintly hear their chatter in the distance, over the rumble of a small generator that was keeping those lights on.

Ideally, this would have been carefully timed, without the need for radios. But they were in too much of a hurry, and there simply hadn't been time to rehearse it, let alone gather the intel on the minefield. If this attack was going to be as coordinated as it needed to be, then they *had* to use the radios.

So, when Gomez finally reached the wire, sheathed his knife, and brought his Galil around to his front, rising up onto a knee next to the triple-strand razor wire, Burgess lifted the radio to his lips. "This is Tomahawk. In position." He had already sacrificed his night adaptation as he scanned the checkpoint, picking his target.

CHAPTER 14

Curtis heard the call from Burgess and settled in a little more securely behind his K3. He didn't remember if he'd ever specifically used a Daewoo K3 before, though as soon as he'd handled it, he'd known it wouldn't matter. He could run this gun in his sleep.

After all, it was basically a South Korean version of the FN Minimi, which Curtis had come to know intimately as the M249 SAW.

Making sure that his belt was straight and clear, he leaned into the gun, loading the bipods as he lay in the prone on the side of the road, just far enough out from the checkpoint that the spotlights couldn't reach him. On the other side, Hank Brannigan was behind the second K3, handling it until they could get Vinnie Bianco out to take over.

Curtis tried not to think about the possibility that Vinnie might not be able to take the reins as the team's second machinegunner. Even if he wasn't dead, it was possible that the locals had tortured him so badly that he wouldn't be able to do much of anything.

He *really* didn't want to think about it. Curtis had been to hell and back plenty of times, but he wasn't the kind of man to dwell on the bad stuff. Not if he could help it. It wasn't so much that he was tough; he just blanked out the stuff he didn't want to deal with.

It still snuck in sometimes, try as he might to keep it out. Those were generally the nights that he went down to the Strip and got hammered. Even being married now, it still happened sometimes, even though he knew it was stupidly dangerous, given his wife's familial connection with organized crime in Vegas, organized crime that was *not* happy that she'd run off with a black guy.

It was trying to sneak in now, even as he picked his own targets on the checkpoint. The machineguns were a last resort, in case the other Blackhearts hadn't been able to eliminate the entire guard force in seconds. Automatic fire was good for suppressing but there were concerns that extended bursts might be heard farther away and draw more attention.

Curtis wasn't convinced of the logic. He could cut that sloppy idiot behind the left-hand machinegun in half in a heartbeat. But it wasn't his call.

He still flipped the safety off and rested his finger on the trigger as he settled his body, his natural point of aim putting the front sight post right on the soldier's chest...

***

Flanagan was sweating bullets, and not just because it was hot and humid, even at one in the morning. He'd been picking the way through the minefield toward the wire on the other side of the checkpoint, and the strain had been terrific. He was generally a quiet man who enjoyed the backwoods and didn't back down from hard living, but playing with explosives was not his idea of a good time, *especially* when they'd been placed by a bunch of Third World soldiers who may or may not have known what they were doing.

He'd heard Burgess's radio call. It was almost time. He got down on his belly on the sandy ground, not before checking carefully that he wasn't about to put a knee or a foot on a mine, and searched out a target.

The checkpoint wasn't particularly fancy. A tent was partially surrounded by sandbags, set back from another pair of sandbag walls where the machineguns were mounted. Those emplacements flanked the drop arm that blocked the only way through the wire and the mines.

They'd counted six soldiers on the checkpoint during the brief time they'd had to observe from the road. Flanagan, Tackett, Wade, and Brannigan were currently much closer to that road than Burgess and his element, for a couple of reasons. Not the least being that they couldn't be sure there weren't more soldiers in the tent, and so they would need to rush in and make sure the entire checkpoint was clear, once the six who were lounging around the swing arm, smoking and talking, were eliminated.

Fortunately, neither of the machineguns, more of the old M1919s from the looks of them, were quite what Flanagan would call "manned." Their crews were standing near the emplacements, but neither were behind them, and one of the old Brownings had its muzzle pointed at the sky, the T&E not attached to the tripod. The checkpoint unit was in no way, shape, or form ready for what was about to happen.

He settled his front sight on the rightmost soldier and whispered, "On target."

Brannigan was behind him, his radio to his lips. That took a gun out of the fight, but somebody had to coordinate this shot.

"Execute, execute, execute."

Flanagan's trigger broke about halfway through the second "execute." The Galil bucked in his shoulder and barked, the unsuppressed muzzle flash bright in the night, but he was in the prone and in a good shooting position, and his target was barely thirty yards away.

The soldier dropped out of sight, though Flanagan was already sure of the shot. The other five were all down as his vision cleared from the muzzle flash, a couple of them still thrashing and moaning, the bullets having missed killing them outright. Another that he could see was still twitching.

Flanagan stayed in place for a moment, just in case, then, with a look over his shoulder to make sure he wasn't about to stand up into another Blackheart's field of fire, he got his feet under him and stood, just as Tackett did the same to his left. Brannigan was already up behind them both, though in the middle of the minefield, going around wasn't a great idea. Flanagan had worked his way back toward the ditch by the road, finding a small bit of cover, so he could get to the road itself quickly, but without following him exactly, movement would be extremely dangerous.

Of course, there was still a chance that he was about to step on a mine he hadn't spotted anyway, but they needed to get in and clear that tent, fast. There could be no radio calls from this checkpoint.

He took the last few steps at a run, almost leaping across the ditch, just in case, and hit the road without blowing up. If he hadn't been so focused on his target, he might have breathed a sigh of relief.

Weapon up, his eyes just above the sights, he sprinted for the tent.

The temptation was there to just bull his way in and clear it, but he'd been in too many fights in too many combat zones. He pivoted first right, then left as he cleared the sandbagged machinegun positions, just before ducking underneath the swing arm. Two of the moaning wounded men had gone silent. The twitching had stopped. And there were no others on the other side of the sandbags, out of sight when the shooting had started and sitting there waiting in ambush.

Tackett and Brannigan had caught up with him, and now he could hear the clatter of a machinegun belt knocking against the receiver of a K3 as Curtis, Hank, or both came running up from their positions farther back on the road. He ignored the noise, trusting to Brannigan to watch his back, as he moved toward the tent, Galil at the ready.

A figure appeared in the tent opening, venturing a sleepy-sounding, if still scared, question. Flanagan didn't give him the chance to react, but simply dropped him with a quick pair. The figure vanished inside the tent, the flashlight dropping next to him, which was when Flanagan realized that it had been zip-tied to an old FAL.

His advance turned into a run. He'd known men who could accurately engage while at a dead sprint, but he knew he wasn't one of them. Still, he needed to get to that tent before anyone else at the checkpoint got on the radio.

Slowing sharply at the entrance, just before reaching the still-twitching body, he forced his breathing to slow as he pied off the opening.

There was no one else in the tent. A couple of cots, a card table—with cards and ashtrays on it, as well as the radio—and some ammo crates that they must have been using as chairs. That was it.

He lowered the rifle, even as he heard Tackett moving around the back, just to make sure there weren't any squirters. "Clear."

Brannigan was already lifting the swing arm. "If there weren't six more sleeping in the tent, then we have to assume they have a relief coming."

"They'll know something's up as soon as the relief gets here and finds the bodies." Hank had set up on one of the machinegun positions, his K3 aimed up the road toward Santa Paz, leaning on the sandbags.

"Can't help it." Flanagan squatted down and picked up his target's FAL, switching off the flashlight. They might want to keep the weapons, just in case. It looked like the junta's soldiers were all using the older 7.62 battle rifles instead of the 5.56 Galils. "Though we might be able to pull the bodies off into the bush, keep them guessing for a little bit. Kick some dirt over the blood pools."

Brannigan thought it over, even as Burgess, Gomez, Kirk, and Puller came out of the dark along the line of the wire, still moving carefully as Gomez probed for mines. "Not sure we have the time. It might be easier to just ambush the relief if we catch them coming out." He checked his watch. "Depending on watch schedules, they could be getting here any minute, or not for another four hours. No way to tell."

"The more we hit 'em, the more likely somebody's going to get a message off." Wade might have been the least likely to be the voice of caution, at least at first glance, but despite his temper, the man was a professional, and he'd been a senior NCO before he'd retired. He knew his business and he knew how these things went. "I don't think we should be over-complicating things. Besides, if we wait to ambush the relief trucks, just in case they find the bodies and alert people, that's going to be, potentially, another several hours that Vinnie and Carlo are getting worked over."

"If we cross paths with them, we'll see if we can stop them." Brannigan was apparently no more interested in wasting time than Wade. "Let's get the bodies out of the light, at least. Wade, Tackett, head back and get the trucks."

Wade waved a hand and turned to jog back down the road into Colombia. Tackett showed even less reaction, but just disappeared into the shadows.

Curtis looked down at Hank. "You know Vinnie's *going* to take that belt-fed. Don't get too attached."

Hank started to say something as Flanagan glanced over, but then he clamped his mouth shut. It didn't take a genius to figure out what had been on his mind. It was on all their minds.

That's going to depend on what kind of shape Vinnie is when we get him out.

If *we get him out.* Flanagan shoved that thought out of his mind. Despairing of accomplishing the objective was a good way to sabotage the op before it ever really got started.

Reaching down, he grabbed the body of the man he'd shot and started to drag it toward the road and the scrub on the Colombian side of the border. There was still a lot to do before they could move on.

CHAPTER 15

Wade hadn't driven a five-ton in a long time, and the Colombian truck was older than he was. It rattled and creaked alarmingly, and he couldn't help but wince at every *bang* as the tires hit a dip in the unimproved road, which had, if anything, only gotten worse since they'd entered Costa de las Joyas. Clearly, the locals didn't put maintenance high on any priorities.

Not that he found that particularly surprising. Hell, the roads in parts of the *US* were awful. In a Third World country with a military dictatorship, they were bound to be worse.

The noise only added to his discomfort. Without NVGs, they were driving on white light, and he felt like they were announcing their presence to the entire country. He was still slightly shocked that they hadn't drawn a quick reaction force like a disturbed hornet's nest as soon as they'd dumped the guards at the checkpoint. The gunfire had echoed across the scrubby desert for what felt like miles.

There hadn't been an immediate response, though, which told him a couple of things. One, gunfire wasn't all that uncommon here, and two, the guards really hadn't gotten to the radio before they'd all been dead or dying.

That still didn't make it any better that he was rattling down the road with headlights blazing in front of them. Somebody was going to notice.

So, when he spotted another pair of headlights moving on the road up ahead, he killed his own with a curse, bouncing off the side of the road and into the scrub, even as several of the Blackhearts in the back cursed as they were knocked around the bed. "Sorry guys. We've got company."

The second truck killed its lights almost immediately, as he cleared the road and gave Tackett a glimpse of the oncoming vehicle. It looked like only one truck, which meant they might be able to deal with it quickly, should it prove to be the checkpoint relief.

Wade watched the headlights, his hand on the Galil at his side, his teeth clenched, feeling more than seeing Brannigan glance over at him. "I know. I didn't want to engage these guys, but it looks like we might not have a choice."

"Agreed on both points." Brannigan opened his door, pulling his own rifle with him. "Let's get out and into position, just in case."

Wade didn't bother with grumbling. The situation was what it was. He didn't slam the door as he got out and dropped to the ground, even though he was pretty sure that as rough as the Colombian truck was, the Costa vehicle was probably even louder.

Brannigan was in back, getting the rest of the team out and spread out in the bush. Wade found his own spot, dropping into a small hollow beneath a scraggly tree, thankful that he didn't gouge an eye out on the branches in the dark.

The truck was getting closer, the glow flickering through the trees and bushes as it advanced along the road, the lights bouncing as the truck shuddered over the rough surface. It wasn't moving quickly, not as if the relief squad was feeling any sense of urgency to get out and let their counterparts go back to base. That probably meant they hadn't been alerted, but it could also just mean they were either lazy, far from eager to go into danger, or both.

Maybe they'll just roll on by. If they're that sloppy, maybe they won't even see the trucks parked off the road.

Wade wasn't entirely sure if he was hoping for that, or not. Despite his earlier protestations, now that he was looking at the relief vehicle, he wondered if it wouldn't be better to just make sure *nobody* came back from that border checkpoint until after they'd gotten into Santa Paz and gotten Santelli and Bianco out.

What was going to happen regarding the main mission after that, he neither knew nor especially cared. The team came first. This wasn't the Army.

The lights slowed, the rumble of the engine echoing through the scrubby woods. Wade gritted his teeth. They hadn't missed the trucks, and either they were suspicious, or they were just curious and in no hurry to get to the checkpoint.

Either way, it amounted to the same thing for the Blackhearts.

"Stand by." Brannigan hadn't bothered with the radio. They didn't have any sort of fancy headsets, anyway, so he would have had to transmit out loud, which would have traveled farther than his faint whisper.

The truck, a truly ancient M35 deuce-and-a-half, creaked to a halt not far away, and the passenger door opened with a squeal of rusty metal. That vehicle must have rolled off the assembly line way back in the '50s. Either that, or maintenance was *really* low on the locals' list of priorities, lower than even Wade had assumed.

One of the soldiers got down out of the cab, not even bothering to look around except to stare at the dim shape of one of the five-tons in the bushes, and then, slinging his FAL over his shoulder, he went to the back, opening the tailgate to let some of the others down. There was still no sense of urgency, nothing to make Wade think they expected any trouble at all.

Several more soldiers, their rifles in their hands, jumped down out of the truck, some of them complaining as they came. The man who'd gotten out of the cab barked something that sounded annoyed and started to chivvy the soldiers toward the trucks.

They moved reluctantly, but as Wade watched, putting his sights on the nearest one, he started to suspect that this wasn't quite the casual curiosity he'd initially thought. After all, they hadn't seen any houses this close to the border, and it was more than likely that there wasn't supposed to be anyone on this road except for National Army soldiers.

There was no choice, now. Time was a-wasting, but they weren't going to be able to just sneak by.

No one had had time to outline a plan of attack, but they all knew how to execute an ambush. So, it really didn't come as a huge surprise to Wade when, instead of calling out a command to fire, Brannigan just opened the ball by dumping the lead soldier with four shots.

Wade opened up as soon as Brannigan's first shot broke, and his first round slammed into the leader's throat. The man fell backwards onto the road, clutching his neck, and Wade was already shifting his aim to the next man over, just as he fell on his face, the concussion from Tackett's muzzle slapping at Wade's side.

The gunfire died away a moment later for lack of targets, but they weren't done yet. Though his ears were ringing slightly, Wade could hear the panicked yelling in the back of the truck. For a moment, he turned his attention to the cab, thinking that maybe the driver had just gotten on the radio, but the windshield was shattered, meaning somebody had thought to take him out at the same time.

Heaving himself to his feet, Wade surged forward, heading for the tailgate of the truck. One of the soldiers on the road was still moving, and Wade shot him through the skull without hesitation. There was no way to be sure he couldn't reach for that FAL, and leaving a live one behind him was a bad idea.

Then he was circling around the back of the truck, his Galil up and his finger resting on the trigger. It wasn't proper weapons handling, but he was sure that those kids back there were about to get mighty trigger happy with those FALs.

Sure enough, as his boot scraped on the dirt and gravel of the road, a flash erupted from the shadows in the back of the truck, the concussion of the heavy battle rifle's report slamming out into the night. The shots were nowhere near him, but it was still enough for him to duck and throw himself out of the line of fire, off the road.

He was about to adjust when Hank Brannigan decided to end the conversation.

Standing up, the younger Brannigan leaned into the K3 and raked the bed with a long, sustained burst that tore through sheet metal and canvas alike. More screams echoed from the back, and two of the National Army soldiers, protected from the bullets by the angle that Hank was shooting at, bailed out over the tailgate.

Wade rolled to his side, leveled his Galil, and dumped half the magazine into them. His muzzle flash flickered in front of his face, and some of his bullets skipped off the road or went haring off into the wilds beyond the road, but enough hit that the two of them crumpled before they could even try to bring their own rifles to bear.

Hank had paused his fire, and was holding his position, wisely deciding not to circle around the back of the truck, since Wade had just shot across that portion. So, seeing that he was the one in position to do it, Wade got back up off the ground and started to pie off the rear of the vehicle.

He thought there might still be some movement back there. He knew that it was more than likely that he was going to take fire as soon as he exposed himself at the back, but this had to get cleared out, and it had to happen fast.

Hank opened up again with a roaring burst, the muzzle blast lighting up the side of the truck, continuing to shred the already tattered canvas topper. Wade saw the opportunity for what it was and straightened, getting behind his rifle as he swung around behind the vehicle, getting tall enough that he could look all the way to the cab.

There were still two back there, cowering on the bottom of the bed to avoid the machinegun fire ripping their vehicle to shreds.

They both still had weapons. Wade shot them both, hammering six rounds into their huddled forms, the low light making accuracy by volume preferable to trying to get precise. He paused, waited to see if either would move, then shot them both again, just to be sure.

Neither had surrendered, so he had no qualms about it. Not that he'd have a lot to begin with.

"Clear." He pitched his voice just loudly enough so that the rest could hear it. They'd just made an awful lot of noise, but the instinct to avoid being seen or heard was pretty strong. Even with the Rangers, back when it had been a matter of flying in, run to the objective, smash the door in, shoot any hostiles, and get out, they still had avoided exposing themselves unnecessarily. As a Blackheart, it had become second nature, since more often than not, being sneaky had been the only way they'd survive.

Brannigan didn't waste time. He came around the front, letting the headlights illuminate him so that none of the other Blackhearts mistook him for a bad guy. "We don't have any more time to screw around. Leave the bodies. Get back on the trucks and let's get away from here. Carlo and Vinnie are on the clock, and it's ticking down."

CHAPTER 16

The outskirts of Santa Paz were dark and silent at that hour of the morning, which was gratifying but also presented its own danger. There was barely any traffic, so two five-ton trucks were going to stand out. Fortunately, they were roughly the same green as the National Army's vehicles, so there was a chance that they'd pass as just more soldiers at first glance.

It wasn't a camouflage that would stand up to prolonged scrutiny, especially if they encountered any of the Costa de las Joyas soldiers face to face. So, they needed to move fast.

Just not fast enough to alert the locals that something strange was going on.

"Turn right." Brannigan rode next to Tackett in what was now the lead vehicle, since he knew roughly where they were going. Unfortunately, there hadn't been time to get eyes on the station, especially when he and Flanagan had known they were being hunted, but map study was—so far—doing the trick.

"I'm surprised we haven't hit a checkpoint yet." Tackett was tense but he wasn't freaking out. "Seems like they should be on just about every streetcorner here."

"Seems like, but it might be that they go home at curfew, too. Just have some patrols out." Brannigan was watching the side streets and the mirrors for those very patrols. Getting stopped could turn out to be very bad, indeed. They'd have to fight their way through, which really *would* wake up the whole city. Ambushing a checkpoint squad on the way to relieve their buddies in the middle of the countryside was one thing. This would be a whole other level of hairy.

Even as he'd said it, a pair of Willys Jeeps came around the corner, three soldiers riding in each. The one in the rear had a machinegun mounted on a pedestal, the soldier manning it holding on as if it were his only lifeline.

Tackett might have cursed under his breath. "Just keep driving. Nice and easy. We belong here." Brannigan didn't want an overreaction to draw attention, and Tackett hadn't even twitched. The man had nerve, that was for sure.

After what Brannigan had heard about his escapades in the South China Sea, that probably shouldn't be too surprising.

The two Jeeps rolled past them, going the opposite direction, the gunner in the rear looking up at them, but one of the right seaters only lifting a hand. Brannigan let out a long, slow breath.

"They think we're with them." He laughed softly. "Holy hell, it worked."

"So far." Tackett hadn't seemed like the kind of guy who would take much of anything for granted, and that confirmed it.

Brannigan craned his neck to watch behind them as best he could, though the bulk of the truck blocked his view of the two jeeps most of the way. When he finally caught another glimpse of them, it was just in the form of red taillights receding down the street.

"They must figure they've got the place locked down hard enough that nobody but them would dare be out on the streets at this hour." Tackett took the next turn, which put them facing the military police station where Santelli and Bianco had been taken. "Jokes on them."

The police station was a three-story adobe inside a fenced compound, an arched portico out front. There was a single guard at the gate leading into the compound, and two more that Brannigan could see under the portico. It was starting to rain, so naturally the relatively undisciplined local soldiers were going to try to seek cover.

That might work to their advantage.

He lifted the radio to his lips as Tackett slowed their roll just a little, allowing some time to take in what they were looking at and what they had to deal with. "We have eyes on three personnel out front. We might be able to bluff our way past the gate guard, but if he takes his job seriously, we're going to have to dump all three and go in fast." He suited actions to words, drawing his Galil up onto his lap and rolling down his window despite the rain.

Tackett accelerated again, starting the windshield wipers going, moving toward the gate. There was a small gatehouse where one man could sit, and then another swing arm like the border checkpoint. That was it. Brannigan suspected that the swing arm was probably wood, much like the border gate, but he still didn't really want to hit it, even in a truck that weighed five tons.

As they got closer and closer, the guard in the shack stood up. Brannigan was careful to keep his rifle below the dash, but he had the muzzle up, the weapon oriented to where he could quickly snap it up and bring it to bear. He might have to shoot through the windshield if it came to it. The guard was on the other side of the vehicle.

For a moment, he thought the guard was going to stop them. The rain must have been too much, though, because the man—who didn't have a raincoat or a poncho—flinched as he stepped out of his little shack, peered up through what was now approaching a monsoon, and then started to lift the swing arm.

Brannigan didn't relax. They were only getting started, and getting in was guaranteed to be easier than getting out. They didn't know how many soldiers were inside that station, and they were probably going to have to clear most of it just to find Santelli and Bianco.

The swing arm rose high enough, and Tackett, keeping his window rolled up so that he wasn't all that visible from outside, started them rolling into the lot, lined with several more ancient jeeps and other small pickups that were all painted in the livery of the National Army of Costa de las Joyas. The two soldiers under the portico looked up as they entered the fence but didn't take their weapons off their shoulders or even move to leave the shelter of the portico to investigate the strange five-tons.

Brannigan had to assume that either the National Army did operate some old five-ton trucks, or else they just didn't recognize the differences between the five-tons and the deuce-and-a-halfs. He'd seen stranger things, and he assumed nothing when it came to knowledge in a Third World military.

The second vehicle was almost through the gate when something struck the gate guard as wrong.

Brannigan heard the yell, then the gunshot. That hadn't been an FAL; even with all the noise the five-ton was making, he could still tell the difference between a 7.62 battle rifle and a 9mm pistol. Wade had probably just shot the hapless guard in the face from a few feet away.

The guards under the portico noticed it, too. They probably had front row seats to the killing, because they came alert awful quick, FALs swinging down off their shoulders. Brannigan cursed, tried to lean out the window with his rifle, got the muzzle caught, then had to back up, open the door partway, and shoot through the V between the door and the frame of the cab.

Tackett had done the same, stomping on the brake and almost killing the engine in the process as he'd almost missed the clutch, but he was as focused as Brannigan on getting a shot at those two before they started putting bullets through glass and sheet metal.

Brannigan took the first shot, just as the soldier on the right fired. The man was shooting from the hip, and the round went nowhere near the truck, while Brannigan put his front sight, as centered in the low light ring as he could get it, right on the local soldier's chest and squeezed off the first round. The bullet smashed into the soldier's chest, and he staggered, throwing off Brannigan's second shot.

Tackett was being somewhat less precise. His Galil rattled as he hammered bullets into the second soldier. The guard, off balance already, toppled backward and crashed to the ground, his FAL falling beside him.

Brannigan's target, despite his wound, had caught some common sense and taken cover behind one of the thick arches. Brannigan threw his door open and dropped from the cab, moving away from the truck, his rifle up and aimed at the portico where his target had taken shelter, pieing off the angle until he had a shot.

The soldier had some guts. Even with a bullet in his chest, he was still in the fight. His FAL's muzzle started to come around the edge of the arch, the soldier leaning heavily against the wall as he started to work his way into the opening, looking for a shot.

He hadn't figured out that Brannigan had moved. He was still trying to get a shot at the truck, and he didn't see the dark, rain-soaked figure in camouflage fatigues and combat gear that had moved into the shadows near a pair of old jeeps next to the fence. He was looking the wrong way, and never saw it coming when Brannigan shot him through the skull from fifteen yards away.

Wade was already on the ground and moving, sprinting toward the front door of the station, his rifle up in the high ready, Kirk and Burgess not far behind him. Brannigan got moving, jogging across the front of the truck to join them.

As he ran, he twisted around slightly. "Hank, Kev, set up defensive positions and make sure we've got a way out of here!" They'd do no one any good if they sprung Santelli and Bianco and still got trapped in the station compound.

He reached the door right behind Flanagan and Tackett. Wade hadn't waited for the stack to really build behind him, and was already pulling the door open, dropping his muzzle level as he went through the opening, moving fast.

* * *

Kirk followed Wade through the door, sidestepping to the right as Wade moved left. He was mildly surprised that there weren't any soldiers with rifles or submachineguns waiting for

99

them already, but the National Army seemed to be pretty complacent. He'd been in enough countries like this that he shouldn't be *that* shocked. The sort of discipline and professionalism that every one of the Blackhearts was used to wasn't universal in the military profession, especially in a place where every young man with a chip on his shoulder joined up because that was the best way to be a bully.

The entryway was relatively clean, though the sort of dinginess that characterized every Third World structure Kirk had ever been in was everywhere, not limited to the peeling paint on the stucco outside. The entire space was lit by two dim lightbulbs in the ceiling and a small, shaded lamp. The lamp was on a large desk that stood to one side, with hallways leading right, left, and behind, and the soldier behind the desk was grabbing a phone as the Blackhearts came through the door. The man was pudgy and unshaven, and he looked up as the two camouflaged figures loomed in the entrance, his eyes widening just before Wade shot him. A puckered hole appeared in the bridge of his nose, gore spraying from the exit wound in the back of his head and spattering on the stucco behind the desk, and then he dropped to the desk, his lifeless skull bouncing slightly as he hit.

The two Blackhearts moved quickly, the rest of the assault section coming in behind them. Wade took up a position on the left hand corridor, which looked like it probably led toward the station's offices, since it was on the shorter side of the building, while Kirk circled the desk, momentarily checking to make sure there wasn't anyone else beneath it—he'd been around these sorts of militaries enough to know that even a soldier on duty here might have brought some extracurricular activity to work—and saw that the dead space was clear, just before Tackett took the coverage from him, allowing him to move to the longer corridor.

The jails were *probably* on the first floor. There was no standardization they could be sure of here, and there hadn't been a plan of the military police station available. The internet was damned near nonexistent in Costa de las Joyas, and so there wasn't much information to go on.

They were going to have to simply flow with the layout as they found it. Fortunately, that wasn't new to any of them, especially those who had been in some hairy places where floor plans hadn't existed, let alone been accessible.

With a bump from Tackett, Kirk took the corner, confident that Wade was going to hook around to cover the other corridor behind him. Wade had been a Ranger. He was better at this stuff than Kirk, who had been an old SF guy early on in the GWOT. Everybody trained CQB, but Kirk had understood that his job as a Green Beanie hadn't been to kick doors and face-shoot bad guys. It had been to train people like these clowns how to do that *for* the US.

The corridor was as dim as the entryway, with every other shrouded lamp hanging from the ceiling being lit. It was also currently empty, and as he paced along it, his weapon leveled and his eyes just above the sights, he saw that this wasn't a jail block. This looked more like offices. Doors with frosted glass windows opened on either side, with names and ranks in Spanish in peeling letters on each one.

Tackett had stepped out to Kirk's left, pacing him just behind his shoulder, his muzzle just visible in Kirk's peripheral vision. Together they moved quickly down the hallway toward what appeared to be a stairwell at the far end.

Kirk found that, despite the fact they were in a close quarters combat situation without body armor—which he knew the Colombians had; Javier had just been either too cheap or not sneaky enough to get any—he didn't feel the elevated tension that he might have. This was just another job, and he was going to do it. He felt detached, perfectly calm.

I must be getting old. He wondered for a moment if it wasn't a warning sign, but then he shoved the thought into a deep, dark hole in his mind. *Focus.*

Footsteps clattered on the stairs, and a shadow moved in the stairwell. "*Que pasa?*" The voice was hesitant and querulous, the voice of a man who knew something was wrong, just not what. The footsteps slowed as the man got close to the bottom of the stairs, and Kirk leveled his rifle at the corner, watching the shadow take on more shape.

The man came around the corner, onto the first landing, a pistol in his hand. He peered at the two advancing Blackhearts for a second, then his eyes widened, and he started to lift the pistol.

Both Kirk and Tackett fired at the same time, slamming the military policeman back against the wall. He hit, the pistol falling from his fingers with a clatter, and then slowly slid down into a sitting position on the landing, leaving a red smear on the peeling whitewash behind him.

The two of them sped up a little, noting that all of the offices to either side were dark and apparently unoccupied. It looked like most of the military police had gone home for the night, and they weren't going to find Santelli or Bianco here. Stepping over the body on the landing, the two of them pivoted as they ascended the stairs, muzzles swinging to cover the unknown above.

The gunfire might have been somewhat muffled by the rain outside and the thick walls, but now that they'd shot a man on the stairwell, the entire building was probably alerted. It was only going to get hairier from here.

CHAPTER 17

Wade and Burgess pushed down the short corridor to the left. Wade wasn't happy, realizing that he'd just picked the short-range dead end, knowing that the others were probably going to get to their objective first and he was going to get stuck holding security. As a professional, he was willing to acknowledge the pettiness of the sentiment and mentally chide himself for it, but as a warrior, it chafed on him.

He was one of those guys who wanted to be in the fight, not hanging out on the edge of it, no matter how much he knew the latter was necessary.

As he took in the hallway and the second stairwell at the end of it, he saw that of the four doors he was facing, two were the same wood with frosted glass windows as Kirk and Tackett were passing by at that moment, but the two closest to the stairs were solid, and appeared to be steel.

And there was light coming from underneath one of them. He moved quickly to stack on that door, while Burgess covered the stairs over his shoulder.

***

Santelli was desperately tired. He might not be the target of the increasingly savage beatings he was forced to watch Bianco undergo, but that didn't mean the junta's interrogator was being gentle on him. Any time his eyes started to droop, he was prodded, and after a few hours they'd brought in a pair of lamps that they set up to shine right in his eyes. He was thirsty, hungry, and tired, and increasingly feeling beaten down by the feeling of utter helplessness as crews rotated out working Bianco over, displayed in as high definition as these people were capable of on the screen in front of him.

A new pair of bully boys had come into Bianco's cell, almost high fiving the two who were leaving. They hadn't had any luck so far, though the younger man was definitely bleeding in places, his shirt sporting dark stains where their truncheons had broken the skin. His head hung while he sat there. If Santelli was tired, Bianco had to be on the verge of passing out, if he hadn't already.

One of the soldiers lifted a baton as he came abreast of Bianco, and Santelli couldn't take it anymore. He turned away from the screen.

He got a sharp slap to the back of the head in response. "You must watch." The fat interrogator hadn't taken a break, which spoke to either his dedication or his sadism. Or both. "You would let your friend suffer alone, while you separate yourself from what is going on?" He pointed his cigarette at the screen. "He is being beaten. The least you can do is watch."

Santelli felt a sudden surge of rage that almost overwhelmed his fatigue. He looked up at the slovenly fat man in the sweaty uniform, and for a moment, he couldn't disguise the anger anymore.

"I'm going to cut your fucking heart out."

If the interrogator was surprised by the sudden venom, he didn't show it. In fact, a faint, crooked smile creased his fat face, and Santelli cursed himself as he looked down. He'd slipped. He'd let his anger get the better of him, and he had given something vital away in the process. Most tourists who were scared innocents getting terrorized by the local government didn't react that way.

The fat man took another long drag on his cigarette as he studied Santelli with flat, unblinking eyes. "Well, now we are getting somewhere."

104

Santelli gritted his teeth, but there wasn't much he could do. He looked up at the screen as he'd been bidden, just as more blows rained down on Bianco's bruised shoulders. The interrogator had an opening now, and he was going to use it.

Just then, he heard faint, percussive reports outside, and his heart began to race. He tried to keep his face from showing it, but despite the fact that the sound was muffled by a couple feet of concrete, metal, and plaster, he knew gunshots when he heard them.

Got to be ready to move. Just don't telegraph it because you're tired.

He was handcuffed still, but the cuffs hadn't been fastened to the table or the chair. That gave him some opportunity to move, but he would have to make it count, since the pistol in the patent leather holster on his tormentor's hip would be more than enough to end this if he miscalculated.

The interrogator didn't seem to notice the first reports, which was strange, since Santelli knew that he didn't have the best hearing anymore, not after a career in the infantry that had spanned nearly thirty years. He must have been entirely focused on the fact that he'd just gotten Santelli to crack.

"So." Another long drag, the cloud of smoke billowing into Santelli's face as the man leaned over the table and exhaled. "You have tried to convince me for all these hours that you are simply an innocent tourist. That you have no connection with your CIA. And yet, now that the pressure is up, you show your teeth. Very interesting. Were you truly innocent, I would expect…"

The man trailed off, straightening and looking up toward the steel door. There had been no mistaking the hammering reports outside that door this time. Gunfire in an enclosed space is distinctive, even to someone who might not have heard it before.

Something told Santelli that this man had heard it before, and not in either a combat or training context.

He tensed, wondering how fast he could push the chair back and clear the table. The interrogator had unsnapped the flap of his holster, and now he pulled out an old, worn 1911.

105

More gunfire sounded outside, somewhat fainter. The interrogator looked back at Santelli just as he started to try to scoot the chair back, the feet scraping loudly on the floor.

That .45 came up fast, and Santelli found himself staring down a muzzle that looked like a cavern. "Do not get any ideas. Whatever is happening out there, you will not leave this room." The interrogator's finger rested on the trigger, and Santelli saw the calculations start behind those black, dead eyes, as the man's knuckle began to lighten with pressure.

***

Wade tested the doorknob. Locked, unsurprisingly. He was about to turn around when Gomez snaked an arm over his shoulder, a ring of keys dangling from his hand. "Took them off the guy at the desk."

Accepting the keyring, Wade looked down at them, hoping he was about to guess right, even as he heard voices on the other side of the door. The voice was speaking English, but he couldn't quite make out the words through the door. He could hear the tone, though, and that alone made him realize that they needed to get through that door *now*.

He didn't know which of the Blackhearts was in there, but he knew that at least one of them was. And that that man's life was currently hanging by a thread.

Here goes nothing. The big key looked like it might be a master, so he stuck it in the lock and turned it.

The knob turned, the door opened, and he threw it out of the way as violently as he could, dropping his Galil level as soon as the handle left his hand.

Training would have driven him to make entry immediately, pushing through the opening as fast as possible to clear the corner nearest to him, just in case there was a threat there. But from where he stood, he could clearly see a fat man in a National Army uniform, pointing a .45 straight at his face.

His own rifle was pointed in the soldier's direction, but not quite close enough, and he was still getting his support hand back on it.

106

The pistol barked, a flash almost filling his vision, and Wade knew he was dead. Except that he felt the bullet whip past his ear, just as a stubby fireplug of a man slammed the soldier against the wall, both of them hitting with a grunt.

Wade pushed directly toward them, even as the soldier tried to bring the pistol down to hit Santelli with the butt of it, though Santelli was doing more than just trying to hold him against the wall, throwing elbows even though he was still handcuffed. Wade's back felt awfully naked as he cross the threshold, knowing that he couldn't see the corner behind him, but he needed to press the fight, and the soldier and Santelli were too intertwined as they fought to get a clear shot from the doorway.

He heard Burgess go in behind him, even as he got within an arm's length of the struggling men, still trying to get a shot. The Costa soldier might have been a fatass, but he knew what he was doing, and he kept working Santelli between him and Wade, even as Santelli kept him pinned against the wall with knees and elbows.

Finally, Wade had had enough. He let his Galil hang on its sling, drew his Cordova, jammed it against the Costa's forehead, and pulled the trigger, just before the fat man's mouth opened to protest, his eyes crossing as they went to the 9mm muzzle.

The concussion was brutal in the concrete interrogation room, and at contact distance, Wade, Santelli, and the wall all got splattered with blood and bits of brain and hair. Santelli cursed as he stepped back, shoving the body away so that it slid along the wall to finally fall onto its side on the cement floor. There was a divot in the wall in the center of the splash of red, where the bullet had gone all the way through the man's head and punched into the concrete.

Burgess was already moving to Santelli to check him for wounds, while Wade quickly scanned the rest of the cell before going to rifle through the interrogator's pockets for the key to Santelli's handcuffs. "You okay, Carlo?"

"Aside from whatever VD I'm going to get from that punk's blood, I'm fine." Santelli joined him in going through the fat man's pockets. "Vinnie's not, though. We need to get to him."

Distant thunder echoed through the building. "We've got guys on it," Wade assured him.

CHAPTER 18

Tackett moved up ahead of Kirk as they ascended the steps, the realities of covering all the angles forcing a constant switching of roles. Kirk held on the upper landing while Tackett circled around him and climbed up toward it, pivoting as he went to hold on the next floor above.

He was about to post up on the next landing, but when he reached the door leading onto the second floor, movement caught his eye, and he snapped his muzzle toward it.

Just in time, too. Three men in the green uniforms of the National Army were jogging down the hallway toward him, Uzis in their hands. One of them saw him, exposed in the glow from the bare light bulb hanging down from the ceiling above, and started to bring his submachinegun up. The guards on duty inside had finally been alerted, probably by the gunfire downstairs.

Tackett's rifle was leveled and a lot closer to the three bad guys than any of their Uzis were to him. He immediately opened fire, though he was still careful to aim at each man in turn as he double-tapped the three soldiers, one after another. He didn't want to get sloppy with his shooting and accidentally hit Bianco in his cell.

The first two went down fast as the Galil thundered in the hallway, bloody holes punched through uniforms and vitals. The first just sort of stopped in his tracks before his knees gave out and he crumpled. The second spun halfway around, dark stains spreading on his shirt front, and fell, tripping the third man, and saving his life. Tackett's bullets only clipped him, one scoring a furrow in his shoulder, the other parting his hair and smacking into the wall at the far end of the corridor, splashing an explosion of pulverized plaster into the air.

Tackett was already moving, clearing the doorway and trying to get out of the fatal funnel, which was the only thing that saved him, as the third man's finger closed spasmodically on the trigger of his Uzi, sending a burst of 9mm into the doorjamb and the stairs beyond. Tackett adjusted and put a single round through the man's brain at about ten feet, and the subgun fell from nerveless fingers to hit the floor with a clatter that seemed loud even after the deafening reports of 5.56 and 9mm fire.

"Kirk, you good?" He didn't dare take his eyes or muzzle off the rest of the corridor, where he could hear a lot of noise as the prisoners started to either panic or yell to be let out. There were only three bodies in front of him, but that didn't mean there weren't more guards on the premises. There was a whole third floor overhead.

"I'm good." The older man sounded grumpy about it, but that was probably a good sign. "That was awful close, though."

"Sorry. He tripped."

"Whatever. With you." Kirk's muzzle dropped into Tackett's peripheral vision, and he resumed his advance down the corridor. "Vinnie!"

"Should we be yelling in here?" As soon as he said it, Tackett realized how dumb it sounded. He'd just gunned three men down with an unsuppressed rifle in a concrete hallway. They were definitely made already. "In English, I mean?"

"I ain't got time to dredge up my Spanish and hope that Vinnie remembers enough to use it." Kirk raised his voice again to be heard over the yelling in Spanish all around them, as the prisoners raised a racket. "Vinnie!"

Tackett looked right and left as they paced down the corridor, between barred cells. Most of the prisoners were in filthy

110

t-shirts and shorts, and they all looked a little the worse for wear. It looked like the guards here didn't spare the rod. One old man, who could have been anywhere between fifty and a hundred in a place like this, had a livid bruise raising one cheekbone to almost half again the size of the other.

If Bianco had heard Kirk and responded, Tackett couldn't hear over the racket the other prisoners were making. "*Cállate!*" he roared. Unfortunately, none of the other prisoners listened, and if anything the noise only increased in volume.

"We're going to have to check each one." Kirk sighed.

"Wait!" The voice coming from the next cell up was speaking English. Thickly accented, but still English. "You are Americans?"

Tackett moved up, covering the man with his rifle. He was middle aged, fairly fit—or at least he had been. Time and mistreatment in confinement had wasted him away somewhat, but he still looked wiry and tough.

"Who wants to know?" There was no way they could trust anyone in this place without being extremely cautious. For all he knew, this guy could be trying to lure them into a trap to curry favor with the guards. He probably had a family to worry about.

"You speak English, and there is another American here. I can show you where he is, but you have to take me with you."

Tackett studied the man. It was hard to make a judgement about him while he was in a cell, but his first instinct was to assume he was lying to get out.

The man looked into his eyes and could tell that he was considering just moving on. "Wait!" He grabbed the bars. "I know you don't have any reason to trust me. But I'm telling the truth." He looked from side to side, up and down the corridor as best he could through the bars. "I am Colombian. I am here for the same reason your friend is. They arrested me three days ago and accused me of being a spy. I am just a businessman."

Tackett still didn't know whether or not to believe him, even as Brannigan picked up Kirk and kept pushing, while Flanagan moved to join Tackett, covering their six. "Even if I believe you, if you've been in this cell, how are you going to know where our friend is?"

The man was clearly getting desperate. "The interrogation room is at the end of the hall. They had me there before they brought in your friend. Please! If you don't take me out of here, they'll put me up against a wall and shoot me in the morning!"

Flanagan stepped up next to Tackett. "If we get you out of here, and you turn on us, you won't have to worry about the National Army shooting you, because we'll do it in heartbeat. Where can we find the keys?"

The man pointed toward the bodies sprawled in the hallway behind them. "The short one was the jailer."

Tackett glanced at Flanagan, and saw his own doubts mirrored in the dark-bearded man's eyes. But while neither of them were ready to trust this guy, someone with some local contacts might be useful.

Even if they needed to be ready to shoot him in the head at any second.

While Tackett continued to hold security, Flanagan proceeded to rifle through the guards' uniforms until he came up with a set of keys. He moved past Tackett, tapping him on the shoulder as he went, moving toward the end of the hall where Kirk was holding on the stairs while Brannigan tried the doorknob.

"Wait!" The Colombian in the cell held out a hand. "Where are you going?"

"We get our guy first." Flanagan didn't even look back as he joined Brannigan. Tackett followed, making sure to turn and cover back the way they'd come as he joined the stack on the interrogation room.

Tackett held on the corridor for a moment as Brannigan took the keys and worked on the door. Reassured that they weren't about to get shot in the back, he turned and joined the stack as Brannigan threw the door open and went in.

Tackett and Flanagan followed, each man splitting off in the opposite direction as he cleared the door. Kirk fell in behind Tackett, unwilling to stay in the hallway by himself.

Tackett couldn't blame him for that.

The room was relatively large, and the four Blackhearts easily and quickly spread out along the walls, weapons tracking across the room, looking for targets. They were all keyed up, but they were aware enough to check for actual threats before they started shooting.

That was second nature for these men, after so long in the business.

There was a small table set up against one wall, a single light hanging from the ceiling, and a chair in the center of the room, bolted to the floor. There were two batons lying on the table, as well as a camera on a small tripod.

Vinnie Bianco was cuffed to the chair, hand and foot, his back to the door, his head hanging, his shirt stained with blood. There was no one else in the room.

"Get Vinnie up." Brannigan had already turned to cover the door. "Kirk, with me."

The two of them moved out into the hallway, while Flanagan stepped over to Bianco. Tackett went past the two of them to the table, where he made sure the camera was off. There would be no disguising the fact that they'd been speaking English, though they shouldn't be recognizable as anything but trained men in camouflage and combat gear.

"Vinnie. Can you hear me?" Flanagan was crouched in front of the chair, already working on the cuffs.

Bianco lifted his head. "Yeah, I hear you. About time you guys got here." He chuckled a little, that turned into a pained gasp.

"Can you walk? Where'd they hit you?" Flanagan got the cuffs off but didn't immediately let Bianco up, instead tilting his head back with one hand while his rifle hung on its sling, taking out a small flashlight to shine it into his teammate's eyes, checking his pupils. If the Costas had beaten him so severely that he was concussed, or even had a fractured skull...

Tackett had come to the Blackhearts after the incident with Childress, but he'd heard the stories. The young man who'd been one of their chief scouts had turned to OSINT support after a bullet to the spine had made him a paraplegic, only to be kidnapped by Humanity Front operatives and beaten so severely that he had incurred severe brain damage. The Blackhearts were still taking care of him, but he was out of the game permanently.

Bianco squinted against the light and lifted a hand to brush Flanagan aside. "They didn't hit me in the head. Seems like they still hoped they could get some information out of me, so they kept it to body blows and my legs." He looked down, took a deep breath, then heaved himself upright as Flanagan stepped back. He winced a little, but he took a step forward. "Hurts like hell, but I think it's just bruising."

"We'll still have Doc look you over once we get out of here. Come on." Flanagan turned to the doorway, where Tackett, seeing that Bianco appeared to be all right, had already set up. "Coming out!"

The radio crackled in his vest. "This is Angry Ragnar. I have Guido and we are moving to the trucks."

"That answers that," Brannigan said. "On me. We're getting out of here."

"What about him?" Kirk nodded toward the English speaker in the cell.

Brannigan eyed the man for a second. "Do you know any of the people around here?"

The Colombian looked scared to death, but he nodded. "A few."

"Will any of them be willing to help you? And us, by extension?"

Tackett started to see where the colonel was going. If this guy had local contacts who weren't especially friendly to the regime, they might be able to find some shelter within the city, without having to fight their way all the way out into the hinterlands.

The Colombian hesitated. Whether he was weighing his options, trying to decide if it were more advantageous to lie in the short term just to get out and possibly have a chance outside of the military police station, or whether he was just concerned about

114

whether or not the people he knew here would stick their necks out, Tackett couldn't tell.

He hoped that Flanagan's threat had been enough to keep this guy from betraying them, but he knew to be ready for it, anyway.

After one of his own team had sold out to the Chinese in the Anambas, Dan Tackett was not the most trustful man.

"There is one family, yes. They might be watched, though. They have been under suspicion ever since independence."

Brannigan looked at Flanagan, who shrugged. Finally, the colonel nodded. "Fine. We'll take you with us, but we need to get off the streets and out of sight in the next few minutes, before the local react force shows up."

The man just nodded quickly, a mix of fear and desperation in his eyes. Tackett glanced at the colonel. He said nothing, but he was far from convinced that this was a good idea.

He wasn't in charge, though, so he'd watch his sector and keep an eye on their new straphanger, ready to put a bullet in him if need be.

That was a little disturbing to him as he thought about it, even as the small group hustled down the hallway, Bianco pausing to bend down and pick up one of the guards' Uzis and a couple of spare magazines, wincing at the movement as he did so. He'd been worked over pretty good, regardless of his protestations that he was fine.

Tackett had taken on a leadership role in the Anambas, after the absolutely horrific reversal that had happened on the assault on Yuan's compound, followed by the raid on the MMPR base in Singapore. He'd needed to rein in some borderline sociopathic personalities, guys who had been willing to go all the way over the line as soon as the opportunity presented itself. He'd clung to his moral compass like a lifeline, and it had saved his soul, if not his life.

But there were wounds left over, and he was recognizing how deep some of them went now. He trusted the Blackhearts, but his own willingness to murder the Colombian at the first sign of treachery was a warning.

It was one he knew he needed to heed, and he had to distrust himself as much as he distrusted the freed prisoner, if he was ever going to be able to look Cassie in the eye again.

CHAPTER 19

Hank Brannigan felt the rainwater soaking into his cammies as he leaned over the hood of one of the National Army jeeps, the K3's bipods resting on the sheet metal, watching and waiting. It still felt a little off, being the guy out on security while the rest of the team went inside and did their thing, but he had to admit that in many ways it wasn't that different from being a captain stuck in the TOC while his boys went out and did the hard work.

At least here he might still get some action.

Another man—and he'd known a few in his time—might have resented his current position. He'd gone straight for OCS instead of spending at least a full contract in the ranks like his father had recommended. His career as a Marine officer hadn't been a bad one, but it had been far from as fulfilling as he'd hoped, and he'd finally gotten out a thoroughly jaded and disillusioned man. He'd drifted a bit after that, but he'd come back to one truth.

He was a warrior at heart, like his father before him, and despite the fact that the Marine Corps had forced him to be more of a manager and administrator than a leader, he still couldn't be satisfied with an average job.

While the Blackhearts had all been admirably closemouthed about what they were doing, he'd grown up around a few of these men, and he'd figured out that his dad was back in

117

the business before anyone had been willing to admit it to him. So, he'd already known what his next career path was going to be even before he hung the uniform up.

That had taken some doing and some proving, though. All of the rest of the team was older and more experienced, despite the rank he'd held in the Marine Corps. By rank, only his father had been higher than he had, but by experience, he was the low man on the totem pole. Even Tackett had stories he couldn't hope to match, and Tackett was the latecomer to the team.

His own time and experience had taught him a lot, though, and he hoped that he'd become a big enough man to have the humility to accept that his place right now was out on the perimeter, behind a K3, covering the rest.

It should be a relief. I don't have to deal with any of that officer bullshit anymore. All I've got to do is tote a gun and watch my sector.

Of course, it was all a little more complicated with the Blackhearts, as they all needed to be ready to pull their own weight in any role at any time. That was the way it had to be in a small team this far from support, but that was another thing he loved about this job.

He glanced over at Curtis, the other man little more than a dark silhouette where he was down in the prone, at least quiet about the wet, though Hank had been around him enough to know that the bitching and complaining would start as soon as he had an audience. Curtis was a study in contrasts, though Hank had commanded enough men like him that he recognized the personality and knew what to expect.

Lights and movement drew his attention back to the street in front of them. It was still a long time before sunrise, and the rain was making everything darker. There were still lights on in Santa Paz, but they weren't nearly as bright or as common as they might be in an American city. Deep darkness, made more intense by the wet as the rain soaked up the light, characterized most of the streets and alleys, so the headlights out there stood out.

He shifted his position behind the gun. The Marine Corps had pretty much phased out the SAW entirely before he'd gotten his commission, so he wasn't nearly as familiar with the platform as Curtis, Bianco, or really any of the other Blackhearts were, but he'd familiarized himself quickly enough. Now, it seemed as natural as breathing to lean into the gun and put the sights on the oncoming headlights, just in case.

The lights got closer, as he heard the radio calls that Wade had Santelli, and then that his dad and the others were coming out with Bianco. Despite the fact that he was probably going to find himself in a firefight in the next few seconds, since that truck was definitely coming straight to the military police station, Hank let out a faint sigh of relief. It sounded like they were both still alive and able to move.

He heard a radio somewhere nearby, a voice sounding stridently in Spanish. He couldn't tell where exactly it was, but there was no one still alive here in the parking lot to answer it. It definitely told him that someone knew things were amiss, and that this truck was probably a relief force coming to investigate.

The truck's cab was invisible behind the glare of the headlights, but Hank could still tell roughly where it was, and he set his sights to where he could walk a burst up into the passenger side, figuring that the leadership was probably riding shotgun, and knowing Third World militaries as he did, he knew that taking the officer out would probably throw the enemy force into chaos.

Not like the Marine Corps. He'd quickly come to understand as a fresh bootenant that if he got killed, his platoon sergeant was probably going to have an easier time getting things done.

With a squeal of badly maintained brakes, the truck lurched to a stop just outside the gate. A voice was raised on the radio again, then the passenger door opened.

Hank hesitated, though. He knew all too well that this was probably more bad guys, and they needed to finish this fast if they were going to get out alive. They'd already ambushed one of these military trucks out on the road. But they were in the middle of the

119

city, and if he miscalculated, if this *wasn't* a National Army vehicle…

Engaging without positive ID was still anathema to him, regardless of the risks.

Then Curtis took the decision out of his hands, his K3 stuttering and roaring, flame spitting from the muzzle as the red streaks of tracers ripped across the pavement at knee level, shredding a back tire and chopping the legs out of one of the figures dropping from the bed, toppling him to the street where more bullets punched into his abdomen, chest, and head.

Yells and screams erupted from near the truck, and figures scattered toward the buildings to either side of the street, one of them running beneath a flickering streetlight to show Hank that these were, in fact, National Army soldiers. He opened fire a split second later, a long burst sawing through three of the soldiers as they ran to cover, including the officer who had just dismounted the cab, pistol in hand. The three of them tumbled bonelessly to the ground, blood mixing with the rain and the flowing drainage in the gutter.

He raked the truck itself with another burst, putting out one of the headlights and clearing up some of his vision. After a second, he corrected his fire, realizing that if they needed to move that truck to get out, they might have a problem. He was pretty sure he'd just put half a dozen rounds into the radiator, and at least one tire was rapidly going flat with multiple bullet holes in it.

"Coming out." He barely heard the radio, since his ears were ringing from the machinegun fire, though both he and Curtis had ceased fire, no more targets presenting themselves on the street.

Hank held his position, watching the street, hearing the distant whoop of sirens. It sounded like a good chunk of the city was now awake, and things were about to get sporty.

I wonder if the mission is still on after this? We're definitely made now.

Figures moved in his peripheral vision, and then Wade was beside him. "Let's go, Junior. We're on foot from here and we need to make tracks." Tackett, Gomez, and Flanagan were already moving through the shattered gate, weapons up, though they were mostly covering the back of the truck, the dead space that he and Curtis hadn't quite covered.

If there were any National Army soldiers still back there, though, they were probably flat on their bellies in the bed, shaking as they hoped the killers who had just torn their buddies to shreds passed them by.

Hefting the K3 off the hood, he fell in with Wade and Santelli, the latter carrying an FAL. Curtis was getting up off the ground, as soaked as Hank felt, and joined them while Kirk and Burgess took up the rear. Kirk was carrying an extra pack, rifle, and LBV over his shoulder, probably for either Santelli or Bianco. They'd stopped at one of the trucks and pulled the leftover gear out.

He noticed the scarecrow of a man trailing behind Brannigan and Doc Puller up ahead. "Who the hell is that? Did we pick up a stray?"

Wade glanced back at him, and he subsided, mentally kicking himself. They weren't off the X, let alone somewhere secure, and he was asking questions already. *What a boot thing to do.*

Instead of moving down the street, back the way they'd come and backtracking the truck that he and Curtis had just turned into a bullet-riddled wreck, they turned immediately off the street and into an alley to the left, bearing east and toward the outskirts of the city, which was also up against a low, rocky hill. They kept to the shadows and moved fast, and Hank found that he was having to struggle a little to keep up with the weight of the machinegun, the ammo, and the sustainment he was carrying in the small pack on his back. *Probably a good thing we didn't leave stuff on the trucks, just in case.* With that wreck of a truck in the way, they'd never have gotten out in time.

For several blocks, all Hank could do was follow along as his legs and his arms burned from the weight and the pace, doing his best to remember to cover the danger areas of cross streets and

121

gates into residential compounds as he passed them. Flanagan wasn't sparing the horses, wherever they were going.

They finally slowed and halted outside a relatively large walled compound, with a two-story, flat-roofed house inside.

While he still didn't know exactly what they were doing, Hank dutifully moved to a corner and took a knee in the wet, muddy street, facing back the way they'd come, ready to put a burst of 5.56 into whatever threat came their way.

CHAPTER 20

Brannigan waited at the gate while Tackett escorted their unplanned companion up. Flanagan had taken some responsibility for the man, but Tackett seemed to be keeping the closest eye on him, as if he were expecting to have to follow through on Flanagan's threat. Having heard a few stories about Tackett's experience before he'd first joined the Blackhearts to go into Kyrgyzstan, Brannigan could understand why the quiet man would have some problems with trust.

It was probably a minor miracle that he'd come to trust the Blackhearts enough to want to join up, but then, he had seen them in action and seen what lengths they'd go to in order to accomplish the mission.

They'd lost Herc on that mission, after all, and hadn't quit. That must have counted for something.

The man moved to the gate and the little call box crudely wired to the outside. He pressed the button and waited.

"*Que?*" asked a tinny, suspicious sounding voice. It was, after all, still dark and raining hard. And if these people were the Colombian's friends, they had good reason to be suspicious of someone ringing their doorbell in the wee hours of the morning.

The man spoke quickly in Spanish, far too quickly for Brannigan to follow with his considerably limited knowledge of the language. He could pick out a word or two here or there, and the sounds did confirm that if this guy wasn't a Colombian, he was pretty good at faking the dialect.

The voice from inside changed, though the man still sounded worried. A minute later, Brannigan heard movement on the other side of the gate, the screech of a locking bar being pulled loose, and the sheet metal gate swung open, scraping faintly on the uneven, rocky ground underneath.

The man on the other side was short and thin. There wasn't much else to see in the dark, but he peered through the gloom at their freed captive. "Baltasar?"

"*Si.*" The man switched to English, possibly because he could feel Tackett's eyes boring a hole in the back of his head. Tackett wasn't the only one watching the two of them carefully; Brannigan was far from relaxed, himself, and Flanagan had positioned himself at ninety degrees from Tackett, so there was nowhere for the man to go if he decided to bolt. "We need to get inside, now. The soldiers will be looking for us."

The small man looked around at the armed men standing in the shadows. He must have realized what Baltasar was doing, and he switched to English as well, though his was halting and heavily accented. "Come in, quickly. If the soldiers see you here, they will kill us, too." He really didn't sound happy at the prospect of having a dozen unannounced guests, armed to the teeth, in his living room, but he seemed to be even less happy about the fact that it was going to make him a target to the regime.

Baltasar led the way as the man turned back toward his house, his shoulders hunched against the rain. Brannigan waved at the other Blackhearts to follow, his weapon pointed at the sky, though he never quite took his eye off the two men as they paced toward the front door. Like both Flanagan and Tackett, Brannigan knew better than to trust this man they'd just met and broken out of prison.

But then, that applied to most indig contacts he'd dealt with over the years, whether on active duty or as a private soldier.

The small man opened the door and went inside, though he had the good sense not to immediately duck out of sight. He took a few steps inside and waited, half turned to face the door, his hands in view. He'd had soldiers in his house before, probably from the National Army.

Gomez had pushed up with Tackett, and now the two of them made entry first, each man hooking to one side, out of the doorway and where they could easily cover the main room. Brannigan followed, though he kept his muzzle high and didn't level it to clear the room, since neither man had opened fire, telling him that for the moment, at least, they were in the clear.

"Check the rest of the house. Secure any phones." Brannigan kept his eyes on their host as he spoke, and he saw a flicker in the man's eyes, though it looked more like fear than resentment. This guy's life was on the line, along with his family's, and he knew it.

In the light, Brannigan could take stock of the man, as well as Baltasar, and he studied both of them as Wade got the rest of the team inside. He heard murmurs behind him as they set security, those who hadn't gone with Tackett and Gomez to clear the house.

"Give me that, Junior." Bianco wasn't demanding, but he was firm, even though his voice was hoarse from what he'd gone through during his captivity. "Blackheart seniority. I get the second belt-fed."

Their new host was an older man, his face deeply lined, though his hair was still mostly black. He wore a mustache like many of the men of Costa de las Joyas that they'd seen so far. He was currently in pajamas and barefoot, and while he'd turned a lamp on, he kept the room somewhat dim, probably to deter any National Army snoopers who might be looking around.

He was watching the Blackhearts as they collapsed into his home, spreading out to cover the windows and doors, but most of his attention was on Baltasar. There was a coolness in his dark eyes. Sleep had fled, and there was a lot going on in that man's head right at the moment.

For his part, Baltasar seemed to be entirely cognizant of the position he was in, and that he'd put the older man in. He

125

turned to Brannigan, seemingly sensing that the towering American with the handlebar mustache was the man in charge.

"Thank you for getting me out of there." Some of the ragged emotion had fled his voice. He was starting to feel a little safer. "I do not think that I had much time left."

Brannigan just nodded. There was more going on here than he knew, and he was getting increasingly angry at Van Zandt for the sheer lack of intel going into this. *Should have turned this one down, but the piracy angle was too much.*

"This is Raul." Baltasar motioned to their stony-faced host. "He has spent his fair share of time in the government's interrogation rooms, himself."

"And I would rather not spend any more, Baltasar." Raul looked at Brannigan. "Who are these men, and why did you bring them to my door?"

"They are the men who freed me from the Hector Ospina military police station, Raul. That is all I know about them, and all I need to know. They are no friends of the generals." Baltasar turned to face the older man, and there was a flinty hardness in his eyes now. Brannigan watched impassively, taking in every detail. What happened in the next few seconds could very well determine the success or failure of their mission here.

"Before you try to throw us to the soldiers, Raul, I want you to consider something." The fact that Baltasar was still speaking English meant that he wanted the Blackhearts to hear, wanted all the cards on the table. "I was in those cells for a week. I could have told them about your connections with Bogota, about the literature you still have in this house about trying to reunite this country with Colombia."

Raul's expression stiffened, his eyes hooded, even though he didn't move a muscle.

"I didn't tell them. Oh, I told them the truth, that I am not a spy, that I don't work for DNI. I told them that I am just a businessman, which is what I am. I didn't ask to get caught up in your movement. But I didn't give you up, either. If I had, then it

126

would have been the National Army knocking on your door tonight, and I wouldn't have been with them."

Baltasar folded his arms, though they were stick thin and Brannigan thought he saw bruises around his wrists. "You can repay my silence with the opportunity to hide here for a day, or you can prove to me that you are every bit as bad as the soldiers and call them. I am sure that these men will not decide to kill you in that case." The sarcasm dripped from Baltasar's voice, even through his accent.

The man named Raul—Brannigan had taken note of the fact that Baltasar had not given his last name, which was probably deliberate, making him wonder just how much of a "businessman" the Colombian really was—looked from Baltasar to Brannigan, then let his eyes move to the other Americans, soaked and loaded down with weapons and ammunition, spread out through his home. He closed his eyes for a moment, then nodded.

"I will trust you, Baltasar, if only because of our mutual friends." The man turned to Brannigan. "You are Americans?"

There wasn't much point in denying it. He nodded.

"You are here because the government has decided to turn to piracy to try to refill their dwindling coffers." It was a statement, rather than a question, and again, Brannigan saw no use in adding any input. Let this man come to what conclusions he might, until they became a threat to the team and the mission.

Raul's eyes moved from man to man, taking in their equipment and their generally unmilitary grooming. Lots of facial hair and less than high-and-tight haircuts. "I am surprised that your government sent you, instead of a full invasion force. Wasn't that what they did in Panama?"

"There were political considerations." That should be enough, and while the man grimaced slightly as he clasped his hands behind his back, he nodded his understanding.

"What did they send you here to do, then? You cannot take on all the National Army by yourselves. Almost half the young men in this little country are in uniform. Are you *yanquis* so confident in your abilities at war that you think that a dozen men can take on an army and win?" He shook his head, in either disgust or disappointment, then he stopped and looked up. "If they sent you here to rescue hostages from the hijacked ships… I am afraid I have bad news for you."

Several of the Blackhearts looked over then, and the tension in the room ratcheted up a notch. No one had mentioned hostages, though Brannigan—and probably most of the other Blackhearts—had assumed there probably were. They hadn't been mentioned in any of the briefings, but Brannigan had figured that they'd try to find them during recon.

Now it sounded like that was a forlorn hope, and that things were much more serious than they'd been led to believe.

"They took no prisoners when they captured those ships. I had friends watching when they returned to the harbor. They brought the ships in, offloaded the cargo, then took them out to sea and scuttled them. There were no people brought off." Raul shook his head. "They want the goods to sell on the black market. They have no other source of income anymore. They have been under sanctions almost since independence, certainly since the massacre at Toledo Point. They are bankrupt and desperate."

Brannigan glanced over at Santelli, then Flanagan. Two of the oldest Blackhearts, two of the only surviving team from the Khadarkh mission. They'd been there since the beginning, and if there were two men in this crew that he trusted to give an honest assessment, it was them.

Santelli was frowning. He looked exhausted, though he hadn't been worked over like Bianco had been. When he met Brannigan's eyes, he shook his head ever so slightly. He wasn't sure.

Even back in the days when Santelli had been his battalion sergeant major, he'd never made any pretentions of being a genius. He had always asserted that he was a simple man, and that was why he was a sergeant major instead of an officer. That had always been a way of self-effacing a lot of simple common sense. Even that was often sadly lacking once men made it to the rarified ranks of senior NCOs, but Santelli had never lost track of his own abilities as he'd piled on the rockers.

He had a good feel for things, one that was almost instinctual, and Brannigan trusted it, probably more than Santelli himself did. And Santelli figured that there was definitely something off about this situation.

Flanagan was somewhat more unreadable. He was watching and listening, trying to put the pieces together.

If this Raul was a dissident against the regime, then he might know who Hierro was. Might even have connections with him. That might be an asset.

Brannigan dismissed the idea almost immediately, though. It was entirely possible that Raul did know Hierro, and he might have some information that could help the mission. On the other hand, if he was already under suspicion, then the National Army could be knocking at his door at any moment, especially after the incident they'd just kicked off at the military police station.

They needed to make themselves scarce, and quickly. Furthermore, they couldn't trust that this man wouldn't talk under torture, especially if it was a matter of his skin or the Americans who had come out of the night unexpectedly. Baltasar might trust him, but they didn't have much reason to trust Baltasar, either.

"We need some transportation." He'd keep it to logistics and avoid letting either of these men find out what their ultimate goal was. "At least one truck, a way to get us out of the city."

"I can get you out, but I can't give you my truck." At the suggestion that all he was going to have to do would be to get the armed Americans out of his house and out of Santa Paz, Raul visibly relaxed. He really didn't want to be involved any more than he already was, and Brannigan's distrust had just given him an out.

One more reason to make sure he didn't know where they were going or what they were after.

"That'll do." He turned as he thought he could hear sirens outside. "We'd better get moving, though."

Raul nodded, suddenly all business. "This way. I do a lot of transport for one of the farmers outside the city, so it won't be too unusual that I am driving out before the sun is up." He turned toward the kitchen and the side door leading back out into his yard.

Brannigan stopped him with an outstretched hand, the other still resting on his Galil's pistol grip. "Just one thing to remember. We'll all be behind you, and all of these guns are loaded."

Raul looked down at his rifle and swallowed. He looked up into Brannigan's eyes, then around at the other Blackhearts who were watching him like hawks. He nodded. "I understand. Please, we need to move quickly."

"Just as long as we understand each other." Brannigan waved at the man to lead the way, then turned slightly and circled his hand above his head.

The Blackhearts, without a word, began to collapse on the kitchen, following Raul toward what they hoped was their way out of the city.

CHAPTER 21

The truck was definitely a farm truck, and it was not a comfortable ride. They couldn't have any of the Blackhearts up in the cab, or even sitting up exposed in the canvas-covered bed. So, they were all lying in the back, piled like cordwood, covered with a musty tarp that smelled like mold and dust.

"I can't breathe. This is bullshit." Curtis's whisper was a hiss barely audible over the creaking and banging coming from the truck's undercarriage as they made their way around another corner.

"If you couldn't breathe, you wouldn't be able to bitch. Shut up." Ordinarily, Flanagan would have been the one to shut Curtis down, but Wade was every bit as uncomfortable, and it was making him angry. He just didn't have the patience for Curtis's shenanigans.

Fortunately, Curtis subsided, though Wade could have sworn he was still muttering under his breath. That was fair enough; Wade was cussing every bump that drove the buttstock of Bianco's K3 into his side. But he wasn't feeling calm enough to be fair, so he just gritted his teeth and tried to choke off Curtis's airway with his mind.

The truck slowed, though not smoothly. Wade was considerably unimpressed with Raul's driving, but after all the time he'd spent in the Third World, be it the Middle East or

Central Asia, he shouldn't have been surprised. The brakes seemed to catch a couple of times, the surging jolts slowing the truck down until it finally lurched to a stop, prompting a bitten-off curse from Puller, who was close enough to the cab that he'd probably hit his head on the front of the bed.

Voices sounded outside, as one of the other Blackhearts hissed at Puller to be quiet. For once, at least, it wasn't Wade. That probably wasn't fair; the team as a whole were professionals, even Curtis and Puller, but Wade was uncomfortable and grumpy.

He could hear footsteps outside the truck, and the driver's door opened. Raul said something in Spanish and got a somewhat harsh response. The Colombian's reply sounded conciliatory and slightly upset, and Wade could have sworn that the answering voice was a little apologetic.

Should have studied Spanish some more, especially with all the narco stuff going on. After we went south with Gomez, that should have been a slam dunk. Just been too busy.

More footsteps came toward the back, and the chains on the tailgate rattled as they were unhooked. Wade grimaced, trying to crane his neck slowly enough not to be noticed as he looked down the line of his rifle's barrel. He had his Galil by his side, pointed down at the tailgate, even though there were several boxes stacked against it, full of fertilizer. They were the other reason it stank under the tarp.

He wasn't going to be able to aim that well if he did have to shoot, but it wasn't like it was a long shot, either, and he was at least sure that there weren't any Blackhearts on the other end of the muzzle.

That was really all he cared about.

The tailgate swung down with a *bang* that shook the whole truck. Wade stayed as perfectly still as he could, hoping and praying that nobody sneezed under the musty tarp.

The tarp moved as Raul lifted it, showing the soldier outside the boxes of fertilizer. Wade couldn't make out the words, but the tone of the man's voice sounded like he was asking the trooper if he was satisfied.

While he couldn't see, Wade could imagine the soldier reeling back from the fertilizer. The stuff stank, there was no getting around that. It made the ride that much more miserable, but it was a good deterrent, keeping the local bully boys from digging too deeply into the cargo.

The tailgate swung up with a screech and a bang, and the chains rattled back into place. Footsteps started back around the truck, and Raul got back in the cab with a friendly-sounding comment, slamming the door and firing the engine up again. With another brutal lurch, they were on their way.

Brannigan had given Raul cash to use for bribes to get them out of the city. Wade had no doubt that not only had Raul used some of it just now, but that some of it had already ended up in his own pocket.

If anything, the ride got progressively bumpier as they kept going. Under the tarp, there was nothing to go on but sound and the sense of movement, and the latter quickly devolved into nothing but a brutal, bruising jouncing.

Finally, after what felt like an eternity in the dark, the dust, and the stench, getting knocked around like a billiard ball, the truck lurched to a stop again. This time Puller did curse out loud, cut off quickly, probably because Kirk or somebody had elbowed him.

There were no voices this time, only the creak of the driver's door opening and the crunch of footsteps outside. Then the tailgate rattled and shrieked open again, and Raul spoke, in English. "We should be safe here. You can get out."

Wade threw the tarp off, which triggered another bout of cursing as it got in Curtis's way. Wade didn't care, but helped Raul get the nearest box of fertilizer off the bed so that the Blackhearts could get out. Momentarily succumbing to a bout of selfishness, he slid off the back of the truck first, dragging his weapon with him, trying to ignore the aches, pains, and bruises from the drive as he moved away, scanning their surroundings.

The rain had stopped, though the ground was still muddy, and the sky was clearing. The sun was up, though still shrouded in clouds. It was bright enough to take in where they were.

The farm nearby blanketed the rocky hills above Santa Paz, which was still visible below, still showing some lights in the morning gray. He had to look through a couple of scrubby trees to see it, taking in the sheer amount of greenery in the city. The locals had tried hard to turn Santa Paz into an oasis in the coastal desert.

He saw no sign of soldiers or military vehicles. Raul had parked the truck in a small grove of trees, half surrounded by crude fencing, with more of the boxes of fertilizer stacked under one of the trees. This must be one of his regular delivery spots. It was also conveniently out of sight.

I wonder how many other enemies of the regime he's hauled out here?

That was actually a good sign, as far as Wade was concerned. It made it seem less likely that he'd turn on them.

Brannigan stood next to Raul as the rest of the team disembarked, most moving stiffly and slowly. It had been a rough ride, and none of them were getting any younger. They still formed a perimeter as soon as they got on the ground, moving to whatever cover was available as quickly as they could.

"You'd better get out of here." Brannigan's voice was low, but Wade was still pretty close. "I don't think I need to tell you that you should probably forget you ever saw us, let alone where you dropped us off."

"I wish that were so." The words might have been insulting, but the man just sounded tired. He was already heading for the cab. "If your mission leads to the downfall of the generals and the return of some freedom and peace to this place, then I hope it succeeds." He paused just before climbing back behind the wheel. "If it does not, then I hope you will not take it badly that I hope you fail."

Wade twisted his head to look toward the truck, but Raul was already pulling the door shut. A moment later, the truck rumbled as the man put it in gear, and with a swaying lurch, it rolled out of the little grove of trees, disappearing around a shoulder of the hill a few minutes later.

The Blackhearts stayed in place, no one speaking, just watching their sectors, listening for anyone that might be coming up on them. They'd kept a close eye on both Raul and Baltasar before they'd gotten into the truck, so it seemed unlikely that they'd called anyone—and the odds that Baltasar, whatever his agenda might have been, was going to call the same army that had been keeping him in prison until only a couple hours before seemed pretty long.

Brannigan waited only about a minute or so after the truck disappeared down the road. "All right. We're not staying here. Mario, you've got point. Find us a hiding place, somewhere off this farm."

Gomez had already anticipated the order, and had stepped back from the perimeter, studying his map. Now he shoved it into his LBV and got to his feet. "On me."

One by one, the Blackhearts fell in behind the taciturn half Apache, as he led the way into the thicker trees around the edge of the farm, putting the adobe house between them and the city, climbing higher up the hill.

**

It was almost noon by the time they set into a thicket overlooking Santa Paz, at least four or five miles from the farm. It wasn't the best hiding place, but it would do, and so far, they'd seen no sign that the local army had working helicopters, so they just needed to be concealed from ground level. Everything in Costa de las Joyas seemed to be roughly frozen in the late '60s, and a dirt poor version at that.

"Bring it in." Gomez and Burgess were on security, the brush and the terrain ensuring that they would at least have some warning before anyone got close. The rest gathered around Brannigan in the center of the little clearing, overshadowed by the branches of one of the scraggly trees. It was brutally hot, the humidity from the nearby Caribbean and the recent rain only making it worse, and there wasn't a breath of wind under the trees.

Brannigan spread his map on a rock. "Okay. They definitely know that we're here now, and they're going to be on the alert." He looked around at his teammates. They were dirty and tired, having been up pretty much the entire night to get Santelli and Bianco out, but they were still game. "Our only potential advantage is that they shouldn't know *why* we're here."

Kirk nodded. "That Raul guy thought we were here to overthrow the junta ourselves. Hopefully they'll think the same thing. Intensify the security around the generals, maybe even strip some guns from our real target."

"Have you seen how *many* guns they've got here?" Puller sounded a little strained. "What did that Raul guy say? That half the young guys in this country are in the army? They could pull an entire regiment and we'd still be outnumbered!"

"Easy, Doc." Brannigan looked over at him, and Puller's eyes fell. "Nobody's talking about running in, guns blazing, hey-diddle-diddle, right up the middle. Not how we operate even under the best of circumstances." He looked back at the map. "We've got to get some rest today, anyway. Time might be short, but most of us have been up one hell of a long time." He rubbed the stubble on his chin. "If we had more of a support structure here, I'd say we fade for a week or two and let the heat die down. Sure, that might mean they take a couple more ships, but we have what we have.

"We don't have that support, though, and the longer we're in this country, the less I like it."

There was silence for a moment as they took it in, eyes mostly on the map. This mission was already going poorly. Brannigan didn't think he was the only one wishing that he'd twisted Van Zandt's arm for some more support, though the Blackhearts' deniability had been the primary reasoning for its lack.

"What's the plan, then?" Flanagan asked. "Wait until late tonight and then try to spring Hierro?"

Brannigan nodded. "We'll keep our eyes and ears open and scout the objective ahead of actually going in. If it looks like

136

it's going to be too hard a nut to crack tonight, well, then we'll have to fade into the hinterlands for another day or two." He grimaced. "We won't be able to hop back and forth across the border into and out of Colombia. Hitting that border checkpoint meant we were committed. We're in here until the mission is accomplished, or else we have to cut and run." He took another look around the team. "If it weren't for the fact that these bastards murdered American merchant crews and stole their cargos, I'd probably have already scrubbed this and gotten us out. This tinpot dictatorship isn't worth any of our lives, if it's just because it's a tinpot dictatorship that broke off from Colombia. Let the Colombians handle it if that's all it is.

"But they killed Americans, Washington's not willing to go all the way in response, so I say we stick it out and give these sons of bitches what they deserve."

He didn't get any argument. They settled down to putting together a more detailed plan before settling down to rest until the sun went down.

CHAPTER 22

Santa Paz was quiet in the late hours of the night. Curfew had hit just after sunset, imposed early by the military government after the breakout at the Hector Ospina military police station. The junta was rattled; that much was obvious by the number of extra troops on the streets. A jeep with four men and a mounted M60 rolled up the road toward a hasty checkpoint that blocked the way deeper into the city.

Those additional patrols and roadblocks were going to be a problem. While they'd needed to break Santelli and Bianco out, they had well and truly stirred up the hornet's nest. That was going to make the main mission that much more difficult.

Flanagan paused in the shadow of the last farmhouse before the outskirts of the city itself, peering up the road, watching the jeep and the checkpoint, thankful that the farmer didn't seem to have a dog. Barking might have given away their presence. Behind him, Kirk, Burgess, and Curtis hunkered down, covering back the way they'd come.

They were already behind schedule, thanks to having to take cover twice to avoid the headlights of a couple of those jeep patrols. It was going to be a long night. Thankfully, Curtis had flipped his "professional" switch as soon as they'd seen the first vehicle. There was no bitching or levity tonight. Tonight was going to have to be all business if any of them were going to survive it.

The jeep stopped at the checkpoint, and one of the soldiers sauntered out from behind the hasty barricade made of tires, random junk, and another jeep, his FAL slung over his shoulder. He didn't seem that worried, which was interesting, considering the dead men the Blackhearts had already left on the ground.

Maybe the junta doesn't want to tell their guys that their "invincible army" might be threatened by an unknown force they don't know the size or composition of. Might be bad for morale. Might signal weakness, more importantly.

Still, the man on foot was obviously checking the guys in the jeep. It might be pro forma, but that didn't mean things weren't going to go severely sideways if the Blackhearts walked up.

As he watched, the man with the rifle stepped back and waved the jeep through, a couple of the checkpoint troops moving their own vehicle aside so that it could get past. With a jerk, the patrol vehicle started moving, almost knocking the gunner off his feet, and Flanagan could hear the swearing in Spanish as they got moving.

"We could take that checkpoint out in a couple of seconds." Kirk's whisper was right at his ear. "They're not exactly the peak of alertness."

"We could, but then we'd probably have half the city's guard force coming down around our ears," Flanagan replied without taking his eyes off the checkpoint. "They might be sloppy right now, but that's probably going to change as soon as anybody hears gunfire."

"I hear you." It surprised Flanagan a little that Kirk had suggested going in shooting, but he realized that there was more to the man's observation. "Not my point. If they're that sloppy, they're not going to be looking much beyond the road. The officers obviously haven't told them everything, so they don't know they should be paying more attention. As long as we don't run into dogs, I think we should be able to get through some yards and get in that way."

140

Flanagan nodded. "Good point." He slipped back behind the compound wall where they were hiding and started to circle around Burgess and Curtis. If they could get into the city without a fight, so much the better.

They were going to awaken all hell in a couple of hours as it was.

The small element peeled off behind him, falling back into a ranger file with Curtis bringing up the rear. He was the shortest, and carrying the machinegun, which might have made him the wrong candidate for rear security, but for once he wasn't complaining.

Flanagan was sure he'd get an earful once they were somewhere that noise discipline was no longer an issue, but for now, Curtis was where he could provide the most fire support the quickest.

Circling around the back of the compound, Flanagan paused just long enough to pick his route. He was looking for shadow and cover from the checkpoints, either the one they'd just observed or the next one about a half mile farther along the line of cramped, cinder-block-and-plaster residential compounds.

The ground between the farm and the city proper was pretty open, but the darkness was also pretty deep, and they hadn't seen any night vision being used by the Costa soldiers. It should be easy enough to cross it without being spotted. Noise was the greatest threat, though the soldiers at the checkpoint were talking, loudly enough that Flanagan could hear their voices across the field.

Keeping low, even though if he *were* spotted moving that way, it would be an immediate signal that he didn't belong there, Flanagan started across the open ground toward the nearest residential compound.

There was more than one way to cross open ground in this sort of situation. He could crawl, but that would take time, time they already didn't have because of the need to avoid other patrols out on the road. He could walk as if he belonged there, broadcasting to any observers that he wasn't a threat by body

141

language alone. Or, he could take the middle road, trying to present as small a silhouette as possible while covering the distance to the wall ahead as quickly as he could.

He reached it without the alarm being raised, and he breathed a faint sigh as he leaned against the wall, facing the nearest checkpoint, the one they'd been watching. Burgess reached the wall a moment later, followed by Kirk and Curtis. Curtis made the most noise, unable to keep some of the clicking of the K3 down as he hustled across the open ground, bent over at the waist.

Flanagan waited a moment, straining his ears for any sound that might indicate they'd been detected, either by the soldiers at the checkpoint or possibly by a resident or a dog on the other side of the wall.

The night was quiet, though. As close to dead quiet as any city Flanagan had ever been in could ever get. The residents of Santa Paz knew better than to defy the curfew order, and the National Army seemed to be confident that they had the city locked down.

He had to wonder just what kind of nasty surprise the junta had up their sleeves. They couldn't think that this bunch of poorly informed, lackadaisical troops was going to be sufficient after *somebody* just kicked in the door of one of their military police stations, killed everyone with a gun, and then exfilled with three prisoners, all without being successfully intercepted or caught.

Turning back to the rest of the small team, he put his back to the plastered concrete wall, going down into a sitting position and cupping his hands in front of him. "You first, Tom."

Burgess didn't hesitate or argue, but slung his weapon onto his back, put his boot in Flanagan's cupped hands, and launched himself up to the top of the wall.

There were times where it would have been the tactically sound thing to do to hold at the top, bring a weapon around, and scan the yard on the other side before dropping down. They were

142

behind schedule, though, and sometimes speed is its own security. Burgess swung a leg over the wall and then he was over and gone.

No yells, no barks, and most importantly, no gunfire. "Kirk." Nobody ever called Kirk "Ignatius."

The older man didn't go over quite as quickly or smoothly as Burgess. He scraped and huffed his way over the top of the wall, then landed with a faint rattle and a thud. Flanagan suppressed a wince. Kirk was doing what he could, but he wasn't in his twenties anymore.

None of them were.

"Come on, Kev, let's go." He was dreading this part a little. Curtis was a pro, and he'd shut down the "class clown" part of his personality for the moment, but he was shorter than any of the rest of them, and that machinegun and ammunition did not make for the stealthiest climbing.

Curtis knew that, though. This wasn't his first rodeo. He hefted the K3 with one hand, muzzle toward the sky, and used his other hand and his foot to boost himself onto Flanagan's shoulder. Flanagan gritted his teeth under his friend's weight, but he held up.

"Psst! Kirk!" Curtis hissed. A moment later, he hauled himself the rest of the way up onto the top of the wall, straddling it while he lowered his chest to the top and then handed the K3 down to Kirk before turning his head and extending his hand. "I got you, Joe."

Flanagan reached up, grabbed Curtis's hand, and scrabbled his way up as Curtis rolled off the top of the wall to provide a counterweight. In seconds, he was over, landing in the dirt at the base of the wall slightly more quietly than Kirk or Curtis had managed. Burgess and Kirk had already moved to the front gate, which was slightly ajar, and were watching the street through the gap.

"Let's go." It went against the grain a little bit to simply push without pausing for a few minutes to make sure they weren't about to pop out in front of another vehicle patrol, but they needed to move. The other element would wait for them, but there was a limited amount of darkness they had to work with, and they would need to be far away from Santa Paz by the time the sun came up.

Kirk reached out and tested the gate. It started to squeal, and he winced, letting go. It figured that a sheet metal gate in this humidity would be rusty and loud. Burgess didn't hesitate, but simply put his back to the wall beside the gate, mirroring Flanagan's stance on the outside of the compound.

It took only a minute to repeat the dance, getting all four of them over the wall and into the narrow street, currently almost as dark as the field outside. The nearest streetlight was on the main thoroughfare half a block away, near the checkpoint, and it was around the corner, giving them the shadow of the nearby buildings to hide in.

They did pause for a few moments, tucked up against the wall, weapons pointing up and down the narrow street—it was almost an alley—while they waited to see if they had made enough noise to alert the soldiers. They didn't even need to be on the alert for Americans. They just needed to be strict enough about enforcing the curfew. If they'd heard the gate, or the bodies and boots going over the wall, they might come around just to beat the snot out of a local teenager sneaking out after allowed hours.

The street was silent and still, though, and Flanagan got up and led the way, angling across the narrow avenue toward what looked like an even narrower alley between two compounds on the other side. If they could slip through there, they could get deeper into the city, farther away from the lights, and closer to their objective.

Like ghosts, the men in camouflage with guns penetrated deeper into Santa Paz, while the guards patrolled and looked in all the wrong places.

CHAPTER 23

A part of Hank Brannigan was bothered by what they were about to do. He knew that necessity demanded it, and that there was a lot more at stake here, but the fact of the matter was, they were about to steal some local fisherman's boat.

He'd known a lot of Marines, enlisted and officers, who had viewed the constant slogans about integrity as just that: slogans. Platitudes to mouth while they did what they could get away with. He'd never been that kind. His father had driven that integrity home when he'd been growing up, and that had held even when he'd left the house, gone to college, to OCS, and then into the Fleet.

Stealing from civilians was something that he'd always believed was wrong. Something that the good guys didn't do. But that was before he found himself working on a small team, far from support, and had to make do, sometimes weighing one moral imperative against another.

The mission had to come first. They had accepted it on the grounds that they believed it was righteous—the Blackhearts got well paid, but he knew and trusted his dad enough to trust that the pay would never be *the* deciding factor—and therefore it was worth completing at risk of life and limb. This mission, at least the punishing the junta for piracy part, had only gotten more righteous as they'd found out that the junta's people had murdered the American crews. Kill Americans, pay the price.

Still, he was glad that he was on security and not actually cutting the boats loose. It was a thin sort of self-justification, but it was something.

"Bring it in." The whisper at his ear caught him slightly by surprise, which pissed him off. Not that Gomez had snuck up on him; that was almost expected at that point. He hadn't known Mario as long as some of the others, but he should have anticipated that Gomez would just appear wherever he wanted to be. The man was a ghost, even more than Flanagan.

No, it was because he'd been thinking too much about the situation they'd found themselves in. He hadn't been paying enough attention to their surroundings and the here and now.

Boot move, Hank. Fix yourself.

He got up and moved to join the rest of the team. Two fishing boats were now floating just off the beach, with Brannigan at the helm of one and Santelli steering the other. Wade and Bianco were at the bows, keeping them straight as much as possible in the faint swell. The others, Puller, Tackett, and Gomez, were wading out and clambering over the gunwales, making the boats tip a little in the water as their weight shifted.

Hank clambered in across from Puller, and then Bianco heaved himself into the bow, where his K3 was already lying against the gunwale. The boat rocked even more violently as Bianco's considerable weight got settled and the big man, beaten up as he was, got his belt fed ready to use.

The locals had worked Vinnie Bianco over pretty good, but they hadn't broken any bones, and now he was fueled by a deep-seated, simmering rage that Hank didn't think he'd ever seen in the slightly baby-faced big man.

Brannigan backed water, pulling the boat out into the warm waters of the Caribbean, as Hank settled himself in with his rifle over the gunwale, scanning the shore. This part of the coast was dark, no lights showing at all. There was a fishing village a few hundred yards back from the beach, up on the high ground

146

where it wouldn't get flooded out by the tides, but Santa Paz seemed to be the only place in Costa de las Joyas with electricity.

That gave them some extra concealment, and the fact that the locals didn't have a watch on their boats meant they had gone completely undetected so far. The junta must have assumed that they were going to stay on land.

The outboards puttering all too loudly, the assault element moved out to sea, leaving the dark line of the coast behind, angling out away from the dim glow of Santa Paz.

They would get into position just outside the range of the lights on the base, and then wait for the signal to start in.

***

Flanagan stopped for what felt like the fifth time in the last hour, ducking back into the darkness of the alley as another jeep rolled past, headlights sweeping across the buildings on the other side of the street.

He shook his head as he moved deeper into the shadows, tempted to glance at his watch but knowing that the glow could give them away. The National Army of Costa de las Joyas hadn't set a particularly high standard of discipline or alertness, even after the hit on the Hector Ospina military police station, but the four Blackhearts sneaking through the middle of Santa Paz couldn't afford to lean on that demonstrated incompetence.

Still, he didn't need to look at his watch to know that they were behind schedule. The patrols had only gotten thicker the deeper they'd penetrated into the city, and while they were all mounted—walking seemed to be anathema to these guys—and they weren't being obviously alert and observant, there wasn't going to be any missing four men in camouflage and carrying rifles if they stepped out into the street in front of a pair of headlights.

"We're going to run out of time." Burgess's whisper was so low that Flanagan could barely hear him, even after the jeep had moved on. "Not only that, if we get much deeper, there's no way in hell we're getting out."

"You've got another idea?" Burgess was a quiet man, much like Tackett, and Flanagan had never heard him complain about much of anything. He was laid back and tended to be the kind of guy who just listened to the plan, nodded, and rolled with it. So, he wouldn't have said anything unless he figured they needed to change their approach.

"Yeah. We fall back a bit then go loud closer to the outskirts. We'd have to stay in place long enough to start drawing their full attention, then we break contact and run for it."

Flanagan thought about it as the red glow of the jeep's taillights receded on the street outside the alley. It made some sense, though it had the obvious weakness that the farther away from the objective they were, the less they were going to be able to aid the assault element if those guys ran into trouble.

Though with only four men, their entire part of the mission at the moment was to draw off the guard force so that the assault element could punch their way into the base, hit the prison, and get Hierro out. There wasn't a whole lot they were going to be able to add, coming from a different direction, if the main force got bogged down.

And Burgess was right. This rescue mission had already turned into two rescues, and they didn't need it to turn into three— presuming the four of them survived if they got surrounded and cut off.

"Okay." The alley was far too narrow for a vehicle, but they could still backtrack without simply turning around in place, which would put Curtis on point. Not a great idea. "Back we go." He did check his watch then, carefully shielding the glow of the watch face with his body. Yeah, they were definitely behind. Unless things had gone sideways for the assault team, they were probably bobbing on the waves out in the night, waiting and hoping that they didn't have to abort and leave the assault for the next night.

The next night might not happen.

He whispered the plan to Kirk and Curtis as he passed them, already thinking ahead in his mind, trying to remember the

148

somewhat tortured layout of the city that they'd already passed through. He knew they didn't really want to be more than a block inside the city when they went loud, not if they could help it. When the time came to break contact and run, they didn't want to be threading through alleys and side streets.

He reached the next street and paused, which turned out to be exactly the right move, as another set of headlights flashed past. The jeep didn't cross their path this time, but the illusion of quiet and normalcy on the edge of the city was well and truly destroyed. There were a lot of soldiers out on those streets, and they were concentrated around the military base.

Looks like they figured out why we're here, even though the Hector Ospina police station is on the other side of town.

That didn't necessarily mean that the junta knew that Hierro was their objective. Or even the prison. After all, while the generals themselves lived in several mansions overlooking the Caribbean, the center of their power was that base. Hit it, and they feared that their grip on the country could crumble.

It said something about how solid their grasp on power was, if they were this nervous.

The light faded, and Flanagan eased out to the corner, peering down the street to catch a last glimpse of the jeep's taillights, the red glow illuminating the man on the machinegun in the back. The gunner was facing forward, ignoring their six, which was just fine by him.

He pivoted, craning his neck to ease one eye out to look the other way. Nothing but darkness and one flickering streetlight about a block down.

Unfortunately, there were no alleys right across the street. They were going to have to either move toward the streetlight, or follow the jeep, and hope that it didn't stop and have someone look back. Either that or go over one of the compound walls in front of them and start to work their way through yards.

Flanagan would rather avoid the third option if possible. They'd gotten lucky on the way in, but he'd heard dogs since then. All they needed was to jump into a compound and get attacked by a local dog. That would not only probably get somebody bitten, but the barking would almost inevitably bring the heat before they were ready for it.

A moment later, though, as he dashed across the street and stopped himself against the wall of the nearest compound, the decision got taken out of his hands.

Another jeep came around the corner, right under the streetlight, and Kirk found himself pinned in the headlights, halfway across the street. Flanagan didn't hesitate, but turned and opened fire, his first shots blowing out one of the headlights and shattering the windshield.

The curfew meant there were no noncombatants on the streets that night.

The driver immediately panicked, slewing the wheel around and almost throwing the gunner in the back off his feet. He bounced over the crumbling curb and slammed into the nearest wall with a bang.

Kirk threw himself the rest of the way across the street to join Flanagan, at the same moment the red taillights of the jeep that had passed earlier flared with a faint squeal of tires or brakes, and that driver started to back up. The gunner on that jeep was already trying to turn around, until Curtis leaned out of the alley and just about cut him in half with a long burst, the K3 braced against the corner by one bipod leg.

Burgess sprinted across the street to join Flanagan and Kirk, but Flanagan was trying to figure out what to do next. There was no cover out there, and they were two blocks—at least—from where he'd wanted to be when they kicked this off.

Kirk sprinted along the sidewalk a half dozen paces, getting out of the glow of the remaining headlight, dropping to a knee on the concrete a moment before the dazed gunner started to swing his M1919 toward him. Kirk's Galil barked, spitting fire, and the bullets ripped through the young National Army soldier, throwing him backward across the short wooden rails on the sides of the jeep's bed.

Burgess had reached the wall, seen that there wasn't much of a fight, and immediately turned to the nearest gate. Dogs or no dogs, this was going to be their Alamo.

The gate wasn't locked, fortunately, and Burgess hauled it open with a squeal as the rusty hinges protested and the bottom of the sheet metal gate scraped on the concrete. Like most Third World countries Flanagan had been in, nothing seemed to be built entirely straight, flat, or level.

Flanagan went in first, blowing past Burgess with his rifle leveled, clearing the nearest corner as quickly as he could, forced to use the flashlight that he'd taped to the rifle's forearm. The lack of NVGs or other modern optics and illuminators was turning into a pain, but light discipline right at the moment played second fiddle to the need to make sure they weren't about to get shot or stabbed in the back.

Burgess and Kirk flowed in behind him, clearing the other corner and holding on the house and the back yard. Flanagan moved back to the gate quickly, leaning out and getting eyes and muzzle on the street. "Kev! Get in here!"

Curtis didn't need to be told twice. The gunfire had died down for the moment, but that just meant Flanagan could hear someone on the jeep that Curtis had lit up screaming on the radio. They might not be as far from the center of town as they'd hoped, but they'd definitely started the planned diversion.

The short, muscular machinegunner raced across the street, the belt flapping and clattering off the side of the K3, and dove through the gate even though none of the soldiers had started shooting yet. Flanagan could hear the moans of one of the men they'd shot. Or maybe it was the driver of the closer jeep, after he'd slammed into a concrete wall.

It didn't matter. "Kev, stay on the gate. Kirk, take the back. Tom, looks like you and I get to wake the family up and get them under control." He grimaced. The next few minutes were *not* going to be fun.

"Pretty sure they're already awake, but I'm with you." Burgess was already stacking on the front door, while Curtis

151

collapsed to the corner of the building near Kirk. He could see out the gate without being too exposed to the street, and his field of fire was narrowed to the point he could turn that gateway into one hell of a fatal funnel. While Kirk barricaded on the corner, covering the back of the house, Curtis got down in the prone, snugged in behind the K3, ready to lay the hate.

Flanagan reached past Burgess and tested the door handle. It was unlocked. He swung it open and followed Burgess into the dark interior.

CHAPTER 24

Santelli sat in the stern of his boat, his hand on the tiller, far more comfortable being soaking wet as long as he was back in camouflage fatigues, wearing combat gear, and with a Galil, thoroughly doused in gun oil, hanging from its sling around his neck. He'd never been in jail before, and the first experience had not been pleasant. Not that he'd expected it to be, but that had been far worse than he could have expected in an American jail. That interrogation room, where that sadistic son of a bitch had forced him to watch Vinnie Bianco get beaten up. Using his compassion and his sense of responsibility for the younger man against him.

Now he sat and watched the lights of the Fortaleza Generalissimo Marto with a white hot anger that he hadn't felt for a very, very long time.

He had Wade, Gomez, and Tackett in his boat. He could count on Wade to be right there with him. Hell, the military police didn't need to have beaten the hell out of Bianco for Wade to get his rage on. Gomez wasn't given to fits of anger, but he was a cold-blooded killer on a level most of them would never reach. Gomez was the sort of guy that had men like Wade expressing their gratitude that he was on their side.

Tackett might have been more of a question mark, except he'd already been along with the Blackhearts on two other jobs, and as far as Santelli was concerned, he'd more than proved

153

himself. He lay next to the gunwale, watching the lights and the harbor as Santelli kept the boat still in the swell.

There was a time where this might let me think about fishing, take a few moments before the shooting starts to get calmed down. Not tonight. Not now. He glanced over at the other boat, all but invisible against the night. The clouds were moving in again. It was going to be a wet, dark night.

Perfect for what they were there to do, at least until they got inside.

He glanced down at the radio. There was no guarantee that Flanagan or any of the rest were going to be able to call before they kicked things off, but they'd hoped to. Santelli was worried about those boys. The assault force could conceivably get away to the sea. Flanagan and the diversionary force would have to fight their way out of the city. Of course, the military base was at one corner of that city, so they might be able to take a shortcut out of town, but they were in for a hell of a fight.

Santelli just hoped that they could hit the base hard enough and fast enough to draw some of the heat back off those four before things got really bad. There was a balance to be struck tonight, and it all hinged on timing.

The clock started as the distant crackle of gunfire echoed out over the water. A minute later, a siren began to wail inside the base in response.

Santelli didn't wait for the signal from Brannigan. He cranked the throttle, though he still had to be careful not to stall the ancient, rattletrap outboard, and started the boat moving in toward shore, the bow bouncing off the waves, trailing a white V of foam in the water as it picked up speed.

Shortly after he got moving, he glanced over to port, to see that Brannigan hadn't been caught napping. His boat was right alongside.

Even at a distance, they could see the activity on the military base. The sirens continued to wail, as jeeps and trucks started moving to and fro like something out of the Keystone Kops. At least, that was what it looked like from out at sea. In

154

reality, Santelli knew that the movement was in deadly earnest, and whether the Costas were remotely competent or not, there were enough of them that they could and did present a serious threat.

A mass of men shooting poorly can still kill the most elite soldier by sheer volume of fire.

The two boats bore down on the piers, the water getting calmer as they passed inside the jetties to either side, entering the calm of the artificial harbor. So far, no one ashore seemed to have noticed the boats coming in, or if they had, they hadn't realized that they were hostile.

A moment later, Santelli realized why the locals were less than concerned with the boats.

The large yacht was blacked out, which was why he hadn't seen it before. Despite what Van Zandt had told them, it seemed as if the pirates were still concerned about American intervention, even if it meant an airstrike or drone strike. That might even be a likely course of action, since it wouldn't involve ground troops.

Nobody would raise too much hell about pirates getting smoked at sea. Only going after their supporters could get sticky, which was why the Blackhearts were here.

The pirate boat coming in could be both a threat and an opportunity. If they were there to put the pirates out of business, it seemed to Santelli as if taking out the junta was only doing half the job.

He fished his radio out of his vest, knowing that this was a long shot. At least he was fairly confident that the noise on shore, not to mention what the outboards were making, would keep anyone from hearing him talk.

"Kodiak, Guido. I've got a yacht on the starboard side, about two hundred yards away, blacked out. Think it might be our pirates. We're going to have some additional opposition on the docks if they come in with us."

It was too dark to tell whether Brannigan was looking over, though Santelli knew he was. "Copy, Guido." There was no other response at first, which was probably because Brannigan was thinking it over.

There weren't enough of them to spread out too much. Hierro was the objective, and even with the entire National Army mobilizing to go after Flanagan and the boys, there were still going to be too many guards on that prison. They didn't dare split the assault up to take the pirates at the same time, but they also couldn't afford to get bogged down on the docks, either.

"We'll see if we can get past them but be prepared to clear that boat before we move in on the prison." There wasn't a good way to approach this, but they also didn't dare back off at this point. Flanagan and the others were committed, and if they didn't push the fight, those boys were dead.

There would be no do overs of this op. It had to happen tonight, or else it wouldn't happen at all.

Brannigan was slowing his boat a little, and Santelli did the same, allowing the yacht to move in ahead of them. Santelli chafed at that a little, preferring to have solid ground under him before a fight started, but he understood the logic after a second. Better not to get caught between the hammer and the anvil.

The yacht chugged in toward the docks, figures appearing at the rails, dimly visible in the wash of light coming from the port. Santelli's night eyes weren't what they'd once been, especially not staring into the bank of lights over the docks, but he was pretty sure the men on the yacht were armed. They couldn't have missed the sirens and the mobs of armed men scrambling into trucks and jeeps and heading for the city, even if they hadn't been in radio contact with the base on shore.

A handful of soldiers appeared on the steps leading down to the docks from the military base side, rifles in their hands as they jogged down the stairs. One of them seemed to be in charge, and he was shouting toward the men in the bow of the yacht, as the big pirate boat snugged up to the pier.

Brannigan's boat was getting closer to Santelli's, and he started to steer aside until he realized what the colonel was planning on doing. The yacht's bulk would present them with

156

some cover, and in fact would give them concealment from some of the port lights as well, as they moved toward the base side of the port.

And if they really were going to go through the pirates on the way to the prison, then the yacht's stern might well be the logical place to dock, board, and clear.

Sure enough, Brannigan was slowing as he got closer, the fishing boat directly astern of the yacht and out of sight of the soldiers on the dockside, who seemed to be the sole focus of attention aboard the yacht itself. There was no one in the stern. Santelli angled his own boat to come in after Brannigan, fighting the urge to rush as more gunfire crackled and hammered out in the night, deeper into the city.

Flanagan, Curtis, Burgess, and Kirk were in it, and the pressure was mounting.

They just had to hit hard enough, draw enough attention, to relieve some of that pressure without getting themselves pinned down and killed in the process.

Brannigan had made contact, and now he was keeping the bow of his boat pressed up against the yacht's stern. Bianco was already starting to climb, reaching up to the rail at the aft end and pulling himself up, his Cordova in one hand and the K3 slung across his back. Santelli wouldn't have picked the machinegunner to be the first one to board, but they had limited options.

With that in mind, Santelli pushed his own boat up next to Brannigan's doing the same maneuver to keep the bow pressed against the yacht's hull. Wade was already moving even before he touched, risking his balance to reach up for the rail.

Wade was halfway over when Bianco opened fire with his K3, stuttering machinegun fire tearing through the night, the muzzle spitting flame in the dark.

CHAPTER 25

Burgess moved fast, knowing they didn't have a lot of time. There hadn't been any gunfire for the last few minutes, but he could hear sirens beginning to wail in the distance. They were made, and this was going to be where they stood, at least for a little while. That meant they had to secure the house's occupants, and quickly. Even if the locals weren't especially loyal to the junta, Burgess and the other Blackhearts had been around enough to know that the local devil you know is always preferable to the foreign devils you don't, and so they couldn't count on the people here to lend them any help, especially if they had just come through their gate in the middle of the night.

It was rough, but it was the way of the world.

There were bars on the doors and windows. It seemed that the locals were still worried about crime, even with a substantial portion of the youthful male population in the army.

Maybe that was the problem.

The door was locked, but Burgess had been in some sketchy situations before, and he had learned a thing or two. The lock was no great barrier, and he had it open in seconds, the door creaking alarmingly as he pulled it open, Flanagan's muzzle dropping level to cover the opening as Burgess stepped back.

Flanagan went in while Burgess shoved his lockpicks back into his vest and got his Galil back in his hands, following as quickly as he could.

The lights were off, but the house's occupants were obviously awake. Burgess could hear low, frightened voices coming from somewhere inside. They'd heard the gunfire, and they were trying to hide.

Flanagan cleared the entryway, as Burgess moved quickly into the living room, his rifle leveled and his flashlight flickering as he strobed it on and off to check corners and dead space. Flanagan was doing the same thing, pulsing his light to avoid giving a shooter too much of a target, though he was doing so much more quickly than Burgess.

Getting old. Can't take in as much as quickly anymore.

The living room was small, and almost one piece with the kitchen. A single hallway led off to the left, where the bedrooms had to be. The entire house was about the size of a postage stamp.

The two of them turned toward that little hallway, weapons leveled, and started down it, though Flanagan gave the back door a little love before turning all the way into the hall.

There were only two rooms on that hall. Burgess turned into the one on the right first. That was where the voices were coming from.

The door was shut, but it wasn't locked, so he didn't have to kick it in. That probably would have only increased the panic he could already hear in the tones inside, as someone heard them out in the hall, and the whispers got sharper and more fearful.

Burgess had been all over the world, but he'd spent a lot of time in the Middle East and Africa. He'd seen terrorized populations in a dozen countries. It wrenched at him a little bit to hear the sounds of little kids' voices in there, kids scared that the big bad men were going to come and kill them, or at least tear their parents away. He'd seen kids in that position before, mostly in Africa, in places where he'd hired on for a pittance to run protection for Orthodox missions. He hated the thought of being the cause of that kind of terror.

160

All the same, he shoved the door open and went through fast and hard, his rifle up and searching for targets, his light blinding the little man and his wife where they were huddled on the floor with their children gathered together around them. He couldn't take the chance. Not as outnumbered as they were.

The kids were already screaming. They didn't know what was happening, but they knew they should be afraid. Their parents were terrified, and that only made things worse.

He and Flanagan quickly swept the room, Flanagan firmly moving the civilians away from the two beds with a short movement of his muzzle and a finger to his lips, which prompted the man to put his hands over his children's mouths.

The plan was for Burgess to search the room for weapons while Flanagan covered the family, but before he could even start the search, a roar of machinegun fire from the front of the house set the kids and the wife to screaming again and announced that their brief respite was over.

***

Kirk had moved to the small shed set against the wall on the north side of the compound, while Curtis had shuffled backward to take up a position covering the gate where Kirk had been kneeling. He had a better view of the back of the house, in case a squirter came out or the army tried to send a team over the back wall, but the truth of the matter was that he'd felt exposed as hell kneeling there with his back to the open gate.

He'd already taken a bullet with this team. As much as he liked being a Blackheart, he didn't really want to repeat the experience.

Some light flickered through the windows, partially obscured by the curtains and the dark of the interior, and flashing rapidly enough that Kirk recognized the quick pulses of weapon lights, intended to reveal the room without exposing the shooters too much. The search was proceeding.

He didn't see the soldiers coming, though he was still glancing over his shoulder toward the gate fairly often, even though it was a bit against his training, as he kept his muzzle

161

pointed at the back wall. The training said, "Eyes, muzzle, target," but he needed to be aware of all his surroundings while he could still engage in his sector.

His hearing was also pretty battered from a long career around firearms, explosives, and helicopters, not always with ear protection, so the first announcement of the Costa de las Joyas soldiers' presence was when Curtis opened fire.

The roar was deafening in the enclosed space of the compound, and the shockwaves battered him, since his new position was actually a little in front of Curtis's muzzle. He flinched back involuntarily as flame spat and thundered, slapping him with waves of hot air, the crackle of the bullets painfully loud.

There was no way he could give up his own sector. Someone had to cover their rear. But if the locals made a hard push, he couldn't leave Curtis to try to cover the entire front by himself.

Flanagan took the decision out of his hands. Glass shattered, though Kirk couldn't be sure he'd actually heard it over the crackling thunder of gunfire, and muzzle flash flickered from one of the bedrooms off to one side of the house. If he yelled anything, Kirk didn't hear it, but a moment later, Curtis had ceased fire and heaved himself to his feet. He shouted something at Kirk, but he still couldn't hear it, watching the rear of the house as he felt himself tense, waiting for the bullet between the shoulder blades that he'd never see coming.

Curtis was suddenly right beside him, muscling the K3 up by main force and sending another long burst rattling through the open gate. "Come on, Kirk! We're falling back into the house!"

That made sense and would probably be better for covering his own personal back a little bit better than this corner of the yard. Flanagan was stepping up the fire from inside the house, even as some return fire started to come through the gate, smacking plaster off the walls and shattering more of the window glass.

This was going to be a hell of a gauntlet, but Kirk hadn't been in this business as long as he had for nothing. He might not *want* to get shot again, but it was always a possibility anyway.

"Go!" He still had to cover the rear, so he and Curtis stayed together, sprinting toward the front door while Curtis sent another burst through the gateway and Kirk kept his own muzzle pointed at the back. Only as he cleared the corner, ducking involuntarily as another bullet went past his ear and struck the wall in front of him, showering him with grit, did he finally lift his rifle's barrel and throw himself through the door.

Curtis, despite all training to the contrary, backed through that same door, taking a step at a time to avoid tripping, still pouring bullets through the open gate. His belt ran out as he got inside, and he ducked out of the doorway to flip open the feed tray cover. "Reloading!"

Kirk had pivoted out of the doorway as soon as he'd cleared it. "Where's Tom?"

"He's covering the family and the back!" Flanagan shouted the update while he kept firing out the front. Unlike Curtis, he wasn't just laying down suppressive fire, but hammering out pairs ever few seconds. Knowing Flanagan, he was picking targets as best he could in the dark, and making those shots count.

After all, they hardly had an unlimited supply of ammunition. Curtis was down to two drums.

He had a couple of options. Flanagan and Curtis could probably keep the front locked down for a while, but if this was where the soldiers were going to push, then they would need all the firepower they had focused on that front gate. On the other hand, if he were the local commander, and he was facing a belt fed directed right into a fatal funnel, he'd try to find another way around, which meant the back or one of the adjacent yards.

And Burgess had his hands full with the family, even if they were cowed. He couldn't even hear the kids crying anymore. With some of the crews he'd been around, he'd start to worry about one of the guys who'd just joined the military to kill people

163

offing the family to keep them quiet, but he'd known Tom Burgess for a lot of years. Tom would never do something like that. Still, they had to maintain security on the family in case somebody did something stupid, even if it was only to keep one of them from running out into the local army's gunfire while they tried to get help.

"I'm going to the back with Tom! Call me if they push!" He waited just long enough to get a wave from Flanagan to indicate that he'd heard. If they hadn't been quite as secure as they seemed to be, he might have simply gone, but communication was important. They all needed to know where the others were, just in case things really went sideways.

Flanagan fired another pair as Kirk headed for the back of the house, checking on the back door leading out of the kitchen first, only to see that it had been hastily barricaded. Flanagan had been busy.

There weren't any other windows on that wall, so he moved to join Burgess, checking to make sure there wasn't another door at the end of the hall. There wasn't; there was just a single bathroom for the whole house.

Burgess clearly had his hands full. He had posted up in the corner, where he could cover part of the window and the family, which was huddled on the bed, the man watching the Blackhearts with wide eyes as he kept his arms around his wife and children. The father hardly seemed less terrified than his kids.

With a bit of a twist, Kirk realized just how easily this could be used against them. While he'd seen enough to know that a lot of the soldiers out there had probably put on the uniform just to be bullies, but there had to be some generally decent kids out there. And they would probably eagerly accept the assertion that the foreigner invaders were holding an innocent family hostage.

They weren't; they just needed to keep them under control for their own safety as much as the Blackhearts'. But that wouldn't change the soldiers' minds out there.

If they had intended to kick the hornet's nest, they'd sure done it.

He moved around the bed, neither turning his back on the man, woman, and kids nor stepping in front of Burgess's muzzle. He stepped up to the window, moving past it as quickly as he could to avoid being silhouetted, even though the lights in the house were still off.

He wasn't a moment too soon, either. Even as he got into position where he could cover the view out the window that Burgess couldn't, he saw the ladder hit the top of the compound wall. A moment later, gunfire thundered out front again.

They were surrounded and about to get hit hard from multiple directions.

CHAPTER 27

Wade dropped to the deck as quickly as he could, getting showered with brass from Bianco's K3 as he almost got his rifle snagged on the railing. For a second, he was too concerned with getting his feet under him and getting out of the line of fire to see just what the baby-faced machinegunner was shooting at. He threw himself behind a spool of cable on the aft deck as a bullet split the air over his head, firing his Cordova at the boathouse in reply. It wasn't particularly aimed fire, but this wasn't a hostage rescue situation right at the moment, and he wasn't going to get broken up about some dead pirates that he wasn't necessarily shooting at right that second.

It wasn't as if the pirates had a good track record of keeping their target ships' crews alive.

Sliding behind the spool, he hastily crammed the pistol back into its holster and brought his Galil to bear. Bianco was hosing down the boathouse, driving any of the pirates to cover, but his ammunition wasn't going to last forever, and the other teammates were already climbing up onto the deck behind them.

Push the fight. They had a certain degree of surprise on their side, but it was burned into John Wade's very genes that the best way to get the tactical advantage was to attack, attack, attack. They simply didn't have the numbers or the ammo to hunker down on the aft deck and trade gunfire with the enemy.

167

And Joe, Tom, Kirk, and Kevin didn't have the time.

Wade couldn't have given less of a shit for their objective at that point. Hierro was a paycheck, nothing more.

Even as Gomez hit the deck next to him, Wade got up, looked for a target, spotted movement through a still-intact porthole, and shot at it, before realizing that he didn't have room to go around the spool until Gomez moved. The smaller man was going to, but Wade didn't feel like waiting.

He went over the spool, keeping his muzzle high, and then he was driving on the hatch leading into the yacht's boathouse, his rifle up and looking for targets, trusting to Bianco's target discrimination to keep from getting shot in the back, and Gomez's own killer instinct to follow him and not let him go charging in alone.

As fast as he was moving, and as completely absorbed in the fight as he was, he still paused at the hatchway, covered from within by the bullet-scarred bulkhead, just long enough to make sure that Gomez was with him. The half-Apache killer wasn't alone, either. Hank was right there with him.

Wade went in fast, ducking low just in case there was a pirate in the aft compartment who was aimed in and hoping for a headshot. None of the Blackhearts were really equipped for close quarters combat, at least not the way they'd all trained in the past. No helmets, no body armor. Speed, surprise, and violence of action were going to be their *only* hope of getting through this.

There were two bodies on the deck already, leaking dark fluid out onto the wood, visible as little more than black shapes in the shadows, occluding the reflections off the shattered bits of glass that littered the decking. The only light inside was coming from the lights of the port.

He could hear voices deeper in, but at least one of them seemed to be on the verge of panic. The pirates hadn't expected to get hit, and from the sounds of it, they were falling back, screaming for help from the National Army soldiers on shore. Only those who had been armed and too close to avoid the fight had gone down so far.

While the op was Brannigan's, Wade was already thinking ahead as he paced toward the next compartment. They'd have to clear this yacht now. There was simply no other choice if they weren't going to leave a sizeable contingent of bad guys at their backs. But that wouldn't be enough.

With the local soldiers already alerted to an assault from the port, the Blackhearts couldn't afford to take the entire team after the prison anymore. Someone would have to stay here and keep the door open, or they'd all be cut off and slaughtered. He didn't think about being captured. That wasn't going to happen.

And he wouldn't save the last bullet for himself, either. He'd *make* them kill him. It would still be better than getting slowly tortured to death in a Latin American military prison.

He paused again at the next hatch, just long enough to feel Gomez or Hank squeeze his tricep. They'd actually been experimenting with how to communicate "the bump" during the shooting package he'd put together. They'd finally decided on the tricep squeeze instead of the shoulder tap or the old school knee to the ass cheek. It was easier to be sure of.

He was moving fast as he cleared the threshold. A little too fast, he realized, as he barely registered the figure crouched behind the small bar forward before he was past and digging his corner. Only the fact that he threw himself forward and onto the deck saved his life, as a stream of bullets chewed into the metal and fiberglass of the bulkhead above him, right where his head and neck had just been.

Rifle fire boomed in response as he twisted onto his side, searching for the target, but finding himself staring at tables and the front of the bar instead. Hank was moving along the opposite wall, his own bullets smashing bits off the bar top as he maneuvered for a shot at the pirate.

Hank suddenly stopped dead and threw himself backward as the pirate stuck his PAF submachinegun around the end of the bar and blindly ripped off a burst, the bullets tracking up the bulkhead in a wild curve.

Wade wasn't going to sit there. His lurch to his feet turned into a lunge, throwing himself around the nearest tables and toward the bar, still keeping low, his muzzle pointed right at the top of the bar itself.

The pirate must have heard him coming, because he ripped off another burst around the opposite side of the bar. Hank was getting up and moving in, but Wade was already ahead of him.

Just like he'd done with the spool, though this was more than a little more dangerous, Wade went over the top.

He had intended to lift his rifle high and just shoot the pirate, but the bar top was slicker than he'd expected, and he went right over and on top of the pirate, the two of them crashing to the deck with a grunt and a clatter of weapons and gear.

The pirate was trying to shove him off, but Wade had switched gears as soon as he'd felt himself start to slide. *Guess we're doing this.* Rather than try to open up the distance, knowing that the pirate's submachinegun was shorter and more maneuverable than his rifle, Wade grabbed the man by the back of the neck with one hand and clamped down, driving a knee into his nuts at the same time, or trying to. The pirate had squirmed enough that his knee strike hit either a thigh or a hip.

There'd been a time when he might have gone for his pistol, though that was on the wrong side. His rifle was trapped between the two of them, as was the pirate's PAF.

But he still had a knife.

Yanking the short, wicked blade out of its sheath on his vest, he started stabbing.

The pirate screamed, right in his ear, but Wade didn't let up. Neck, side, whatever he could reach, he set about punching holes in it, while the pirate squirmed, yelled, and tried desperately to get a hand on his wrist. By the third stab, though, as he felt hot liquid spilling out and down the man's body, the struggles started to get weaker.

By the time he let go and stood up, the man was already shuddering out the last of his life. Blood soaked Wade's trousers, but he ignored it.

Gomez and Hank were already moving past, pushing toward the yacht's bridge. Wade moved up to join them, though not before he ripped the PAF out of the dying pirate's hands and threw it toward the aft deck.

Gomez hardly paused at the entrance to the bridge, waiting just long enough for Hank's squeeze, which came before he'd come to a full stop. Then he was moving in, hooking left while Hank went right. Wade followed them, going left after Gomez.

The bridge was deserted, but they got a better view of what was going on down on the docks.

More and more soldiers were coming down the steps, spreading out on the docks as the pirates went running down the gangplank, yelling for support. Some of them weren't even fully dressed, let alone armed. They'd figured they were in for some R&R, protected by the National Army of Costa de las Joyas.

Wade took the scene in and quickly adjusted the plan that had been forming in the back of his head while he'd been fighting through the upper deck of the yacht. They still *should* clear the whole boat, but they might not have the time or the manpower.

"Kodiak, Angry Ragnar. We're going to have to hold this boat if we're going to keep the back door open. We need Gamer up here. I'll send Chico to back you up while you go after the objective." It was the only way he could see to still make the mission happen without over penetrating and getting cut off.

Apparently, Brannigan thought the same. "Copy. Gamer's on his way."

Gomez had already started back toward the stern on his own after the radio call. Wade and Hank moved to the windscreen, keeping low, preparing for what came next.

They were about to make Flanagan's position out in the city look like fun.

171

CHAPTER 28

Brannigan had been at the rail when Wade's radio call had stopped him. He quickly recalculated, realizing that Wade was right. If they'd managed to sneak ashore and make first contact as they hit the prison, the earlier plan might have worked. But they were committed now, and there were only going to be more reinforcements descending on the docks. They could get to the prison, break Hierro out, and return to find the port held against them.

"Good copy, Angry Rangar. Tell Chico to step it out." He held his position, one hand on the rail, the other on his Galil, as he scanned their surroundings, trying to rework the plan on the fly. Going through the port wasn't going to work anymore.

That was when he noticed something, something he hadn't seen on their initial recon.

The fence around the base wasn't entirely complete. There was a stony promontory thrusting out into the Caribbean, and just above it, though it was flanked by guard towers, there was a gap in the fence. Either the ground was too rocky to get the fence posts in, or they had just gotten lazy, figuring that the rocks and the ocean were sufficient defense.

The two guard towers would still need to be dealt with, but that gap looked like it was about fifty yards from the prison. Right where they needed to go.

Gomez called out from the hatchway. "Chico, coming out." As pressed for time, outnumbered, and outgunned as they were, nobody wanted to chance a blue on blue.

"Bring it out, Chico." Bianco had already disappeared forward. There was a chance that there might still be pirates aboard, belowdecks, but they had to take some risks.

This entire op was one huge risk, one that was getting worse by the minute.

Gomez went over the rail quickly, landing in Brannigan's boat, where Puller, Tackett, and Santelli had already transferred, leaving the other boat tied to the rail for Bianco, Wade, and Hank.

Santelli had taken over the outboard, and now he backed water as Brannigan dropped back down into the boat, letting go of the rail. The former sergeant major had a surprisingly deft hand at the tiller, and in seconds, as Brannigan pointed the way, he had them moving toward the point and the fence.

The Blackhearts got low in the boat, weapons up and pointed toward the guard towers. Bianco was laying the hate from the yacht's bow, though, spitting tracers across the docks and forcing the National Army soldiers to cover, and that seemed to be drawing all the attention.

It wasn't a long movement, though it did require them to go back out around the jetty, hopefully disappearing into the dark for a short time. Santelli quickly steered into the shadows, turning tightly around the end of the jetty and then moving in along the outside, close enough to the long pile of rocks that there was a significant risk that the boat might get caught by the waves and slammed against the stones.

They were getting close to the promontory, and Brannigan was looking for a spot to land. Looking, and so far, not really seeing.

I hope I didn't miscalculate here. If the rocks were too sheer to land the boat, they might be stuck. And those boys in the city or on the yacht didn't have a lot of time for the assault team to be screwing around trying to get ashore.

There. It was a small gap in the rocks, but it should be enough. He pointed, and Santelli steered the boat in, while the other rifles all turned to cover the guard towers looming above.

The sheer volume of gunfire over at the port, however, seemed to have drowned out the putter of the outboard and the slap of the waves against the peeling sides of the boat. There was still no sign that anyone in either tower had noticed them.

While Santelli held the boat up against the rocks by the force of the outboard's thrust, Brannigan clambered out and onto the rocks, helping to haul the boat up out of the water, even if only a short distance. He was looking for a rock to wrap the mooring line around, and found it a moment later, as Gomez and Puller scrambled into the water to climb the rocks and help.

Brannigan waved them off as he gave the rope a couple of turns around the base of a boulder that looked like it weighed twice as much as the boat. Gomez immediately scrambled up higher to hold security, while Puller just looked around for a moment before he realized he should probably do the same thing.

Tackett was on shore by then, already moving up past Puller, scrambling over the boulders with his Galil held muzzle high in one hand. He was almost level with Gomez by the time Santelli levered himself out of the boat to join Brannigan on the rocks.

"I hate to leave it here, but we're gonna need every gun we've got in there."

Brannigan just nodded, though the movement was probably close to invisible in the dark. Without NVGs, the contrast between the bright lights of the port and the city and the darkness down there on the shore, sheltered by the jetty, was stark.

With Gomez and Tackett leading the way, they started to work their way up the steep and rocky slope, close to a cliff in some places, while the battle on the docks raged on the other side of the point.

***

Gomez all but slithered up the rocks, having slung his rifle across his back for the moment so that he could move better. He had his Cordova in his hand, and it made rock climbing difficult, but not so much as the Galil would have.

He paused about halfway up to the fence. There was indeed a gap there, and he was pretty sure that it was because of the ground rather than just local laziness. The rocks got rough, and the two guard towers were well situated to cover the gap, though it would take someone pretty dedicated and crazy to try to climb these rocks to get inside the wire.

Gomez had been a Recon Marine. He was that dedicated and crazy. It was in his blood.

He didn't look straight at either tower, but let his eyes sort of drift to one side, letting his eyes' rods do most of the work. It wasn't quite so dark that he needed to do that to see details, but there was also the fact that he didn't want a guard in that tower to sense that he was being stared at.

After a moment, he began to frown. Tackett was almost even with him now, and Puller, Brannigan, and Santelli were close behind. Gomez glanced back, then looked up again.

Tackett had sensed something was off, and he paused now, as well. He looked up, a little more directly.

When his eyes came back down, he met Gomez's look and nodded. He'd noticed the same thing.

The guards in the towers hadn't just been ignoring the movement around the base of the cliff. They hadn't even been there.

Gomez had noticed that there didn't seem to be any movement from the towers at all. It looked like either the National Army guard force had decided that the seaward side with the cliff and the rocks wasn't the way any attacker might try to come, or they figured they had the port locked down enough not to have to worry about it. Or maybe the guards had all decided to join the sweep going into the city after Flanagan and the others.

Either way, they had their opening. Gomez crossed himself briefly and then he was clambering up the last few yards of rocks.

He still crouched behind cover, sprawled as close to prone on the rocks as he could get, bringing his Galil around so that he could engage any of the Costa de las Joyas soldiers who might have realized they had a gap and be moving to cover it. But the line of warehouses was dark and still, and so was the ground between them and the prison. The handful of lights around the concrete structure weren't enough to light up the entirety of its surroundings, though they were still enough to make this dangerous.

Satisfied that he wasn't about to walk right into hostile gunfire, Gomez carefully got to his feet. A ripping burst of 5.56 sounded down in the harbor. The gunfire down there had died down a bit as the soldiers and their pirate companions realized that they weren't in a good position and took cover, but Bianco was doing what he could to keep them honest—and focused on the pirate yacht.

He moved quickly across the open ground toward the nearest warehouse, taking a knee at the corner of the building and leaning out slightly to check beyond it. Still no movement, though now he could see a pair of very nervous and agitated looking guards at the entrance to the prison. They obviously wanted to go join the fight, either because they were young and excitable and just wanted to get stuck in, or because they were worried that they'd be considered slackers if they didn't.

They'd have to be dealt with. Fortunately, they were the only soldiers in sight on this part of the base.

Tackett, Puller, Brannigan, and Santelli had joined him at the side of the building, Santelli over at the other corner to cover that side. It was now or never.

He still didn't move just yet. Shooting the two of them from the corner might well alert the entire base. The junta wasn't stupid, even if a lot of their soldiers appeared to be classic Third World bullies. Once shots were fired near the prison, they had to know that their political prisoners were really the target. Or one of them, at least. And there were still several guards in towers who hadn't abandoned their posts to go get in on the action elsewhere.

But taking two men out with knives, under a light, wasn't going to work that well, either.

So, he braced his Galil against the corner of the building, hoping the barrel wouldn't glint too much under the lights all around them, and lined up first one, then the other guard. He rehearsed the shots briefly, shifting his muzzle back and forth, his finger resting lightly on the trigger. He waited, listening for another burst of machinegun fire, whether from out in the city or down on the docks. Then, as another stuttering roll of thunder echoed across Santa Paz, he leaned into it, settled the sights on the first man, and fired.

The rifle barked deafeningly, the flash momentarily brilliant in the dimness, but Gomez was leaning into the weapon and had it clamped against the side of the building, so he was able to clearly see the guard jerk as the bullet punched through his left lung and his heart. He swayed for a second, then crumpled.

Gomez had already shifted his aim, though, and the second man took a bullet through the vitals, slightly more off center, before the first had even hit the ground. Before he'd even registered what had just happened. The second guard toppled backward, crashing onto the ground to stare sightlessly at the stars above.

None of the Blackhearts needed to be told that was the signal. With Gomez leading, checking his flank one last time before he surged out into the open ground, they raced to the front of the prison in two elements, Tackett right on Gomez's heels, Puller and Santelli forming a small wedge with Brannigan as soon as the first two had set up at the entrance to the prison.

Gomez didn't see any cameras. That didn't mean they weren't there, but he'd seen enough of Costa de las Joyas' tech that he didn't think they had any. They had a little bit of breathing room. He waited until Tackett and Puller were holding security, then started to go through one of the dead guard's pockets, while Brannigan took the other.

Brannigan came up with the keys first. This wasn't a fancy, high-tech facility with electronic ID cards or anything.

They turned toward the twin steel doors, two men each taking up the stack on either side while Brannigan unlocked the doors and then stood with his muzzle high, his off hand on the handle, looking to each man to see if they were ready.

Then he swung the doors open and stepped aside as five muzzles were leveled inside the most secure prison in Costa de las Joyas.

CHAPTER 29

The doors creaked open, letting dim incandescent light out of the entryway. The Blackhearts stayed off to either side, weapons trained on the entry.

If the guards had had cameras on the outside, then Brannigan was sure that they'd be met with gunfire. However, as it was, they only heard a querulous call from inside, a guard wondering what was going on and who was coming in.

Gomez and Tackett led the way in, Brannigan falling in right behind Gomez while Santelli and Puller held security on the outside for the moment. They found themselves in a narrow cement room, with two dim ceiling lamps hanging from the overhead and a smaller, hooded lamp on the steel desk set a couple yards back from the doors. The guard at that desk looked up in shock, his eyes widening as he saw the weapons being pointed at him, though his brain didn't catch up for a second as the Blackhearts flowed in, clearing their corners except for Brannigan, who advanced on the man, his own Galil pointed at the guard's face.

When he realized what was happening, the guard started to move, but froze again when Brannigan twitched the muzzle of his rifle slightly to warn him against doing anything stupid. He signaled the man to get up and move away from the desk.

The guard was no fanatic and no fool. His face looked ashen as he raised his hands and stood, very slowly, backing up from the desk, though his eyes were still moving from side to side, looking for an escape—or a way to call for help.

"Mario, if you'd do the honors?" Gomez was the one who spoke the best Spanish, though he knew that Santelli was relatively fluent as well.

He pressed the guard back against the wall and handed security on him off to Gomez before he circled around the desk. Sure enough, there was a radio and a panic button, but the lack of interior alarms suggested that the guard hadn't had a chance to press the latter. They knew they'd gotten to him before he'd been able to use the radio. He turned back toward the guard, who was up against the wall, his hands high, swallowing hard as he looked Gomez in the eye.

Mario Gomez was a killer's killer. Brannigan didn't know how many cartel *sicarios* and mules he'd buried out in the New Mexico desert, aside from the fighting he'd done with the Blackhearts, and he didn't think he wanted to know. The man was half Chiricahua Apache, and a man who looked in his still, dark eyes could easily see that heritage, along with the barely leashed violence that came with it.

He spoke in a low, even tone, interrogating the guard. When he didn't like the answer, his hand didn't move to lift his Galil, but dropped from the forearm toward his knife.

The guard's eyes widened still further, and he jabbered desperately. Gomez didn't take his eyes off the man, but he moved his hand back to his rifle. "He says that the warden has the keys. None of the regular guards do."

"Where's the warden?" The last thing Brannigan wanted to do was go on a wild goose chase for the warden and the keys, but they didn't have a torch that would get them through a prison cell door, so they didn't have much choice.

Gomez rapped out the question in Spanish. "He says that he has a room on the top floor, here in the front of the building. That he's probably there right now."

182

Brannigan wished for a flashbang, but there hadn't been any in the cache that Javier had sold them. "Doc, keep an eye on this guy. Carlo, hold the door. I don't want to leave anyone by themselves. Dan, Mario, you're with me."

The three of them turned toward the stairwell on the left side of the entryway, Brannigan taking the lead despite the look he got from Gomez. He was used to it. He'd adopted a "lead from the front" philosophy as a Marine officer, one that was easier for his subordinates to swallow since he'd been a Gunny before he'd gone to the dark side. It often chafed, though, when the enlisted who knew that their place was at the front of the stack got pushed aside by the Old Man.

Some of that was professional pride. With a lot of his Marines, and with the Blackhearts, it was a combination of that and a desire not to lose the Old Man to some goat herder with an AK.

He mounted the stairs carefully, determined not to do something stupid and leave Flanagan leading the team. It had happened before, when he'd gotten shot up on the Tourmaline Delta gas and oil platform, but they were too spread out and too outnumbered to be able to afford it here. He pivoted as he climbed, twisting his torso like a tank turret to keep his muzzle pointed at the next landing up.

The stairwell was dark, lit only by a single light bulb at the top. The prison wasn't that large, being only two stories tall, so he was covering the hallway on the top floor by the time he rounded the landing and started up the last flight.

There had been a large, heavy steel door between the entryway and the main part of the prison, so he hadn't been able to hear any noise from the cells when he'd been on the first floor with the guard, but now that he came up, he figured there had to be a balcony overlooking the main cell block, because the noise was getting loud. The prisoners could hear the shooting, even through the thick concrete walls, and there might have been a riot in the offing if they hadn't all been locked in their cells for the night.

He slowed as Tackett caught up with him and came alongside, the two of them advancing up the steps with both rifle muzzles trained on the doorway ahead. The hall was dark, though Brannigan could see some movement off to the left, where the presumed balcony stood.

Sure enough, there were two guards with FMK-3 submachineguns on the balcony, overlooking the cell block. One of them had a megaphone in his hand and was bellowing in Spanish, probably warning the prisoners to quiet down or they would be shot. Brannigan could only pick out a word or two here and there, and the local dialect was a lot different from what little Spanish he'd learned in the States.

There was a glass door immediately to their right, housing what looked like a small office or guard post, and then a large double door straight ahead, with what looked like a corner window overlooking the cell block. That was probably the warden's quarters.

Brannigan and Tackett, still unnoticed by the guards, stepped out into the hallway, Tackett pivoting just enough to clear the nearest corner before turning back toward the two guards and the warden's door. Gomez, meanwhile, moved up and joined Brannigan, both of them pointing their Galils at the pair of guards.

One of them must have sensed movement behind them, because he started to turn, though he didn't lead with his muzzle, probably thinking that one of the other guards had come up to reinforce them, since all hell was breaking loose across Santa Paz. Gomez barked at him, and he froze. The second man started to move, and Brannigan stepped up closer, setting the cool metal of his rifle muzzle against the back of the man's neck.

It wasn't the smartest thing to do if the guard had been a trained fighter. Brannigan himself had trained in martial arts enough to hopefully be able to knock a barrel aside and at least grapple the gunman for it if it was touching him. This guy didn't seem to be much of a martial artist, though. He was fatter than the other, and he hadn't even been aware enough to notice his buddy starting to turn around.

184

Gomez barked more instructions, and both guards lifted their gun hands, slowly lowering their FMK-3s to the floor by the handguards. Brannigan lifted his muzzle, reaching around to take one of the guards' handcuffs.

It was the matter of a few seconds to get both of them secured. Gomez even ripped a part of each of their uniforms to gag them. It wasn't really necessary, but he probably just didn't want to listen to them yell, especially given the rising cacophony from down in the cell block.

A glance down there didn't show Brannigan very much. It was pretty dark. The one light above the balcony was the only illumination except for the dim glow of another at the far end. The block was two levels, with a catwalk running around the outside of the large open room, accessible by stairs from the lower level at the far end, and a gate off this balcony.

They'd get to that. The warden came first.

Tackett was already stacked on the warden's doors. They were wood, and they didn't appear to be reinforced. The warden was probably relying on the bars and the steel doors lower down for his own security. After all, he was the supreme authority in the most secure prison in this tiny hellhole of a country. What did he have to fear?

Brannigan had seen enough to know that often the most secure of tyrants were the most fearful. They would have to move fast and use that fear to their advantage.

As soon as Brannigan had his own weapon leveled at the doors, Tackett turned his back to the opening and donkey-kicked the right hand door, just beneath the doorknob. It cracked but held. He kicked it again, something splintered, and the door juddered open, driven the rest of the way into the room by Brannigan's shoulder as he and Gomez made entry, guns up and looking for targets.

The warden was up. That wasn't surprising; it was probably impossible to sleep with everything going on that night. He must have been watching the cell block, the same as the guards, because he was next to the window, though now his back was to it, pressed against the glass and the wall, staring at the men who had just barged into his rooms with guns.

He was dressed, though his uniform shirt was partially untucked. He was fat enough that Brannigan wondered if that shirt ever stayed tucked in. His hairline was receding, and his jowly features were already greasy with sweat.

Brannigan had quickly turned toward the warden, his rifle trained on the man's midsection. There was a pistol on the desk another two steps inside the room, and the fat man's eyes flicked to it for a moment, but then they focused on the Galil in Brannigan's hands, and any thought of going for the weapon evaporated, as the warden started to shake.

He might not be able to speak enough of the language, but Brannigan had taken this "ground," so he had to hold it. "Clear the rest of the rooms, make sure we're not going to get shot in the back."

Tackett had already been moving on the bedroom, while Gomez went around the desk to join him. They flowed into the back quickly, and Brannigan watched the warden's eyes as they moved toward the room, then back to the 5.56 muzzle trained on his vitals.

There was a scuffle and a high-pitched scream from the bedroom. Brannigan kept his eyes on the warden. Gomez and Tackett could handle themselves, and neither man had spoken or fired a shot.

They came out a couple of minutes later, Tackett hauling a disheveled woman wrapped in a bedsheet by the arm. He pushed her, somewhat gently, toward the desk and then put her down on her knees. She'd stopped screaming, though there was stark, animal terror in her eyes as she looked from Blackheart, to Blackheart, to the warden.

"Looks like she was either one of the prisoners or picked up off the street." Gomez looked at the warden, his eyes flat and hard. "I don't think she's here willingly. She only screamed and struggled because she thought we were going to do worse to her."

186

The guns and the military gear were probably pretty frightening in a place like this. Brannigan stepped back to let Gomez do his thing with the warden.

Gomez stepped up in front of the man, looking him in the eyes. The warden wasn't able to hold that unblinking gaze for long. His eyes dropped as Gomez began to speak, his voice low but sharp. Brannigan could hear the name, "Ernesto Hierro," and the warden blinked at the sound of it. He started to shake his head, but Gomez spoke even more sharply, and the man winced.

Brannigan was getting a read on the warden as Gomez continued to question him. Faced with two rifles, the man's answers were hesitant, and he seemed to flinch at every word coming out of Gomez's mouth.

The warden's cruelty could be seen in the bruises on the cowering woman wrapped in a sheet on the floor. Yet, when faced with force, he seemed to fold like a cheap suit.

It fit the mold. The kind of man who would usually rise to the position of running a high-security prison in a military dictatorship was probably the sort who enjoyed throwing his weight around with people who couldn't fight back. This man was a bully, probably a sadist, and a coward.

Gomez took a step back and jerked his muzzle toward the door with a curt command. The warden was shaking, and said something in a low, frightened voice.

Tackett picked up on it and grabbed the key ring off the desk, tossing it to Gomez, who barely took his eyes off the warden to reach up and catch it. "*Vámonos*."

The warden looked up at Brannigan, but he saw no more mercy than he saw in Gomez. He shuffled toward the door, still shaking, and Gomez followed, giving him a prod in the back with his Galil's muzzle, just to keep him honest.

Tackett spoke quietly to the woman on the floor, and Brannigan glanced back over his shoulder to find the quiet man watching him. "We can't leave her here."

They weren't in a good place to rescue everybody, but the man had a point. From the looks of things, the warden would take out his loss of face on her once they were gone, unless they killed him first. He'd probably kill her. Tackett was right. They couldn't leave her.

"Bring her along, but make sure she keeps quiet. We'll have to let her go as soon as we can once we get clear."

Gomez and the warden were already on the stairs, retracing their steps. Gomez said something to the warden, and the man flinched, just before he called down, "Friendlies coming down!"

"I got you." Santelli was waiting, and as Brannigan started down the stairs, he thought he saw the warden deflate a little bit more, his shoulders slumping as he realized that his hope to make a break for it on the steps would not end well.

Puller and Santelli were holding security on the doors in the entryway, the reception guard now handcuffed the same way the two upstairs were. Puller hadn't gagged this one the way Gomez had silenced the two up on the balcony, but it looked like the man wasn't all that eager to attract attention.

The warden looked down at the guard and said something that sounded vicious. Gomez prodded him hard with the Galil muzzle, warning him to keep his mouth shut.

The repercussions of this op within the National Army could get interesting, provided Hierro took any length of time to rally the resistance to the junta.

With a rattle of keys and the shriek of metal that wasn't well maintained in a coastal, tropical environment, the warden pulled the doors to the main cell block open.

Pandemonium met their ears. The prisoners were raising one hell of a racket, banging cups and eating tins against the bars and yelling, mostly in Spanish.

For a moment, Brannigan considered firing a shot into the ceiling, in the hopes that it might cow them into quieting down. It might not, though, and a shot would definitely bring more reinforcements down on them, once whoever was in command that night realized what the real objective was.

Plus, they couldn't really afford to spend much more ammo. They were almost through the crates Javier had provided, and there wasn't much in the way of resupply here in Costa de las Joyas. They needed to make every shot count.

So, he tried to ignore the prisoners' racket as they paced down the middle of the block with the warden leading the way, his head down and the keys rattling in a shaking hand.

A few of the prisoners did quiet down as they saw what was happening. Saw the warden, a man they probably all saw as a monster, marched down the line of cells by unfamiliar men with guns. They had to be wondering just what was happening.

The warden led the way to the back of the building, where the barred cells gave way to solid steel doors. He stopped in front of one of the ones at the very back.

It took a couple of tries with his shaking hands to get the key in the lock, opening the cell door. It didn't screech as much as some of the other doors in the prison, but it wasn't all that smooth, either.

The inside was dark, but Tackett turned on his flashlight, held to the Galil's forearm with tape, and the man sitting up on the cot inside lifted a hand to shield his eyes.

That hand was missing a finger.

Brannigan shoved the warden into the cell with them. There wasn't much room in there, but he wasn't going to leave that fat snake at their backs, especially not when Tackett had the girl on the floor outside.

He and Gomez shone their lights on the man on the cot, trying to see his face. The photos they'd had to look over had been old and grainy, and if this was Ernesto Hierro, then he had clearly been through hell since they'd been taken. His hair had been shaved, and not gently. His scalp was scarred, though not all of those scars could be put down to a rough haircut. He was emaciated, his cheeks sunken and his eyes set in dark pits. Several days' stubble stood out on his jaw, most of it gray.

"Ernesto Hierro?" Brannigan decided that they just needed to ask. This guy was a rescue, not an HVT.

"*Si.*" The man peered up at the glaring weapon lights. "Who are you?" His English wasn't great, but it seemed to be better than anyone else's in Costa de las Joyas. He must have noted the men's size and the accent.

There was also no way in hell Brannigan was going to identify himself or his boys where this fatass of a warden could hear. "We're here to get you out. Come with us."

Hierro started to get up. He wasn't moving very well, and as he stood into the light, the scars, bruises, and barely bandaged open wounds spoke of his treatment at the junta's hands. Getting him out was not going to be easy.

He wasn't all that aware, apparently. "There are others here. Other members of the movement. We need to get them out."

Brannigan shook his head. "You're the contract. We can get you out. Let's go."

For a second, he thought that Hierro was going to argue. Fortunately, he just nodded and straightened to his feet.

Brannigan looked at the warden, thinking. Then he stepped out of the cell, turning to face the fat man as he began to follow. "No, I don't think so."

He shoved the warden back into the darkened cell and swung the door shut.

It probably wouldn't accomplish much in the long run, but it would keep the fat bastard from calling reinforcements for a while.

"Let's go. We have no time."

CHAPTER 30

Kirk leveled his rifle out the window as the first figure topped the compound wall. He had to admit that he was getting older, and he really would have preferred a red dot on the Galil, but the irons were what he had, so he did his best.

His first shot shattered the window glass and missed the soldier, but the man ducked out of sight anyway. Then a small object sailed over the wall and Kirk ducked back out of the window. "Grenade!"

The frag detonated with a *thud* that shook the house and broke what was left of the window. Smoke and dust billowed in through the opening, though everyone inside the bedroom was low enough that any frag pattered off the ceiling and the opposite wall instead of hitting either the family, Burgess, or Kirk.

More gunfire erupted out front as Kirk swung back to the window. If the National Army thought that they could keep their heads down with one frag while they climbed over the wall after it, they were in for a surprise.

The soldiers had gotten a move on. Two of them were already at the top of the wall, while the smoke from the grenade explosion was still swirling upward. Kirk had a better shot this time, and he double tapped the one on the right, dropping him onto the top of the wall. He hit just right that his rifle fell inside while his legs dangled over the outside.

Burgess had swung out, momentarily taking his eyes off the family through sheer necessity, and dumped the one on the left. That one hadn't gotten quite as far up, and his head snapped back as the bullet punched through his brain, sending him over backwards to disappear on the other side of the wall.

Two more frags sailed over the wall then, though Kirk couldn't tell which was louder. The grenades, or the long burst as Curtis must have just about emptied his drum out the gate.

The house shook even harder as the twin thunderclaps slammed against the outside wall, and more smoke and dust billowed into the room. Flanagan suddenly appeared at the door, shouting at the top of his lungs to be heard over Curtis's fire.

"We've got to push! There's a truck out front and we're gonna take it!"

Kirk's first thought, even as he stitched a few more rounds across the top of the wall, was that trying to break out right at that moment was insane. They were under fire from at least two directions.

But there weren't a whole lot of other options. They'd done what they'd set out to do, and that was draw attention. If they stayed in place, they were inevitably going to get overwhelmed. There was only so much ammunition left.

And that was assuming that the father of the house didn't try to do something stupid, if only because they were getting the shit shot out of his home.

No, Flanagan was right. They needed to move. "Go, Tom!"

Burgess might have argued. The two of them had covered each other's backs so often over the years that they'd been contracting overseas that it was a bit of a running joke as to which of them was on the tab the next time. But it was too hot, and there was no time, so Burgess turned and ran to the door, disappearing out into the hallway.

The government troops weren't giving up, though. Another pair of grenades came over the wall, and Kirk ducked, except the hammer blows to the side of the house didn't come.

192

Instead, thick, choking smoke began to pour from the thrown objects, quickly obscuring the backyard and the top of the wall.

Kirk paused before turning toward the door to stitch the top of the wall with the remaining rounds in his magazine, just to keep the local soldiers honest. He reloaded as he turned to follow Burgess, who had paused at the door, turning and barricading on the jamb to face the window.

They were going to run out of ammunition before too long, and it didn't look like the National Army used 5.56 much.

He swept past Burgess and headed for the front door. Curtis and Flanagan were already outside, holding on the gate, though that was going to leave them vulnerable if more of the government soldiers came through the smoke billowing at the back of the house. They were out of options. They had to move, or die.

"Tom! On me!" Kirk kept going through the front door, pivoting to one side to make sure they weren't about to get flanked. He hoped that his last burst at the wall had slowed the attacking soldiers down long enough to buy them the seconds they needed to get clear, but he couldn't be sure.

There were no targets coming up the sides of the house yet, but that couldn't last. He saw Burgess burst out of the door through the corner of his eye, and then he was closing in on Curtis, slamming into the wall behind the shorter man, as Curtis swept the street with machinegun fire. "We're up! Let's go!" He had put his back to the wall to face the house and the backyard, and just in time, too. Thick white smoke was still billowing out from behind the house, and shapes were starting to come out of it, men with rifles, half bent over as they tried to get close to the Blackhearts without exposing themselves too much.

Unfortunately for them, there really was no cover in that yard, and Kirk was already all but aimed in. He fired twice at the first silhouette on the left, then tracked toward the second when the first jerked and went down to a knee. His next pair took the second man high in the chest. The National Army didn't seem to have body armor, and the man stopped in his tracks before crashing over onto his back.

That seemed to have given the rest of the assault force pause, and that was when Kirk realized Flanagan was yelling at him. "Kirk! The truck's right outside, on the other side of the wall from you! Let's go!"

"On you, Kev!" He didn't dare drop security on the back of the house until the last possible moment.

"I'm supposed to be the base of fire, not the damned point man!" Curtis was still up on his feet, the belt dangling from the K3, and he surged out of the gate, turning sharply to clear the sidewalk right outside. Kirk followed, right on the other man's heels, though not before one last glance at the back of the house and the drifting smoke cloud. No one had followed the first two yet. They were being cautious.

That made sense, given the bloodletting these four men had already wreaked.

There wasn't just one truck on the street. Two jeeps and an ancient deuce-and-a-half were parked at angles to the gate. There were bodies littering the street, and one of the jeeps had been riddled with bullets, the gunner's body slumped over the back in such a painful contortion that there was no doubt the man was dead. Any of the National Army soldiers who had exposed themselves to the open gated had died quickly, going down to Curtis's firepower or Flanagan's marksmanship.

Kirk found himself and Curtis facing half a dozen more soldiers, all huddled against the compound wall, waiting for the assault force to divert the Blackhearts inside so that they could close the jaws of the trap. He caught sight of the lead man's eyes widening as the two of them burst out of the gateway, just before Curtis opened fire from what was effectively point blank range.

The K3 roared, the noise echoing off the buildings and the deuce-and-a-half, as he cut the stack of men down, tearing the one in the front almost in half. Blood splashed the whitewashed wall and the street, as men tumbled to the ground, their screams drowned out by the thunder of gunfire.

Kirk didn't even have a shot before Curtis had wasted the lot of them.

They were far from out of the woods, though. He could see the glow of more headlights coming their way. A lot more.

"Take one of the jeeps!" Burgess was thinking, even as he and Flanagan swept the street in the opposite direction, killing a few more of the Costas who had been content to sit tight while they waited for their fellows to storm the house. "They'll be easier to maneuver!"

Flanagan was already on it, pulling a bloody corpse out from behind the wheel of the less ventilated jeep, letting the body hit the street with limp finality. "Somebody get on the gun!"

"Come on, Kev!" Kirk grabbed Curtis and turned to run toward the jeep, remembering at the last second not to get too focused on their way out. They still had to get across that gateway. He let go of the other Blackheart and dropped his muzzle level as he moved into the gate's fatal funnel.

He'd barely stepped into the gateway when he spotted a shape ducking around the corner of the house, on the opposite side from where he'd shot the first two. His finger tightened on the trigger, but the light was bad enough that he hesitated. He had to be sure. If one of the owner's kids had snuck out and tried to run...

A muzzle flash blossomed in front of him, and bullets crackled overhead, a few smacking plaster off the wall above him while the rest climbed into the sky. If the soldier hadn't been firing from the hip on full auto, Kirk and Curtis probably both would have been dead.

He leaned into the gun and kept his muzzle level as he dumped half his current magazine into the man and anyone behind him, even while he and Curtis swept across the gateway toward the jeep, where Burgess was already up on the M1919, sending long bursts of .30 caliber fire down the street toward the advancing headlights.

Kirk pivoted toward the other side of the house as the compound wall cut off his view of the corner where he'd just taken fire. Another figure was coming out of the drifting smoke, and he double tapped that one before turning and sprinting for the jeep.

Curtis was already in the passenger's seat, his K3 laid over the dash, the windshield having been dropped flat on the hood already. Kirk clambered up behind Burgess, covering their rear. "Let's *go!*"

Flanagan ground gears to put the old vehicle in reverse, and pulled a J turn to get them pointed away from the oncoming National Army trucks. Stomping on the clutch and brakes, he quickly worked through the gears to get the jeep moving down the street.

Kirk just hung on as Burgess pivoted to take up rear security. It was going to be a wild ride to get out of the city, and hopefully reach their rendezvous point.

CHAPTER 31

Hierro wasn't in great shape after what he'd been through in that prison. He still did what he could to keep up as the Blackhearts hustled out of the concrete building and toward the gap in the fence. He'd adjusted quickly to the idea that he was being rescued, and he was as focused on survival as any of them.

Brannigan had hesitated as the man had bent to pick up one of the FMK-3 submachineguns they'd taken from the guards. He didn't know anything about this guy except for the fact that he was a political dissident who had been imprisoned and tortured by the military junta that ruled this tiny excuse for a country, and that someone Stateside thought he was a good candidate to take over a resistance and overthrow that junta. But the way that he checked the subgun told Brannigan that this man knew weapons, far better than any disaffected politician he'd ever seen.

Most of the kind of people who would have been broken out for the purpose of rallying a political movement tended to be charismatic but ultimately somewhat soft. Political theorists, activists, that sort of thing. Actual fighters were rare, though many of the "political dissidents" Brannigan was familiar with usually didn't have a lot of scruples about using other fighters to kill people in job lots to accomplish their goals.

Under different circumstances, he might welcome a rescuee that knew how to take care of themselves in a firefight.

Something about this whole situation, though, made him wary. Made him not want to have this man at his back with a weapon.

He couldn't place what was warning him just yet, aside from the fact that this was Latin America, and genuine, American-style democratic politicians were astonishingly rare. Usually, it was either brutal militarists or some flavor of Communist. They hadn't been told that Hierro was a Communist, but then, they hadn't been told much about him.

They got to the door, where the bodies of the outside guards were still lying where they'd fallen. Santelli and Puller had set up on the doorway itself as soon as the other Blackhearts and the package had come out of the cell block, and now they moved out, though not before Santelli had told Brannigan that they hadn't spotted any reinforcements so far. From the amount of noise coming from the direction of the port, that wasn't that surprising. They'd only fired a handful of shots near the prison, so the bulk of the enemy's attention should be focused elsewhere.

They just needed to get moving before that attention swamped their buddies.

With Puller and Santelli in the lead—not the men he would have immediately picked to take point, but they had limited time and options at the moment—they hustled toward the fence in a relatively tight diamond around Hierro.

Brannigan had made sure he was directly behind their package. Just in case.

They reached the fence without incident, and started clambering down the rocks toward the boat, which fortunately looked like it was still tied up. Brannigan stayed atop the short bluff for a moment, taking a knee beneath one of the unoccupied guard towers as he drew his radio out of his vest.

"Angry Ragnar, Kodiak. We have the package and are coming back to you."

***

Wade watched the docks over the yacht's gunwale and his rifle's sights. Things were still moving on the other side of the fence, as the National Army tried to get a new assault put together.

198

There were still a few of the pirates and the original react force hiding behind some of the equipment and crates on the pier, but most of them were either lying still on the concrete, or shuddering as they finished bleeding out. Wade hadn't wasted any ammunition on the ones that hadn't been killed outright, but he and Bianco weren't letting anyone get to them, either.

Bianco twisted in his position, an arm's length away, and sent a stuttering burst at the nearest building above the port, where Wade had last seen movement, mostly in the glow of headlights that were coming from behind that building. Judging by the panic in the sudden scramble, Wade was pretty sure that if they'd been close enough, they would have heard a lot of swearing in Spanish.

"Angry Ragnar, Kodiak. We have the package and are coming back to you."

Wade grimaced as he grabbed for his own radio, hoping he'd heard the whole message, and there hadn't been vital information drowned out by Bianco's machinegun fire. "Copy you're on your way." He really wished they'd had some proper headsets, but it wasn't the first op the Blackhearts had done on a shoestring.

He turned aside to check on their positions on the yacht. The boat was too big to hold entirely, and the need to keep the troops on the docks at bay had precluded a proper clear. He was all the way in the bow with Bianco, while Hank held on the entirety of the rest of the yacht, covering their backs. If there were more pirates on board, somewhere below decks, they hadn't showed themselves, but they might have set ambushes on the way back to the stern.

Assuming they hadn't already cut the boat loose.

"We're going to have to fall back!" Someone down on the docks was trying to move, and he interrupted himself to lay his Galil over the railing and drive the man back behind a stack of cargo containers with a trio of shots, the reports echoing across the port.

"Go, Vinnie!" Wade was already rising from the railing, his own weapon pointed at the sky. They had a moment's

199

breathing room, but they needed to use all of it. "Hank! Take us along the right side!"

For a moment, Hank stutter stepped. "The starboard or port side?"

"Fuck!" Wade moved up next to the former Marine officer, cursing all things nautical, and pointed toward the port side and the dock. "That side! We need to knock that damned gangplank in the drink."

Hank got it, then, and they were moving, Hank in front and scanning not only the stern and the flanks but also every opening they passed just over his sights. Wade had to grudgingly admit that the junior Brannigan knew his business. Bianco tried to maneuver the heavier K3 to follow suit, but the light machinegun wasn't really designed for close quarters.

The gangplank was about halfway to the stern, and as they got closer, Hank moving to the gunwale and taking a knee, even though the thin sheet metal wasn't going to provide any decent cover at all if one of the pirates or government troops tried to get a shot at them, Wade saw that it wasn't going to be nearly as simple as shoving it off to one side. It was a fixture on the side of the yacht, held in place by chains and apparently run out from a slot beneath the deck. He was going to have to either find a way to remove the chains and run it the rest of the way out—which didn't seem likely—or pull it in.

Either task was going to take too long, he realized. Speed was their only security, now that they'd given up the bow and the covering fire they'd been able to bring to bear against the docks, and they needed to move.

"Push, Hank." He glared at the gangplank, then turned to follow the younger Brannigan just before Bianco opened fire again. Wade pivoted to see what was happening, in time to see one soldier topple and the others run for cover.

They really didn't have any time left.

Hank was moving again, pacing toward the stern behind his rifle. They probably should have gone through the boathouse, if only to make it harder to target them, but speed was security.

It was probably the only reason they didn't run into serious opposition earlier.

They came out onto the aft deck to see one of the pirates sawing away at the mooring line that Wade had tied to the rail. Hank shot the man twice, sending him crashing over the rail to disappear off the stern, but then another pirate lunged out of the boathouse and slammed into him, his momentum carrying both of them against the rail, the pirate holding onto Hank's rifle and trying to wrest it away from him.

Wade took a split second to check that he wasn't about to get jumped by another one from the same direction, then he slung his own rifle, drew his Cordova 9mm, and went in.

The pirate was small and wiry, but he was tough. Hank had to outweigh the guy by thirty pounds, but he kept moving, wrestling with the Blackheart for the rifle. From the looks of things, he was strong enough that Hank didn't dare take his hands off the Galil to reach for another weapon.

Wade was not interested in wasting time. With his own Galil hanging from its sling in front of him, he grabbed the pirate by the hair at the back of his head, wrenched his skull back, put his Cordova's muzzle to the man's temple, and pulled the trigger.

The pirate didn't even have time to register what was happening before a good portion of his brains was blown across the aft deck in a spray of gore.

Wade redoubled his leverage on the man's head, prying his now limp form off Hank. "You good, Junior?"

Hank levered himself to his feet, pushing off the rail. He started to speak, but Bianco fired another burst at the same moment, stitching rounds across the pier. Instead of waiting for the noise to die down, the younger man just nodded and headed for the stern.

Wade followed, all but pulling Bianco with him. The National Army soldiers were trying to push from cover to cover along the pier, trying to get to the gangplank before the Blackhearts could get off the boat. They were a day late and a dollar short, though, as Bianco drove them back again, just before his belt ran out.

Then he and Wade turned and ran for the aft rail.

The mooring line was still holding, though it had been half cut through. Wade took a look over the side, to see that Hank had already just jumped into the water and was now hauling himself into the boat. A glance to the west showed the faint white of the other boat's wake. It was now or never.

Wade vaulted the rail, as bullets began to crackle overhead, taking the short plunge into the warm waters of the Caribbean. He wasn't the greatest swimmer, and his musculature tended to make him sink like a rock even without a rifle and a chest rig still half full of magazines, but he kicked savagely to the surface, reaching for the boat and barely avoiding Bianco's bulk as the big man splashed into the water beside him, not quite managing the graceful step off the side of the boat that he'd probably trained for once upon a time.

He grasped the gunwale and pulled himself up, tipping the boat alarmingly and forcing Hank to lean to one side to keep it from capsizing. That made his current task of starting the outboard more difficult, but after it coughed a couple more times, it finally caught.

Bianco was struggling to swim over. The weight of his weapon and ammo was worse than what Wade had, and it was all dragging him down. Wade got a leg over the gunwale and half rolled into the boat, holding out a hand for Bianco.

Two flailing strokes didn't seem to bring Bianco any closer. Wade cursed and leaned out farther, catching the third, increasingly panicked swing and grabbing a handful of Bianco's sleeve.

He rolled back into the boat, hauling on Bianco's arm as hard as he could. He got it far enough that the bigger man got a grip on the gunwale, and he turned to yell at Hank, but the junior Brannigan was already backing water, getting them away from the pier and the yacht, dragging Bianco through the water as they went.

"We're gonna need some fire!" Wade craned his neck to look up as Hank yelled over the growl of the outboard and the rush of the water against the hull. Sure enough, the local troops were running down the pier, now that they weren't taking fire from the yacht anymore. With Bianco holding onto the gunwale, Wade hitched himself up, grabbed the machinegunner's vest, and heaved, pulling him halfway into the boat with a single pull and almost capsizing it again. Hank cursed, trying desperately to correct, though his own weight wasn't anything near the combined mass of Wade and Bianco.

Wade rolled to the other side of the boat, going over his rifle painfully in the process, and fought to get it up, trying desperately not to flag either Hank or Bianco with the muzzle as he did so. Muzzle flashes started to flicker from the pier, the *snap* of the bullets passing overhead beating the crackle of the gunfire by fractions of a second.

Getting the rifle over the gunwale, Wade tried to return fire, though his own shots weren't any more accurate than the soldiers'. At least he had the excuse that he was on a boat that was moving on the waves, and was rocking from side to side as Bianco got himself and his weapon the rest of the way in.

Hank was turning as he backed water farther, presenting Bianco with the full broadside, even though he was still reloading the K3. "Last belt!"

That wasn't what Wade wanted to hear, but there wasn't much they could do about it.

Hank got them pointed out into the dark water of the Caribbean, as Bianco got the light machinegun up and sent another long burst at the pier. Then Hank was laying on the throttle, following the other boat out to sea, and Wade reached over to grip Bianco's shoulder. "Cease fire. Only going to give them something to shoot at from here on out."

Bianco nodded, slumping down into the boat, even as more bullets cracked overhead, though the sound of their passage was getting fainter as the government troops' aim got worse with distance and darkness.

Now they just had to hope that Flanagan and the others could get out of the city.

CHAPTER 32

Flanagan gritted his teeth as he drove, squinting into the wind as he got the old jeep moving as fast as he could without throwing Kirk off the back. Burgess was crouched behind the old Browning right behind him, while Curtis leaned into the K3 over the hood and bitched.

"Can't you drive a little smoother, Joe? I can't hit shit with how bouncy this ride is."

"Would you like to drive?" Flanagan usually had a better comeback for his friend's runaway mouth, but he was trying desperately to avoid the potholes that were everywhere, threatening to bounce them off the street at best, snap an axle at worst. All the while getting pelted with brass as Burgess hammered away at their pursuers.

That they hadn't been cut off yet was a miracle, one that Flanagan didn't trust to last. The three jeeps behind them were starting to back off a little, since Burgess had shattered at least one headlight and probably more than that with full auto .30 cal fire.

It was another minor miracle that their teammate had managed that, given how violently the jeep was moving.

He took the next right turn. The last one had almost gotten them caught and killed, since he'd been halfway into the turn before he'd realized that the alley dead ended. They'd been pushed east, farther away from the edge of the city, where they wanted to go, and he had to get back on course.

It was less likely that the army could get someone ahead of them if they kept moving toward the outskirts.

He saw the white cones of headlights on a crossroads just ahead as he made the turn, and he floored the accelerator, wishing—despite his lifelong desire for an old, all-mechanical Willys Jeep—that he had a Hilux or something. Something with a bit more get up and go. That was almost certainly a National Army vehicle moving to cut them off, and he needed to get them past it before it blocked the narrow street.

The front right tire hit another pothole he hadn't quite seen, bouncing them all halfway out of their seats, throwing up a fountain of filthy water, and rattling the entire vehicle so hard that Flanagan was almost sure that it had broken something and that they were stranded. But when the wheel hit the pavement again it kept turning, and they kept hurtling down the street.

The intersection ahead was coming up fast, and so was the National Army truck. Flanagan didn't doubt that that was what it was. There was no one else out on the streets that night.

He cleared the intersection a bare few feet in front of the oncoming truck. The Costa driver stomped on the brakes at the last second, apparently unwilling to risk a collision, even if his orders had been to stop the jeep.

It was probably a little unsure which jeep they were supposed to stop. In the dark, one gun truck probably looked much like another, and the Blackhearts' camouflage wouldn't be immediately obvious in contrast to the locals' plain green.

And Flanagan intended to take full advantage of that.

He kept going as the truck's driver leaned on the horn, reinforcing his guess that there was plenty of confusion on the streets at the moment. "Tom! Don't open fire unless you have to!" He kept his eyes on the road while twisting his neck to yell over his shoulder. "They can't be sure they're not going to shoot their own guys, so let's just make tracks!"

206

"Gotcha!" Burgess had to roar at the top of his lungs to be heard over the wind, as Flanagan was driving as fast as he dared push the old jeep through the narrow and rough streets.

There was another block ahead, the street ending in a T intersection. He gritted his teeth as he dodged another gaping pothole that had suddenly loomed in his headlights, knowing that if he'd hit it, it almost certainly would have snapped an axle and put them afoot. Which was not where he wanted to be tonight. There was a time and a place for evading on foot, and in the middle of an unfamiliar city swarming with hostile troops was not it.

"Somebody get on the radio to Kodiak, let him know that we're heading out of town!" Coordination had kind of gone to shit since they'd made contact, and at that point he could only really hope that the assault had gone according to plan. Rendezvous was going to be tricky, especially since they needed to lose the Costas first, but he needed to do what they could, especially since stealth was currently out the window.

"Already on the radio!" Kirk wasn't in a position to engage anyone following them—and the truck they'd passed had turned and lumbered in pursuit, though the deuce-and-a-half didn't have anything close to the speed or maneuverability to close the distance with the jeep, especially when it was being driven in as daredevil a manner as Flanagan was currently pushing it. He was holding onto the jeep with one hand and his radio with the other. "They're exfilling now, heading west to link up on the beach!"

Flanagan just nodded, though Kirk probably couldn't see it. He had his hands full as he took the right hand turn as fast as he dared, actually feeling the jeep's right wheels come off the road a little bit as he went around the corner.

The street ahead was clear, at least for the moment, though lights appeared behind them, glaring in the side mirrors. The noose was tightening.

He spotted another cross street heading out of the city ahead, and headed for it, even as yet another set of headlights swung onto the road ahead. A voice came over a megaphone, shouting in Spanish. Even if Flanagan's Spanish had been better than it was, he was too absorbed in driving to note what was being said. The wind and the rattle and roar of the jeep didn't help, either.

Fortunately, neither the truck ahead nor the one behind opened fire, the soldiers wary of hitting their comrades. The Blackhearts were in the middle of a pincer that was actually keeping them safe, at least for the moment.

He threw the jeep around the corner hard and fast, once again almost flipping it, and he heard Kirk swear as he was nearly thrown clear. Curtis was just hanging on for dear life, his K3 now stuffed next to his leg under the dash. Getting a glimpse of his old friend, Flanagan thought that if he'd been a little lighter of shade, he would have been deathly pale.

Curtis's knuckles were definitely lighter than normal where he was holding onto the dash and the door next to him.

He got the jeep under control on the far side of the turn, and they were looking at open farmland.

The road actually ended in another T intersection, with a crude post and wire fence on the far side of the ring road that appeared to go at least partway around the outside of Santa Paz. Flanagan didn't slow down or turn to right or left, and Curtis swore even louder as he leaned back and tried to brace himself.

The jeep actually left the ground for a second as it crashed through the fence and into the field. It was past harvest time, apparently, as there wasn't a lot of growth, and the dirt was dry and hard. They hit with a savage impact, almost bouncing all four of them out of the vehicle and making the jeep emit a *bang* that sounded catastrophic, though it kept rolling as it hit the ground again. Flanagan worked the gears as he killed the lights, hoping that they could hide in the darkness while they got some distance from the city.

The Costa drivers were a bit more cautious negotiating the turn onto the road behind them, and the headlights didn't spill out onto the fields until the jeep was already almost halfway across. Speed was no longer much of an option, as the broken, tilled ground was bad enough that even walking across it would have been miserable, let alone driving.

Flanagan fought the terrain and the vehicle alike, turning north as best he could, toward the ocean. The furrows were running the wrong way, and soon the ride was not only getting rougher and rougher, it was slowing severely.

"We can run faster than this." Burgess was holding onto the gun mount for dear life, as the jeep rocked violently from side to side while Flanagan tried to steer over the furrows. "We've got some space, Joe. Let's get out and beat feet."

Flanagan kept going a few more yards, but the creaking and banging was getting worse, and lights were starting to sweep over the field behind them. Burgess was right. If they got away from the jeep, they might disappear into the dark, but if they kept with the vehicle, there was a good chance that it would get spotted in the headlights and taken under fire. It was just making them a target, now.

He let off the gas, almost killing the engine despite having used the clutch. The jeep had taken a beating on the way out of the city, and it probably didn't have long. Leaving it in neutral—he couldn't quite bring himself to just let it die—he shut the engine off and bailed, joining the other three Blackhearts in the dirt, as Burgess and Kirk hustled around to his side of the jeep. Curtis was already on a knee in front of the hood, his K3 pointed back toward the city and the headlights. Flanagan almost warned him not to open fire, but he didn't need to. Curtis was a clown most of the time, but he wouldn't still be a Blackheart if he wasn't smart enough for the job.

"Let's go." Keeping low, despite the aches in their legs, the four of them stalked toward the line of low, scrubby trees at the edge of the field, and the Caribbean beyond.

As he passed Curtis, he heard a hoarse whisper. "I take back what I said before about you turning into an old woman, Joe, but only if you promise to *never* drive like that again. At least not while I'm in the car."

Despite himself, Flanagan grinned in the dark and gave Curtis's shoulder a brutal squeeze before he got moving toward the trees, risking a twisted ankle with every step.

Behind them, the soldiers started to spread out, lights sweeping the dirt as they began their search.

***

The beach was dark and silent, and Brannigan peered through the night, scanning as best he could with eyes that were only now starting to get their night adaptation back after the fight at the port and the military base, straining his ears for any sound that might indicate pursuit. They hadn't seen any other boats besides the pirate yacht, but he didn't doubt they were out there somewhere.

They needed to link up with the diversionary team and get moving toward the rendezvous. The sooner they handed Hierro off and got out of Costa de las Joyas, the better.

"Kodiak, Woodsrunner. We are five hundred yards out. Be advised, the opposition is in pursuit, but they have lost ground and are unlikely to catch up with us."

Brannigan lifted his own radio to his lips. Even with no one around, they needed to be as quiet as possible. Sound travels far at night, and even more so over the water. "Copy, Woodsrunner. We are moving in toward the beach now." He would have preferred to take the boats, as tight a fit as they would have been, to the rendezvous, but the point they'd been given in the briefing materials was too far inland.

Entirely too close to the Venezuelan border, to Brannigan's way of thinking, but they didn't have direct comms with Hierro's people, so they had to use the RV point that Van Zandt had given them.

Unfortunately, when he checked his watch as the bottom of the boat scraped on the sand, he realized that it was going to take more than what was left of the night to get there. He jumped out and helped pull the boat higher up onto the beach before turning to meet Flanagan and the rest as they appeared at the top

210

of the low bluff, looking down to make sure they were in the right spot before turning and getting down in the prone to hold security.

With a deep breath, all too aware of how dead tired he already was, Brannigan started the climb to join them, while the rest either helped Hierro or started to push the boats back out to sea.

CHAPTER 33

The rendezvous was at another small farm in the hills, not unlike the one where Raul had dropped them off. In fact, it looked enough like the other place that if he hadn't been paying attention to their navigation, Tackett would have thought that they'd circled right back around. But they were miles to the south and east of where Raul had taken them, and the hill behind was different.

They'd holed up in an abandoned hut for the day, despite the risk that it had presented. Tackett suspected that all of them had been bitten at some point, taking an "abandoned" house as shelter in a combat zone only to find out that it wasn't nearly as abandoned as it had seemed. The sunrise had almost snuck up on them, though, bearing testimony to just how exhausted they all were. That, plus the fact that there simply hadn't been another viable hide site in the scrubby desert outside of Santa Paz for over a mile as the sky had started to lighten.

It had been a long, hot, miserable day, crammed into a space barely big enough for half their number, but they'd endured and made it. Curtis had bitched, of course, but he'd kept it to a low roar, and had finally shut up when Wade had glared at him. Flanagan might have grinned in the dark when that had happened. Tackett hadn't been with the team that long, but he was picking up on the dynamics, and the big brother/little brother antics between Curtis and Flanagan were a good sign.

That they'd happened in the hide was also a sign that they were keeping things together, despite the strain and the exhaustion.

Now, a couple hours after midnight, if he was keeping good enough track of time without checking his watch and risking light exposure, they were nearly at their destination.

He crawled forward toward the next outcropping. He and Gomez had taken one finger on the south side of the farm, while Flanagan and Hank had taken the other. Brannigan had wanted to take no chances, directing overwatch to set up before they even tried to approach the farm itself. He'd issued his orders out of earshot from Hierro, too, while Puller had once again gone over the man's injuries.

That Hierro had been worked over pretty hard was obvious. After what Santelli and Bianco had gone through, it really came as no surprise to any of the Blackhearts. But there was something about the man that Tackett found disquieting, and from the looks he'd seen cast at their package, he knew he wasn't alone.

There was an edge to Hierro, a sense of violence. Every one of Brannigan's Blackhearts was a predator, and they recognized kind for kind. There was more to it than that, though. There was a distance, a coldness that rubbed Tackett the wrong way, and he could tell he wasn't alone.

It made Tackett wonder just what kind of "resistance" this man was supposed to rally against the junta. Was this just a matter of trading one devil for another, in the hopes that the new one would be more amenable to leaving Americans alone?

It was possible. It had certainly happened before. It was a cynical, gangsterish bargain, but one that could work under some circumstances.

Those circumstances almost always ended up backfiring, but that was neither here nor there.

There were no lights out in the countryside of Costa de las Joyas, at least not for the most part. The tiny country was crushingly poor, even more than Iraq had been. At least there

214

people had kept generators for the inevitable blackouts. This place seemed more like rural Afghanistan. No lights at all after dark.

Except for this farm.

The lanterns out front were old, but they shed light on the porch of the small stone house. And as Tackett and Gomez crept up to a vantage point above it, they could also see the figures sitting or standing a little way outside the circles of golden illumination.

There were guards on the place.

Tackett peered down at the dim, shadowy shapes of men, one of them lit up suddenly as he struck a match and lifted it to a cigarette. These guys didn't act like the National Army, as generally sloppy and undisciplined as the junta's soldiers were. These men were even lazier, from the looks of it. They were on guard, but they weren't that alert. Especially not if they were lighting up in the middle of the night.

Gomez was an arm's length away, watching the guards. Tackett was pretty sure the man was listening to every sound in the night, too. Gomez might be quiet and calm, but there was something about him that sometimes made Tackett's hackles stand up.

"Guerrillas?" He didn't whisper, but almost subvocalized, keeping his tone so low that it wouldn't travel more than a few feet.

"Looks like it." Gomez didn't take his eyes off the house or the men near it. He nodded toward them. "See the one closest to the house on the left?"

Tackett let his eyes drift toward the figure Gomez had indicated. The man was leaning against the wall, near the corner, a rifle at his feet.

The weapon was close enough to the lantern—and Tackett's dark adaptation had gotten far enough along since the sun had gone down, as much as he might have wished for night vision—that he could make out the silhouette. Especially the curved magazine that definitely was not one of the National Army FALs'.

215

Tackett knew a Kalashnikov, even at a glance in bad light.

That pretty well confirmed that these were not National Army soldiers waiting in ambush. That niggling feeling that something was wrong, though, the same feeling that he got when he studied Hierro, who occasionally watched one of them with the same burning stare that drifted off into the distance from time to time, was still very much there.

He shifted his rifle, even though he only had two magazines left. He'd drop that one first, if things went sideways.

Gomez glanced over at him, then nodded and rolled partway onto his side to access his radio. Pulling it out, he keyed it with his lips almost touching the mic.

"Kodiak, Chico. We have four exterior guards on the house. They're acting lazy, but they're all keeping out of direct illumination from the lanterns. They're also carrying AKs, and do not appear to be government troops."

"Good copy, Chico. Are you in position to support?"

"Affirm. We have overwatch, and we'll take the two to the south first." Gomez laid the radio down next to him. The volume was turned so low that if there had been so much as a breath of wind off the Caribbean, Tackett didn't think he could have heard Brannigan's voice.

"You take the one on the left, I'll take the one on the right." Gomez carefully laid his Galil in a cleft in the rocks, leveling it down at the guards outside the house. Tackett shifted his own position to get as close to his natural point of aim on the second guard.

"Woodsrunner, Kodiak. You and Newb in position?" Tackett had gathered that Hank really detested that callsign, which, of course, was why it had stuck.

"We're set, Kodiak. Just be advised, Newb thinks he heard movement higher up the mountain. I've got him covering that direction."

"Copy. We're going in." There was only so much they could do with the numbers and the ammunition they had.

Brannigan had made it clear that they needed to be ready to lay the hate and run if anything went wrong. None of them could quite put a finger on why they thought this was all about to go sideways, but maybe it was just their own long-standing paranoia keeping them on their toes.

After the Anambas, Tackett was *always* ready for things to go south.

One of the guards shoved off the wall, coming to his feet as he pulled his AK up into his hands. He said something to the others, and soon all four were on their feet, spread out a little bit wider, none of them far from cover.

They were ready for trouble. That might just be because they were guerrillas in a country ruled by a brutal military government. That would only make sense. But Tackett thought that all of the Blackhearts—except maybe Curtis—had to be thinking that they were *awfully* close to Venezuela.

The same Venezuela that had declared itself a socialist republic and had supported not only the FARC but the Green Shirt militia that the Blackhearts had fought a little before Tackett had come fully onto the team.

Footsteps crunched in the dirt and gravel down the valley, and the two guards he and Gomez were watching repositioned themselves just a little. Then one of them spoke into a radio, getting a reply that was all but inaudible up on the finger.

It might have just been to contact whoever Hierro's primary was. Or maybe it was something else. Tackett shifted his position still further to track his target.

The other Blackhearts appeared near the gate leading into the farm, though they were spread out in a wedge, with Hierro in the middle. Brannigan had taken point, probably to the chagrin of the rest of the team, and he halted at the gate itself, in a position where he could quickly take cover. None of them were showing lights, though they all had somewhat makeshift weapon lights on their Galils.

Brannigan didn't call out. For a long few minutes, no one moved or said anything. Tackett felt his heart rate start to go up.

217

Something was going to go down. Either this was an ambush, or both sides were so paranoid at that point that somebody was going to get trigger happy just to be on the safe side.

The door to the farm opened, and a man stepped out, though he quickly closed the door behind him and moved away from the lanterns. Everyone down there was being extra cautious.

With the amount of activity the National Army had been engaged in over the last twenty-four hours, that was probably wise.

Tackett still wasn't going to relax, especially since the locals down there weren't going to. Those AKs weren't quite aimed in, but they were pointed toward the other Blackhearts.

After another long pause, the man who'd just come out spoke up, his voice echoing down the little valley. "Ernesto? Is that you?"

Hierro stepped forward. "I am here, Quito." His voice was a bit of a rasp, though that wasn't surprising after what he'd been through in that prison.

No one on the farm moved. Tackett let out a long breath, his finger hovering near the trigger. Why wouldn't they stand down if the Blackhearts had brought them their prize, as agreed?

"*Yanquis.*" Quito's voice reverberated off the nearby hill. "You have brought our comrade, as promised. Why don't you come up and join us?"

Tackett glanced at Gomez. The other Blackheart was still on his sights, completely still. There was something very, very wrong here. The guards still had their weapons pointed, and they hadn't moved from their defensive positions.

He took his eyes off his particular target, knowing that he probably shouldn't, since it could all go to hell in the next few seconds, and scanned the hill above the farm. It was a good thing he did, too.

Gomez sensed it a moment later. He twisted around in his position, bringing his rifle to bear, just as Tackett registered the half dozen dark figures moving down the finger toward them in

218

crouched stances. It was impossible to see much detail in the dark, but he was pretty sure they were armed.

Initiate now, or wait? He decided to key off Gomez. This might have just been a precaution. After all, the Blackhearts had set in overwatch.

The two of them lay there in the dirt, waiting and watching, as the six men moved down the slope, staying below the crest of the hill, covered from the main body of the Blackhearts as they went. The longer they watched, the more convinced Tackett was that this wasn't a precaution. This was a flanking maneuver.

Brannigan hadn't replied to Quito, and everyone below seemed to be waiting for something. Tackett was pretty sure that Brannigan was waiting for exactly what they were looking at. And Hierro's guerrillas weren't going to go down into the kill zone they'd set up.

Finally, even as the flankers got closer to Tackett and Gomez, Brannigan spoke up. "We've been paid. We just want to finish the mission and go home."

"We can help you. The National Army is hunting you. Come up." Still, none of the guerrillas so much as took a step to join the Blackhearts.

Tackett turned slightly to continue to follow the flanking element, and as he did, he dislodged a rock that skittered away from his boot, raising a slight cloud of dust.

Under different circumstances, it would have been nothing. He'd seen and heard a lot worse on patrol in equally dangerous places. But these guys were wound tight, and one of them was a little tighter than others.

Without being able to see, the guerrilla skidded to a stop and fired a burst at wherever he thought he'd heard the noise.

Muzzle flash strobed in the darkness, bullets crackling far enough overhead that Tackett knew there was next to no chance of getting hit where he lay flat on the ground. Rolling to his back, he brought his Galil to bear between his knees, his finger tightening on the trigger, even though the sights were nearly invisible in the dark.

***

Everyone froze as the gunfire echoed across the little valley. Standing next to Brannigan, Hierro had gone utterly motionless, probably all too aware of just how thin a thread his life currently hung by.

"You up there." Brannigan's voice cracked across the open ground as the echoes faded. From the direction the sound had come from, he figured that some of the guerrillas had run into Tackett and Gomez, though the lack of follow up fire was strange. He doubted that those two had been caught completely flat footed. "If you want your boy back in one piece, I suggest you back off."

"It was a mistake." Hierro hadn't spoken much on the movement so far, but he seemed to be awfully sure of himself now. "Wasn't it, Quito?"

"Yes." Something about the tone of the man's voice didn't sound that sincere, but Brannigan realized that he was so keyed up that he was ready to put a bullet in their principal just to be sure. "It was an accident. Please, let us all be calm."

He kept an eye on Hierro as he reached for his radio. "Chico, Kodiak. You guys all right?"

"We're intact, but we've got a bit of a Mexican standoff going on up here." Brannigan breathed a faint sigh of relief. He hadn't been impressed with anyone's tactical acumen in Costa de las Joyas so far, but all it took could be one lucky burst, and he might have lost two of his best teammates. "One of them shot at noise, and they just figured out that we've got them covered."

Brannigan looked at Hierro, who was watching him, unmoving in the dark. "It was a mistake," the other man repeated. "Things are tense right now. You should know."

That was the truth, but Brannigan didn't think that the other guerrillas had simply stumbled on Gomez and Tackett. There was more going on here. He would have expected the guerrillas to be set up as a welcoming committee when their leader was returned, not an ambush.

Because that was what this looked like. He knew a defensive setup when he saw one, and this wasn't quite it. These

220

guys wanted the Blackhearts to come into what could easily turn into a pincer, and they were being extra careful to stay out of the light in the process. Without any sign of the National Army being near the place, that meant they were hiding from the Blackhearts.

Where they were right now, the playing field was relatively even. The maneuver element, with Hierro, had some cover and could quickly get behind it. The flankers held the high ground to either side, even though Gomez and Tackett seemed to be currently staring down their sights at some more of the guerrillas.

"So they are." He decided to cut through the static. "But that's not our problem. We were hired to get you out and get you to your people. We did that." He waved toward the farmhouse. "You join up with them, do your little revolution, and we disappear."

The look he got from Hierro was hard to read in the dark. Maybe he was just being paranoid, but it really seemed as if there was something more going on, something that Hierro knew that he didn't, and he didn't like it.

But the former political prisoner just nodded, made some kind of signal with his hand, and turned to continue toward the farmhouse on his own.

The guerrillas stayed where they were, none of them even coming out into the light to greet Hierro until he had nearly reached the house itself. Then a man with a radio in his hand stepped out to greet him. The two of them spoke briefly, Hierro glancing back toward the Blackhearts as the man with the radio talked. He nodded, then, and the man with the radio lifted it to his lips.

Brannigan was already doing the same. "Maintain security but let's start moving back to get out of here."

He still held his own position as the others began to fade back toward the open ground below the farm. Hierro and the other man were still watching them, as the other man continued to talk into the radio.

The guerrillas were starting to move. Not to fall back to the house, but they were spreading out, some of them starting to move up the hill.

"They're going to hit us." Santelli had his own rifle leveled, braced against the other post on the other side of the gateway. "Question is, why?"

"My guess is that they don't want anyone to talk about Hierro being back in circulation." Wade was somewhere up behind Brannigan and to his left.

"Maybe." He was watching the guerrilla who was standing next to Hierro. The man was still outside the circle of illumination from the nearest lantern, but there was something about him that didn't match the others. Something about the way he stood. He was too straight-backed, too soldierly, compared to the others.

Then the shooting started.

CHAPTER 34

Flanagan watched the four men with weapons as they crept down along the length of the finger, moving more slowly after they'd frozen following the eruption of gunfire on the other side of the farm. He and Hank were well concealed among the rocks and the scrub brush that topped the finger, which was why they hadn't been spotted yet, and probably why the guerrillas were still moving.

He couldn't rotate his position without giving the two of them away, and something told him that they needed to stay undetected as long as humanly possible. He didn't know it, but he was already hitting the same conclusion that Tackett had: this was a maneuver element attempting to catch the Blackhearts in a pincer.

He didn't know why, but there appeared to be a double cross in the works.

Moving nothing but his eyes, he followed the group as they scrambled through the desert growth just below them. One seemed to be lugging a PKM. The other three all had AKs.

The calls between the guerrilla leader and Brannigan were audible even where he and Hank were lying on the other side of the finger. It was a quiet night, except for the recent spate of gunfire. Sound would travel far, even over rough terrain.

Those four were still moving while the conversation was happening on the other side of the terrain feature. They slowed somewhat as they started to climb toward the top of the ridgeline, the man with the PKM in the lead. It didn't look like they were slowing down because the terrain was particularly difficult, either. The rocks were looser than might be ideal, but they could climb well enough.

No, they were trying to be quiet. Trying to avoid being heard or spotted from the main Blackhearts position down by the farm gate.

The man with the machinegun carefully deployed his bipods before he settled down in the prone, getting set behind the gun while he pointed it down the hill and toward the gate.

Flanagan carefully and deliberately rolled over so that he could face that position, leaving Hank to cover up the hillside behind them. He was close enough that he needed to move achingly slowly to keep from making noise, even though the guy with the PKM was making more as he pushed himself up higher, loading the machinegun's bipods. He could see just enough to see that the others were spreading out and aiming in with their rifles, except for the fourth, who appeared to be prepping a grenade.

There wasn't a good reason for the movement unless they were planning an attack. If they'd been set up defensively, they would have been up there already.

He leveled his Galil, carefully slipping it off safe, though the *click* was unavoidable and disturbingly loud. None of the men farther down the finger seemed to notice.

The one with the grenade pulled the pin. That tore it. Flanagan opened fire.

He didn't have a lot of ammunition left, but he raked the four man position with most of the remainder of his current magazine. The Galil thundered in the night, the muzzle flash brilliant in the dark, as he dumped the grenadier first, just before switching to the machinegunner, even as the two other riflemen twisted around at the deafening reports. The guy with the grenade spun halfway around and started to roll down the hill, the frag

224

falling from his hands and bouncing down the rocks, and the machinegunner jerked and fell over the PKM's receiver, just before the grenade went off with a brief flash and a rolling *boom* that echoed off the hillsides and down the valley.

One of the two riflemen got off a burst, but he'd just pointed at Flanagan's own muzzle flash rather than aiming. Flanagan shot him next, putting the front sight in the middle of his night aperture right in the center of the AK's flash. Without much more precise aiming being possible, he just shot at the man until he went sliding down the hill, his AK clattering away into the shadows.

Hank had rolled over by then, come up onto a knee to where he could shoot over Flanagan's head, and dumped the last one with four shots that slapped at Flanagan with their concussion.

Flanagan slid down the slope about a yard, just far enough that he could clear Hank's field of fire before he got up. He was already turning to check their rear again as he did so, but the hill above them was empty. The bad guys didn't have a bottomless supply of manpower, anyway.

At least, not on this side of the farm.

The sheer volume of fire that erupted below, on the other side of the finger, was deafening. Flanagan scrambled down toward where the second man he'd shot was slumped over the PKM. Whatever had just happened, it wasn't good, and unless they got some fire superiority fast, they were probably all going to die.

He knew what his own loadout looked like. They didn't have the ammunition for this kind of a fight.

Hank was following him, his boots slipping on the sandy, rocky slope, but Flanagan got to the belt fed first, hauling the dead body off of it before dropping behind it, laying his Galil on the dirt next to him. It was based on an AK; it would be fine.

He had to shift his body to the right quite some distance to get the machinegun trained on the farmhouse below. The other Blackhearts were behind cover, down by the fence, returning fire as they could, but it looked like close to a platoon sized element had come pouring out of the farmhouse and the outbuildings, and while they were behind cover themselves, they were dumping bullets at the pinned Americans, muzzle flashes like strobe lights on the hillside.

Racking the PKM's charging handle just to be sure, Flanagan leaned into the gun and opened fire.

He didn't have a good shot at many of them. But sometimes the whole point of a machinegun is to get the enemy to put their heads down. The fire reaching out for the mercenaries slackened considerably as he stitched green tracers across the front of the farm buildings, kicking up dirt and fragmented rock where he couldn't hit meat.

Hank was already on the radio. "This is Newb! We have the flank covered!"

Flanagan didn't hear the reply, as he sent another burst roaring across the guerrillas' front. He couldn't tell if he was actually killing any of them, but at least he was keeping their fire down. Then Hank gripped his shoulder.

"We need to hold for a minute, then fall back! We don't have enough ammo for this fight, and Dad's pulling us out!" Hank had to be rattled to have forgotten to refer to Brannigan as anything but "Dad."

Flanagan just leaned to the right a little more and fired at a pair of silhouettes running through the dark for the base of the finger where the two of them were set up. He couldn't get a shot at one of them, his tracers going over the man's head, but he caught the second one in the neck, nearly decapitating him. The body and head spun out of sight behind a rock.

For a few seconds, that felt like hours, Flanagan's entire world closed in until it was him, the gun, and the targets. He couldn't hear past the PKM's rattling thunder, and the muzzle flashes had done a number on his night adaptation. He had to rely entirely on Hank to pass the word when it came.

"Let's go, Joe!" Hank was practically screaming in his ear. It was time to fall back. Flanagan held down the trigger one more time, until the belt ran the rest of the way through, the bolt locking back one last time, and then he grabbed his Galil, paused just long enough to scoop up one of the dead men's AK and a couple of spare mags, and then he turned to go, following Hank down the side of the hill. The shooting had all but stopped, hopefully because the rest of the team had gotten some cover between them and the guerrillas.

Despite the beating his ears had taken from the PKM, he thought he heard movement. Pivoting back toward the top of the ridge, he saw a head silhouetted against the sky, little more than a slightly darker shape against the dimness. He fired at it, and it disappeared.

Then he was scrambling down the slope after Hank, leaving the farm, Hierro, and the guerrillas behind.

And wondering what they were going to do about this betrayal.

CHAPTER 35

The way Burgess had trained—and he was sure most of the Recon Marines who were now Blackhearts had trained the same way, as had Kirk and probably Wade—a break contact drill was a fast but furious flow of bounding overwatch, elements laying down cover fire for each other as they moved back in waves, sprinting no more than a few seconds at a time.

This wasn't that. The dark, the terrain, and the way they'd been split up to cover the farm had rendered it almost impossible.

There was an old saying in the profession of arms: "Speed is security." And after either Flanagan or Hank had laid the hate on the farm and driven a bunch of the guerrillas back, the darkness itself seemed to have convinced Brannigan to take that route.

So, they just turned and ran.

There was no radio chatter to say where to go. That wasn't necessary. They'd worked out their rally points beforehand, never quite getting around to telling Hierro the entire plan. He'd been the package, not one of the team, even after he'd picked up that submachinegun. If they'd needed to break contact and bring him along, one of them would have towed or carried him.

Now it was looking as if they should have just put a bullet in him and done the junta that ran Costa de las Joyas the favor.

He shook the thought off as he ran through the desert, dodging cactus and brush, praying he didn't turn an ankle in the

229

dark. They'd seen enough to agree that the junta needed to go down, but for some reason their current employers had decided to back a pretty treacherous horse.

Burgess thought he knew what kind of "dissident" Hierro was, now, but it was too late.

He slowed, the breath burning in his throat, his heart hammering, and found some cover behind a boulder, turning and checking his six. He could hear a couple other Blackhearts to either side of him, but linkup needed to wait until the rally point. If they made too much noise, or showed any light, they'd just bring the hunters onto them, either the Costas or the rebels.

He'd regained some of his night adaptation as he'd run. It still wasn't great, but he could see more, though the overcast that had moved in while they'd been turning Hierro over to his comrades meant he couldn't see very far. It was still possible to make out movement behind them, movement that he was pretty sure wasn't other Blackhearts.

The chase was on. For whatever reason, the rebels didn't want the Blackhearts getting away.

Taking stock, he figured he had about half a mile left to go before the rally point. Getting to his feet, careful not to let his sling rattle against his rifle, he started to run again.

It was a little easier than it would have been before they'd hit the prison. He had a lot less ammunition now. That was not a good thing.

Somewhere off in the distance, gunfire crackled. It sounded too far away to be one of the other Blackhearts, but he couldn't be sure. He wanted to go check, just in case it was, and somebody needed help. Hank and Flanagan had been off in that direction, toward the north.

But if it wasn't, then he might just end up in the same boat, being the guy that the *rest* had to come and rescue. He hated it as a justification, but he just put his head down and kept running.

***

The rally point wasn't much. A thicket set into a cleft in the hills that overlooked the southern border with Colombia, it

230

would have been entirely too easy to miss it in the dark, but so far, they were all there. Brannigan had counted the men in as they'd arrived, though he'd stayed back in the bush as much as he could, facing the only workable approach to the hole in the vegetation where they could crawl in and be as hidden as they could.

Flanagan and Hank were the only ones still out. And that worried him.

He'd wrestled with the fact that his son had wanted to follow in his footsteps, first as a Marine officer, then as a Blackheart. Hank's mother was long gone by now, but that just meant that the younger man was all the blood family he had left. Every op that Hank came along on, Brannigan had to clamp down on the instinct to try to protect his boy, the fear that this was going to be the time that the natural order was reversed, and the father had to bury the son instead of the other way around.

A part of him was proud of Hank. The kid had made mistakes, but he was a warrior, and a smart one. He'd taken his licks when he'd joined up, endured the cracks about being the new guy—especially since a few of these men had known him when he'd been a little kid—and had soldiered on. He didn't shrink from the fight, and never acted as if he thought he deserved special treatment because of his last name.

But times like this made his blood run cold and wonder if his wife was watching disapprovingly.

The bursts of weapons fire in the distance didn't make him feel any better. Even though he knew Flanagan was a predator, a hunter of men as well as animals, this was not a night to go looking for trouble, and he knew Flanagan knew it. Which either meant that gunfire was elsewhere, or he and Hank had gotten cornered somewhere.

"Flash." The whisper was entirely too close, and he almost jumped out of his skin.

"Thunder." He let out a shaky breath as Flanagan and Hank came out of the rocks nearby. "You about gave me a heart attack, Joe."

"Didn't want to go yelling the sign and countersign all over tonight." Flanagan slipped down next to him, watching their back trail as Hank slithered into the hide site, though not before Brannigan reached out and gave his son's shoulder a squeeze, one which Hank returned. It was all he dared do at that point, but the relief was so strong that he thought he was going to start shaking.

"It's going to be dawn soon." If Flanagan had noticed the brief byplay, he ignored it. There wasn't a Blackheart who would have raised any hell over it anyway. "We won't make the border before then."

"No, we won't." Now that he had everybody, Brannigan was able to switch gears. "I think we need to find a place to lay low. A better spot than here."

Flanagan might have nodded in the dark. He definitely did point. "Agreed."

Following the silhouette of Flanagan's pointing finger, Brannigan spotted the movement a couple of hills over. Someone was following them.

"I've got an idea of where to go." He'd been thinking about it for a while. "It might not be the most welcoming spot, but it might get us some answers."

It would have been possibly the smart decision to just lie low until they could make a run for the border. Get across into Colombia, ditch the weapons and gear, and get back Stateside. The job was done, even though the people they'd been hired to help had tried to kill them.

But that last part made him angry. It was obvious now that Hierro was not what they'd been led to believe, and it had sure seemed as if the betrayal had been in the plan already. Why else would the guerrillas been set up the way they had been?

He knew that he had enemies in the dark corners of government offices in the States. He had come to grudgingly trust Mark Van Zandt, despite their rocky history, but this job hadn't come directly from Van Zandt. And even Mark had seemed a little ambivalent about it.

No, they weren't going to go to the border. He was going to get some answers, and then he'd decide what to do.

Even if it meant burning Costa de las Joyas to the ground.

CHAPTER 36

The farm was as dark as the rendezvous point with Hierro's people. Darker, actually, since the farmer didn't have any lanterns outside, and no guards. The eastern sky was probably getting lighter, though the overcast was going to keep the predawn twilight dark a little bit longer.

The Blackhearts had spread out in pairs, covering their back trail as well as the other approaches to the farm. Meanwhile, Brannigan headed for the door, accompanied by Santelli, Wade, and Bianco. He wanted Bianco's size and Wade's unblinking, icy stare.

The presence of Raul's truck had made things simpler. The original plan had been to get the farmer to put them back in contact with him, but now they didn't need to add that step.

He didn't know exactly where Raul stood, but the man had been noticeably uncomfortable. At the time, Brannigan had figured that it was because of the American involvement. Now, he wasn't quite so sure.

They were going to find out.

With Wade standing to one side of the door, Bianco stacked behind him, and Santelli holding rear security next to him, his own rifle slung and his Cordova in his hand, Brannigan knocked on the door.

There was no response at first. That probably stood to reason, given the time and the amount of activity across the tiny country during the night. If he'd judged things right, a knock on the door in the middle of the night, or even the very early morning, was something to be feared in Costa de las Joyas.

He waited a minute, then knocked again. He imagined Raul, the farmer, and his family inside, staying perfectly still and hoping that whoever it was just went away.

Finally, just as he lifted his fist to knock again, the door creaked open.

It was dark inside. The face that peered out was almost invisible except for the faint whites of his eyes. "*Que?*"

"Hello, Raul." Brannigan's voice was low and hard. "Open the door." He was not going to be nice about this.

It was hard to tell in the dark, but Raul's eyes might have widened, white in the dimness. For a second, Brannigan thought he was going to argue, or try to close the door, but instead he backed up and pulled it farther open.

Decades of military rule had their effects. These people were mostly cowed by physical force. He'd seen it before. They all had.

They'd also seen the flip side, where the lack of the threat of physical force was met with contempt. This place was not a place where they could afford that. Even if it felt a bit wrong, they had to make it clear that to defy them meant instant death, or none of them would get out of Costa de las Joyas alive.

The Blackhearts made entry, collapsing on the house and spreading out to the windows to watch the outside, while Gomez and Wade swept the building itself to make sure there were no nasty surprises waiting. They found only the farmer and his wife and children, the oldest being a teenager who glared at the men with guns while they herded the entire family into the living room, the youngest crying sleepily, and watched over them.

Brannigan sat down at the table and motioned for Raul to sit across from him. The older man did so, though slowly and reluctantly.

"What do you want?" Raul's voice was low and flat, the voice of a man without options.

Brannigan leaned back in his chair, his weight making the chair creak. He was less relaxing than he was making sure he could get to his Cordova easily if he needed it. He didn't think he would, but desperate men did desperate things sometimes.

"Where is Baltasar?" The search of the house hadn't turned up the man they'd freed from the Hector Ospina military police station.

"I do not know. He left not long after you did." Raul wasn't looking at him, but at his clasped hands resting on the table.

"Did he say anything before he left?"

Raul only shook his head.

Eyes narrowed, Brannigan leaned forward, putting his elbows on the table. Gomez was looming nearby, presenting all the threat he needed to keep things from getting out of hand. "Well, let's cut to the chase, shall we?" Raul's English was pretty good, but he might not understand that particular idiom, not that it mattered much at the moment. "Baltasar brought us to you for a reason. I figure it's because you're no great friend of the military government in this country. Which tells me that you might know a thing or two about their enemies."

Raul looked up at him finally but said nothing. Brannigan continued to watch the man coolly, taking in what information he could from body language and the look in his eyes. Raul was wary, that much was obvious. With good reason, from what they'd seen so far.

"Okay, I'll lay it out." He realized that he was going to have to take a chance here. He didn't know that he could trust Raul. The threat of force might be the only thing that would get him to cooperate. But this was the one thread he had to pull on. "The junta that rules this country killed Americans. We got sent to break out a man that our employers think could be a rallying point to overthrow that junta. We've accomplished that mission, except for one little detail. His friends just tried to kill us as soon as we handed him over."

237

A frown creased Raul's forehead between his eyebrows. "Who was this man?"

"His name is Ernesto Hierro."

Shock was written across Raul's face, and he looked from Brannigan, to Gomez, to Santelli, both of whom were standing behind him. "*Hierro*? Why would *yanquis* break *him* out? Do you know who he is? What he is?"

"Apparently not enough." Brannigan kept his tone even and cool, even as his temper flared. Not against Raul, but against the senator who'd sent them here, and the shadowy or careless intel that had backed up the job. "We were told that he was a political dissident jailed by the regime, and that if we got him out, he stood a good chance of overthrowing it, punishing them by proxy for killing Americans."

Raul blinked as he shook his head in disbelief, once again looking around at the angry American mercenaries. "I… I do not believe it. They had to have known more."

"There wasn't much about Costa de las Joyas that we could find out up there," Santelli said, his arms crossed over his barrel chest.

Raul took a deep breath, looking down at the table. "No, I suppose there would not be. Still… Ernesto Hierro…" He gathered himself. "His father was the entire reason this country accepted the generals' rule in the first place."

"Keep talking." Brannigan saw Wade look over toward them, one eyebrow raised.

"No one knows exactly what Carlos Hierro's real name was, but he took the first name 'Carlos' in honor of Ilych Ramirez Sanchez."

There wasn't a man in that room who didn't know that name. "Carlos the Jackal."

"The same. He named his son after Ernesto 'Che' Guevara." When no one said anything more, Raul looked up and continued. "Whether he was an actual agent of Cuban DGI, no one ever could say, but it was obvious that he was being sponsored by them. There was a lot going on throughout South America in those

238

days, so I probably shouldn't be surprised that his murders went unremarked in the north, but he killed so many and caused so much destruction, all in the name of the People's Front for the Liberation of Costa de las Joyas, that no one mourned when he was killed.

"His wife and son were never found. Twenty years later, Ernesto came out of the jungles of Colombia and Venezuela, once again at the head of the FPLCJ. Their support went from DGI, to FARC, to SEBIN." The Venezuelan Bolivarian Intelligence Service did seem to be flexing its regional muscles with the decline of the Cuban support of international revolution. "He was caught two years ago, and despite the brutality of the generals, every decent man and woman in Costa de las Joyas breathed a sigh of relief."

"And we let him out." Puller sounded haunted.

"He probably would have tried to find a way to use you, but the Venezuelans must have wanted American bodies for something." Raul didn't elaborate, but Brannigan could imagine some possibilities.

"So, we've got a Commie sympathizer with deep pockets somewhere back home." Wade looked more pissed than usual.

"We'll worry about that when we get back." Brannigan needed to keep focused. "Right now, I'm interested in cleaning this mess up."

Raul looked up at him, a glint of some combination of fear and anticipation in his eyes. "What about me?"

"That depends. You can cooperate, or else we need to take steps to make sure you don't double cross us the same way Hierro and his friends already did." There was no pity or give in Brannigan's stare.

The older man turned to look toward the room where the farmer and his family were being kept. With a deep sigh, he nodded. "What do you need?"

"Ammunition, information, and a way into the city."

"I can get them for you."

CHAPTER 37

Wade hated being a passenger. Not that he would have wanted to fly the helicopters that he'd once ridden into insert, but driving was another matter. Especially when the driver was some local farm kid who barely knew which end of the stick shift to use.

What made it even worse was the fact that he was crammed into the back of a truck, covered with a tarp and a bunch of trash, so he couldn't see, either.

The truck hit another pothole and slammed him into the floorboards again, and he gritted his teeth to keep from cursing out loud. If he hadn't known the state of the roads—and the state of the truck—he might have determined to beat the ever living fuck out of the driver.

He still might.

Bianco *was* cussing, even though it was under his breath, where Wade could barely hear it, even though the two of them were pressed together in the cramped quarters of the back of the truck.

There were four of them in this vehicle, and while the old truck had plenty of room in the bed for that many, the need for camouflage had ended up leaving them no choice but to pile on top of each other like cordwood, along with their weapons, which made the entire thing much more uncomfortable.

Wade hoped that he was counting time right, and they were very nearly at their destination. They'd already been stopped twice, but the trash in the back had deterred the National Army soldiers from searching the truck too thoroughly, which was a blessing and a curse.

Trash that was nasty enough that the local bully boys didn't want to sift through it even after a massive firefight right on their own doorstep was also something no one wanted to be buried under for any great length of time.

The truck stopped suddenly, with a lurch and a screeching creak of brakes and strained suspension. As little as Wade usually cared about cars—his interests tended to lean more towards women, guns, comic books, and collectibles—he really didn't want to know how much rust had eaten away chunks of the truck. Not so much because he hated to see an old vehicle go to hell, but more because he didn't want to know how close it was to completely falling apart at the wrong time and killing them all.

This was going to be risky enough without their insert platform going all Keystone Kops.

A voice hissed from the front, near the back of the cab. Wade couldn't tell if the kid driving had opened the rear window or was just leaning in to where he could speak into the bed from behind the cab. *"Estamos aqui."*

For a few seconds, Wade waited for the kid to clear out some of the trash and the tarp, giving them a way out, but nothing happened. The kid must have beat feet. *Of course.* With a silent snarl, Wade pushed on the tarp over his head, feeling and hearing the junk shift and rattle as he pushed it aside, finally getting his head above their camouflage, his Cordova in one hand, just in case.

There were no soldiers at the tailgate, looking in with their rifles aimed. In fact, it was dark enough that he thought he really had miscounted the time, and that they'd kept moving until night.

No, they were in a shed. Perfect.

With Bianco's, Tackett's, and Santelli's help, he shoved the rest of the trash far enough aside that at least one of them could

242

climb out. Dragging the ancient, battered National Army FAL that he'd replaced his Galil with after him, Wade moved to the tailgate, his boots slipping noisily through the detritus, bent almost double to keep underneath the canvas top. It was not a comfortable movement, even without the smell, an all too familiar mélange of rotting trash and diesel oil, and took far longer than it should have, even as the others began to disentangle themselves from their disguise.

He stayed at the tailgate for a moment, listening. Aside from the sounds of traffic outside the shed, everything was quiet. He had to assume that the traffic level was fairly normal. Less than a comparable American city, let alone some of the Middle Eastern cities where he'd worked, but loud enough that he could be fairly sure there wasn't a cordon already around the shed.

Yet.

If he'd had time, he might have waited a full ten minutes, but there were too many moving parts, and therefore there wasn't time. They needed to be ready to go when things started to move. He swung a leg over the tailgate, checked beside the truck with his pistol, then dropped to the dirt floor, reaching in and retrieving his FAL after he had both of his boots on the ground.

The shed was barely big enough for the truck alone. He checked the flanks while Tackett and Bianco got out, followed by a grunting, visibly angry Santelli. Not that he had any particular reason to be angrier than the rest of them, but the former sergeant major was just getting to the limit of his patience.

Peering through the crack in the double doors that the driver had shut behind the truck, Wade couldn't see much. A narrow slice of the street outside didn't tell him whether they were even in the right place or not. He could mainly just see that it was still very much daytime.

That was less than ideal, given what they'd slipped back into the city to do, but it had been necessitated by the curfew, which the National Army was going to be even more strict about enforcing after the last few nights.

"Here." Tackett was at a small side door, his own FAL tucked under his arm to point the muzzle at the opening. They were all packing the old battle rifles, even Bianco and Curtis. Having all but completely run out of 5.56, they'd needed to resupply, and the cache of old National Army equipment that Raul had taken them to—probably squirreled away for an eventual resistance fight, either against the junta or against the Communists—hadn't had any, either. Curtis, of course, had complained as loudly as he dared that there were no belt feds in the cache, but there was nothing they could do, so he'd shut up after Brannigan had finally glared at him.

Santelli was closest, so he joined Tackett at the door, while Wade and Bianco covered the exit leading onto the street. The two of them disappeared through the opening, while Wade waited for something to go badly.

Nothing happened, and he tapped Bianco before turning to follow the other two.

They found themselves in a small compound, with some dying grass in patches around the small adobe house, the plastered concrete block walls just high enough that they didn't need to worry about being spotted from the street. Tackett was already peering in a window, keeping low and just barely easing his eye into the corner.

He turned toward the others and nodded. They were in the right place.

Raul had known where Baltasar had been staying, but he had guessed, though he couldn't be sure, that it wasn't where the man would have gone. There was another house, he'd said, where some of the quiet resistance gathered, men known to the FPLCJ, the kind of men that Hierro would probably do his utmost to pressure into joining him. Faced with the wrath of either the National Army or the FPLCJ, they would have to make a choice, and from what Raul had said, faced with torture and murder now versus torture and murder later, most of them would choose to cooperate with the People's Front.

Tackett's nod had confirmed that Baltasar was here. Now they only had to wait.

Wait, and hope that the other Blackhearts got into position to play their part in the plan without getting caught.

***

Flanagan could only shake his head. While he'd been in the city, he had gotten a pretty good idea of what the fight on the docks had been like, only a couple of days before. Now they were going right back into the lion's den, within sight of the military base up on the bluffs.

According to Raul, the boat was expected, one of the regular fishing trawlers that delivered its catch to the base. Costa de las Joyas was a tiny country with no real friends, and another reason young men joined the National Army—other than getting to be aggressive bullies—was to get three square meals a day. A large part of the country's produce, either from farming or fishing, went to the Army.

That would give them their way in.

Flanagan wasn't sure about this. While he was in full agreement with Brannigan that they needed to deal with both the Army and the Communists, he would have preferred to confront one at a time. That might not have been doable, given what Raul suspected, but it would have been more tactically sound.

Unfortunately, Raul had confirmed that there had been a lot of talk that seemed to expect *something* to happen to overthrow the junta, and soon. None of it had been specific enough to pinpoint that it had anything to do with Hierro, but in context, there was no avoiding the conclusion. Someone connected to Braxton, back in the States, had been in communication with the FPLCJ, laying the groundwork for the coup.

The boat was a decent-sized trawler, though it was hardly top of the line. It wouldn't have looked out of place among the dhows off the shores of Somalia, even if its hull was slightly different. Peeling paint, weatherbeaten wood, and rusty steel made up most of it. The hold, down where the Blackhearts were hiding, smelled like mold, seawater, and fish.

245

Lots of fish.

The trawler's captain had agreed to the plan, though without a great deal of explanation. Gomez was watching him, just in case. None of the Blackhearts trusted him. Flanagan suspected his eagerness to help infiltrate the port and the base was because he was a FPLCJ sympathizer.

It had certainly seemed as if there wasn't much of a third option in this benighted country. Raul insisted that most people just wanted some peace and stability, and neither the junta nor the Communists offered that. It raised some questions about what the end state was going to be after the next twenty-four hours, but Flanagan couldn't quite bring himself to care that much.

So long as the message was received loud and clear that you don't murder Americans, and the Communists weren't allowed to step into the vacuum, that was about all he cared about at the moment.

He knew it was going to be more complicated than that for the locals. Yet, despite all the suffering he'd seen over the years, in various hellhole countries torn apart by civil war and terrorism, he had come to understand something.

Either these people took charge of their own country and their own lives, or the same thing would happen over and over again, no matter how many tinpot dictators went down to American arms.

Their future was in their own hands, whether they liked it or not.

A faint bump reverberated through the hull, announcing that they'd arrived. It was time.

Brannigan held up a hand. He was close to the ladderwell leading up to the deck, near the pilothouse in the stern. Most of the Blackhearts were back there, except for Gomez who was just out of sight on the bridge, and Kirk who was forward, ready to engage if something went haywire.

Curtis was fidgeting. He was probably about to get sick from the stink of fish, or at least that was what he'd say. Flanagan

246

almost said something, but he knew his friend would be all right once they got on mission.

With Curtis, his constant bitching was more often than not a manifestation of impatience and anxiety. The man didn't like to wait for the action to start. It got on his nerves. It had taken a lot of years of knowing Curtis, with his big mouth and his tendency for trouble, to realize that. Many of his more annoying traits were coping mechanisms.

They had to wait, though. Once the unloading had started, they could slip out onto the deck, and from there into the port.

Part of the cache had included uniforms. They were old, none of them fit the larger Blackhearts all that well, and they had no insignia, but they should hopefully act as camouflage just long enough to get them past the docks.

Voices sounded above, and after a minute a crane appeared over the main cargo hatch leading down into the hold. The captain's crew came belowdecks, pointedly ignoring the armed men in the shadows, and started to hook up the baskets full of fish.

Curtis made a faint gagging sound, drawing glares from Flanagan, Burgess, and Brannigan. He subsided, looking a little apologetic.

Footsteps rattled on the deck above, and then the basket was rising out of the hold and swinging toward the dock. Brannigan nodded. It was time.

Moving carefully but trying to look casual, the Blackhearts started to climb the ladderwell.

It came out on the starboard side of the trawler, with the pilothouse between them and the docks. Brannigan led the way astern, where there wasn't much activity. The others followed, though not without a glance toward the sea, looking for the inevitable National Army patrol boats that should have been on station after the fight earlier.

Flanagan didn't see any, at least not close in. There was a boat moving along at a pretty good clip some distance out, but it

247

was too far away to see much detail, and they would just appear to be National Army soldiers at that range.

The tricky part would come once they got on the docks.

They came out to the port side, where the unloading was happening, to see that there were only a couple of the National Army's goons standing guard while several others in uniform but with no weapons worked on getting the fish onto the trucks lined up on the pier.

Those trucks were going to make for some decent cover and concealment, though they still needed to get past not only the guards, but also the working party loading the trucks.

There was no gangplank at the stern, but there was a mooring line running to a hard point on the pier. It wasn't ideal, but they also didn't want to just walk down the plank amidships, right in front of everyone. They needed to get on the ground where they wouldn't necessarily stand out.

Brannigan still signaled that they should stay low, out of sight as much as possible for the moment. They had a better view of what was going on and could time things a bit better from on deck, but to try to head out now would only expose them needlessly too soon.

Timing was going to be everything here. There was some uncertainty, of course, especially given that they were trying to coordinate between the main effort and the ambush team that Wade had led to the house where they expected Hierro and his FPLCJ guerrillas to stage. But unless they wanted to go loud right then and there, on the docks, they needed to step lightly for a while and exercise some patience.

If the strike got compromised here in the port, it was all over. They'd have to exfil and get out of the country, leaving their targets unmolested. It was likely that both factions would still tear each other's guts out, but Flanagan knew that he wouldn't be satisfied at that, especially if Braxton's plan of a new government headed by Ernesto Hierro came to pass.

Minutes turned into an hour, as the tropical sun beat down on them on the boat's stern. There wasn't much shade, and they were going through water a little too quickly, especially Puller. Flanagan glanced at their medic. Puller had been a decent operator when they'd known each other back in the day, in the Marine Corps. He'd been through a lot since then, though, and while he'd held up under the last couple of jobs, he was still a little shaky.

Finally, one eye just above the gunwale, Brannigan signaled that it was time. Flanagan got to his feet, though Gomez was ahead of him. There was a friendly rivalry between the two of them, echoing a similar competition between Flanagan and Sam Childress, before the latter had been crippled on a mission, for the foremost fieldcraft hand, and therefore the point position. Gomez had to take this one for another reason, though. He had the potential to blend in with the locals at least more than Flanagan did. It wouldn't hold up for long—his accent was wrong, for one thing—but it should last long enough for Gomez to get within knife range.

If it came to that. Hopefully the locals wouldn't be paying that much attention. Eager to get the job done and get out of the sun, they'd already showed signs of getting sloppy as they'd loaded the trucks.

His FAL slung, Gomez swung a leg over the gunwale, wrapping his ankles and hands around the mooring line, shimmying down the cable as quickly as he could. In seconds, he was on the dock, straightening as he stepped up behind the rearmost truck, his FAL back on his shoulder, looking around the truck's bumper while doing what he could to stay out of line of sight of the side mirror.

Flanagan followed, though it felt like he didn't get down the line quite as fast or as smoothly as Gomez had. He joined their teammate, feeling his heart rate go up, resisting the powerful urge to unsling his rifle and have it ready. He preferred the woods, somewhere where there was cover and concealment. Standing out on the docks, with nothing but a couple of trucks to hide behind, he felt as exposed as a bug on a plate.

By the time the rest of the team was on the docks, the trucks were already rolling. The Blackhearts followed behind, heading for the stacks of containers near the steps that led up into the military base, to one side of the road that circled around several buildings before reaching the gate on the east side of the base perimeter. There was no way to stay quite close enough to remain completely out of sight, but by the time Curtis made it to the containers, the trucks leaving them behind as they rumbled up the side of the bluff and into the city, there had been no alarm raised, no sign that anyone had noticed anything out of the ordinary.

Now they had to wait.

CHAPTER 38

It was getting oppressively hot. Santelli wanted a rag to wipe the sweat off his face, but he simply didn't have one, and his sleeve was almost as soaked as the rest of him. The walls of the compound seemed to be focusing the tropical sun, making it almost an oven.

He was taking his turn out in the yard. After Tackett had confirmed that they'd been dropped at the correct house, the Blackhearts had faded back into the shed rather than taking the house. Baltasar had been sighted inside, but they didn't know exactly where the man's loyalties really lay, and the objective wasn't the house itself, but Hierro and his strike force. So, they had to settle in to wait. Rather than simply retreating into the shed and the truck, though, they had to keep someone outside, so their lookout crouched in the junk piled against the inside of the wall, watching for their quarry to show up.

The day was moving along, and Santelli was really starting to wonder if this was going to happen before nightfall. It had appeared that the FPLCJ was prepped and waiting on their leader, but who knew how long it was actually going to take them to launch their offensive? Santelli had seen "prepared" forces dawdle for days before.

While the Blackhearts did have some food and water with them, he really wasn't sure they had enough to get them through more than a day or so in this position.

Blinking the sweat out of his eyes, he froze. The rumble of traffic outside the sheet metal gate had been intermittent but generally regular, the cars and trucks—few as they were in this poverty-stricken country—going about their business without stopping at this particular house. The rumble of a heavy truck was much closer to the wall this time, though, and brakes squealed as he saw a white canvas topper just over the top of the wall itself.

The front door creaked open, and Santelli shrank down behind the pile of detritus to hide as a figure stepped out onto the porch. He keyed his radio once, unable to send a voice message. He could just barely hear the others moving in the shed behind him, getting stacked up on the door to move in and intercept Hierro. He had to get a little bit lower and a little bit farther back behind the corner of the house to stay out of sight, though he leaned out just far enough to get a sliver of a view of the gate.

At first, he didn't recognize the man standing in the gateway. He hadn't seen Hierro in daylight, so it took a moment to register that it was, in fact, the Communist revolutionary standing there waiting, dressed in plain clothes but with a pistol in his waistband and the same FMK-3 that he'd taken off one of the prison guards in his hands.

Santelli was about to shoot the man, knowing that it was going to kick things off before the rest of the team was out the door and in position, but Hierro disappeared back out onto the street after saying something sharp to the man on the porch. He had no shot.

There was some rustling and thumping out front of the house, and then he got a quick glimpse of two men lugging duffel bags out to the truck. Then the gate swung shut again with a creak and a bang.

Santelli cursed, just as the others heard the noise and the shed door was carefully opened, a rifle muzzle immediately appearing in the gap. Santelli had moved to the corner of the building, but the porch was abandoned, the gate closed, and the truck outside was already surging into motion with a rattling growl.

"They just blew on out of here, didn't they?" Wade bit out.

"Yeah." Santelli was already digging his radio out. "Kodiak, Kodiak, this is Guido. The target did not stage at the objective house. I say again, they did not stage. They picked up some gear and moved on. We have no target."

He looked at the others as he waited to hear back from Brannigan. Wade had moved to where he could cover the front door, in case there were any more guerrillas inside the house, though Santelli thought that they'd already have come out if there were. The big man was obviously chewing nails in rage. Bianco looked almost as upset, while Tackett, who had simply turned to cover the door into the shed, in case they got company from the street, seemed unperturbed.

Santelli turned back toward the gate, his FAL braced on the corner of the house, wondering just what the hell they were going to do now.

***

Brannigan didn't hear the radio call. His radio was turned down so that the sound wouldn't travel, as the rest of the Blackhearts waited in the shadows behind a stack of ancient, rusty cargo containers, pinned in place for the moment by a pair of National Army soldiers at the top of the steps, smoking. Unless they wanted to kick this off with gunfire early, they were going to have to wait the two local troops out.

Unfortunately, he knew that they didn't have a whole lot of time. They needed to get close to the command building if they were going to have a chance to take the junta in the confusion once Wade and the others ambushed Hierro and his followers. It was almost a repeat of the plan for the prison raid, except that they weren't nearly as interested in extracting anyone alive this time.

Plus, all Wade and his team needed to do was to kill Hierro and most of his inner circle, then run. There wasn't much need to hold the way Flanagan and the others had the other night. The remaining guerrillas would take care of that part.

But they had to get past these two jokers first. And they didn't look like they planned on moving anytime soon.

Brannigan wanted to watch them carefully, but that was dangerous. Even exposing himself enough to see what they were doing might get him spotted, and a guard might wonder why someone was hanging out down by the pier, after the fishing trawler had pulled off to go about its business again. If they got close enough to see any detail, the game was up, and it was going to be a fight. He had to be patient, at a time and in a place where it didn't come easy.

Then the first explosion echoed across the city.

Brannigan frowned, turning to glance at Kirk, who was closest, watching the approaches from the other side of the port. The bearded old Green Beret tilted his head slightly, listening, as yet another *boom* rolled across Santa Paz.

That's not our guys. They didn't have any explosives. Just the FALs and a few mags per man. The ambush should have been an eruption of gunfire.

Unless things had well and truly gone sideways.

He looked back up toward the two guards. They were both looking toward the west, cigarettes forgotten. A third explosion sounded, seemingly much nearer, and then the gunfire started.

Both guards disappeared, hustling out of sight and toward the west, unslinging their rifles as they went. Brannigan saw their opening, whatever had gone wrong. "Go," he hissed, as he pulled out his radio and turned it up just far enough that he could hear. "Angry Ragnar, Angry Ragnar, this is Kodiak."

***

Wade fumed as he looked around the tiny residential compound, but he was thinking all the same. The plan had gone badly, and now his four-man team was out of position and behind schedule. If they didn't intercept Hierro, the whole plan might not work. With the Blackhearts' numbers, the right pressure at the right place and the right time was vital. They simply didn't have

254

the manpower for any sort of all-out assault without it being very, very carefully planned and executed.

"We need to get to the port." It meant effectively abandoning the idea of killing Hierro first and then moving on the junta while the National Army charged in to deal with the FPLCJ. But without knowing exactly where Hierro was going—not to mention without wheels with enough speed and maneuverability to get ahead of him—they were going to be a day late and a dollar short either way.

He had started to move back to the shed and the truck when the first bomb went off.

All four of them froze. Probably all thinking the same thing. If this attack had been planned well in advance, then the FPLCJ would have had plenty of time to plant the bombs, and from the sounds of it, as another *boom* rolled out across the city, they'd been busy.

Wade was feeling very played at that point, and it pissed him off even more. Hierro was going to die. The junta that had had Bianco and Santelli tortured was going to die.

And then whoever had sent them on this bullshit mission was going to pay the price, too.

He got into the shed and climbed behind the wheel while Bianco moved to open the doors to let the truck out. The rattling grumble of the truck's engine starting almost drowned out the radio, but he grabbed for it as he realized that had been Brannigan.

"This is Angry Ragnar." Light streamed in behind him as Bianco got the doors open. He was going to have to move soon, but fortunately, he could do two things at once, no matter what the Army had once said.

"Give me a SITREP." The colonel had heard the explosions, but rather than demanding to know why the plan had gone south, he just asked for an update.

It also meant he hadn't heard Santelli's radio call, either.

"The target barely stopped at the objective house, and we didn't get a shot at him. We are moving out to pursue, but he's on a mission and he's moving fast. Already ahead of us, from what I can hear."

"So it would seem." A third explosion sounded, somewhere closer than the other two. Wade was looking through the mirrors, watching the other three Blackhearts climb into the back of the truck.

Come on, come on.

"We are moving to the primary objective," Brannigan continued. "Pursue Hierro as best you can. Assume he's heading the same place we are. Don't try to take him at this point unless you see a good chance to do it without getting pinned down. If they get to the base before you do, set up a blocking position and be prepared to cut him off if he tries to retreat." There was some background noise, barely audible as Wade backed the truck out of the shed. The colonel was moving and moving fast.

He braked, ground gears getting the truck back in first gear, and almost stalled the truck as he lurched toward the street in the direction that Hierro's truck had gone. "Good copy." The rage was settling down, giving way to the coldness of combat mindset. The plan had gone to shit, but they were adapting.

These bastards were going to pay after all.

CHAPTER 39

Kirk was right behind Brannigan as they moved up the steps, still moving carefully and tactically despite their haste. The gunfire was getting more intense, punctuated by the occasional *bang* of an RPG. From what he could hear, though the surrounding concrete buildings, guard towers, and the bluffs themselves, which he and Brannigan were still beneath, distorted the sound somewhat, it seemed as if the attackers were hitting the main gate of the Fortaleza Generalissimo Marto.

The bombings must have thrown the National Army into some disarray. Given the security that they'd seen even *before* the assault on the prison that had broken Hierro out, Kirk could only imagine how locked down the Army had Santa Paz now. And yet the FPLCJ had managed to penetrate all the way to the base perimeter.

Brannigan slowed ahead of him, and Kirk returned his attention to the immediate tactical situation. They were coming up on a guard post, though there was no real gate, just a small guard shack. There was one guard there, crouched down to try to stay behind cover, his FAL clutched in his hands. He was facing the wrong way, his back to the port and the steps behind him, trying to watch the fight up by the gate.

After a second, Brannigan faded to the side of the steps, crouching down by the slight bluff that still covered them from the firefight above. Kirk followed suit, though he wasn't sure why they were pausing, at least until Gomez stalked up beside them, staying low, his rifle already slung across his back. Then he got it.

Gomez moved like a ghost, his boots making almost no noise, and any sound he did make was easily drowned out by the gunfire and explosions. He was on the guard in an instant, his black-bladed knife in his right hand. His left went over the guard's mouth and nose. The blade came down once, twice, three times. Red sprayed on the dingy white panels of the guardhouse, while he held the guard down with an iron grip.

Kirk had actually started moving just as Gomez passed him, figuring out what the play really was. He wasn't rattled by the violence. He'd been on too many continents, in too many wars, and while knives weren't his thing, he'd seen what they could do, too much to be bothered by Gomez's up close and personal approach.

He didn't go all the way up the steps, exposing himself to the open ground around the guard shack, but paused about three steps down, where he could still cover Gomez's back.

It was a good thing, too.

A small truck came around the corner about a block away, moving fast and squealing tires as it made the turn. The four men in the back had their faces covered, their green fatigues marked by red armbands. Kirk didn't imagine anyone was going to mistake these guys for anything but FPLCJ.

That guardhouse, now painted with the hapless National Army soldier's blood, hadn't just been set to watch the port below. There was a pedestrian gate, currently closed, right next to it. Kirk didn't need to have the Communists' plan spelled out for him.

At that range, he could hardly miss. He opened fire.

His first round took the driver high in the chest. He kept shooting, even as the dying man slewed the wheel around and ran the truck into the nearest wall, bouncing over a curb in the process and scraping the vehicle down the plastered line of cinderblock, crushing at least one of the passengers' arms in the process. One of the masked gunmen fell out of the back of the truck, even as more of Kirk's bullets punched through glass, sheet metal, and flesh.

Brannigan joined him, a step lower but still with a clear enough shot, his FAL's muzzle blast hammering at the side of Kirk's head. He ignored the discomfort, even though the first round made him flinch, throwing his own shot high, but he corrected and put a final round through one of the last guerrillas, a man who had jumped off the tailgate of the now smoking truck, but had ducked around the taillight to try to put a few rounds on his tormentors before he fled. Kirk's bullet punched through his eye, spraying gore from the back of his head, and he flopped limply to the already bloodied street.

"Hold here for a minute. Keep that road locked down." Brannigan stepped around him, a brief tap to his shoulder to let him know the colonel was there.

Kirk wasn't going to just nod and stay there with a mostly empty rifle, though. "Reloading." He didn't shout it, like he might have twenty years ago, but he got the message across. Brannigan's muzzle reappeared in his vision, pointing over his shoulder.

"Covering."

He quickly stripped out the partial mag, stuffing it in a cargo pocket—they were probably going to need every round before the day was done—and rocked in a new one. "Up."

Brannigan trotted the rest of the way up the steps, then, joining Gomez at the gate. It opened without trouble; the dead soldier that was now slumped in a puddle of his own blood next to the guardhouse had been the only real safeguard.

Single file and moving fast, the others followed, Flanagan, Puller, Burgess, Hank, and Curtis. Curtis reached down to give Kirk's shoulder a squeeze. "Last man." The constant patter had ceased once again as the battle had been joined. Kirk had to admit that he was grudgingly impressed. He had not thought much of Curtis when he'd first come along on a job with Brannigan's Blackhearts, wondering why such a clown would be allowed in an outfit that required such a high degree of professionalism. He'd known soldiers like Curtis back in the day, and few of them had really lasted.

Now he knew.

He came the rest of the way to his feet, levering the one knee off the concrete step where he'd rested it to give himself some more stability. The knee twinged, and he stumbled a little.

It was the only thing that saved his life.

The burst of fire from down the street, beyond the corner where the truck full of FPLCJ fighters had appeared, was so close that he felt the first bullet part his hair.

Without seeing where the shot had come from, he dropped flat on the steps. Curtis swore, the profanity disappearing in the roar of his FAL as he dumped half the magazine down the street. Kirk didn't think they could really afford to throw suppressing fire around like that, but Curtis *was* a machinegunner.

Dropping down below the top of the stairs, Curtis cursed again as he turned to Kirk, only to stare a little wide-eyed as Kirk picked himself up and turned to bring his own rifle to bear down the street. "I thought you were dead!"

"I damned near was. Now, let's kill these bastards before we both buy it." He spotted a man's head and weapon coming back around the corner that the truck he'd shot to pieces had turned around, and he put a quick shot into the wall, forcing the man back. "Fuck." He hadn't been trying to suppress the guy.

"Come on." Curtis popped his head up for a second. "We're going to get left behind."

Kirk highly doubted that Brannigan would just leave two of them, especially not when every gun was as needed as it was. But hiding on the steps wasn't going to work either.

Not if the locals thought to use that gap in the fence where the Blackhearts had gone in to get Hierro to hit them from the flank.

Keeping his rifle aimed down the street, Kirk got back on his feet and started up the last few steps again. This time, he had an almost perfect shot as he planted his lead foot and the man on the corner popped out again.

His FAL bucked and thundered, and the top of the guerrilla's head split open, spilling blood and brains onto the street as the man fell on his face.

Curtis was already moving around the guardhouse and to the open gate, pausing on the other side of the shack to take a knee. "Move!"

"Moving!" At the last second, Kirk realized that Curtis hadn't taken the best spot, being drawn to the illusory cover of the thin-walled shack. He was going to have to run across the man's muzzle to get past him.

Curtis realized it at the same time and stood up, moving across the gateway and deeper into the base compound, giving Kirk enough room to move through and get inside the gate and behind the cover of one of the buildings just inside the fence.

With some more cover, he was able to take some stock. The rest of the team was spread out for the moment, set in on security between the warehouses that were lined up on the side of the base closest to the port. They were in a small island of calm at the moment, despite the oncoming Communist guerrillas trying to flank the National Army.

From where he was barricaded on the corner of the building, Kirk had a decent view of the street they'd just left, including the wrecked truck up on the crumbling sidewalk. There was movement out there. The guerrillas hadn't given up. But he didn't have a shot yet.

The fight over at the main gate was getting louder, but Kirk had to hold his sector and wait for the next move. Leaning into the gun, keeping it clamped against the wall with one hand, he watched the shadows move on the street and got ready to continue the fight.

***

Flanagan found himself out front again, flanking Gomez as the two of them moved up between buildings, keeping the warehouses between them and most of the National Army soldiers that were still hustling to join their comrades at the gate, trying to repel Hierro's guerrillas. They still needed to cover the windows and doors as they passed them, just in case there was someone inside with a gun who was hiding from the violence at the gate but might summon up a little courage facing a smaller element.

He reached the corner, taking a knee. They were nearing their objective, but the rattle and thunder of gunfire was only intensifying, and while speed and violence had their place, charging into the middle of that without appropriate caution would only get everyone killed.

It was a good thing he'd paused, too. There were two more warehouses ahead, just before the main road that led from the front gate to the main parade ground in front of the National Army headquarters building, where the entire administration of Costa de las Joyas was run. The mansions where the generals lived flanked the massive building, all surrounded by walls and fences.

Just after he'd popped the corner to make sure no one was coming up the side passage between buildings, the resistance at the main gate collapsed completely.

Gun trucks reversed and started falling back toward the parade ground, the gunners still laying on the .30 caliber fire, though while one of them passed the gap between warehouses, it took a direct hit from an RPG, disappearing in a dirty fireball before slowly rolling the rest of the way out of sight, no sign left of the gunner behind the M1919 as the truck burned. Bodies littered the street, as tracers skipped off the pavement to sail into the distance.

"Move right." Brannigan was at his elbow. "We don't want to get caught up in the middle of this." Flanagan nodded, as Gomez took point, moving between the warehouses and parallel to the guerrilla assault. Flanagan followed, cross covering with Gomez as he moved up to the opposite wall, Brannigan momentarily taking over the sector he'd been covering.

A few seconds later, the entire team was gathered in that gap between buildings. The parade ground had become a battlefield, as those National Army troops that had fallen back from the gate had hastily set in a new defensive line, using the concrete barriers that formed the decorative boundary of the parade ground for cover. Some of their comrades had set up machinegun nests behind those barriers already, and they were pouring fire down the main avenue toward the gate. They were taking fire, as well, but for the moment, the two sides seemed to have hunkered down behind cover to shoot at each other.

That told Flanagan that things were going to start moving out on the flanks soon, including the flank where the Blackhearts were currently set up.

Brannigan pointed over his shoulder. "See that building?" It was a small office building or something, a nondescript cube of cinderblock with a few small windows. Flanagan nodded. "Get us there. We can maneuver around that motor pool to get behind their line there."

Gomez and Flanagan just got up to move. Flanagan thought he could see what the colonel had in mind, getting around the line of resistance and away from where they might get stumbled upon, compromised, and slaughtered. Just for the sake of staying alive, the plan was sound.

It also might put them within striking distance of their targets. Hierro was another problem, but that was why Wade and his team were still out there.

With Gomez in the lead, they started to sprint toward the building Brannigan had pointed out.

Gomez was nearly to the wall, Flanagan a couple paces behind him, more out of habitual dispersion in combat than any difficulty keeping up with the shorter man, when the National Army fireteam came around the corner, running from cover to cover from the motor pool.

He barely slowed down, though shooting on the move is always a tough proposition, even at close range. Dropping his muzzle level, he shot the first man in the throat before it could even register with any of the locals that there was a threat much closer than they'd expected. The soldier spun halfway around at the impact, throwing a hand to his neck as blood spurted, his rifle clattering to the street, while Flanagan kept shooting, slowing down a little as he leaned into the FAL, the booming reports

263

reverberating off the nearby buildings, bullets tearing into men and dropping two more, one of them screaming loudly as the 7.62 round ripped through his guts.

He reached the wall of the building a second later, slamming into the concrete just behind Gomez, who was facing the corner and put a single bullet through a head that just barely appeared around the corner, the soldier not quite having arrested his momentum in time to get behind cover. The soldier collapsed, falling to his side and spilling his life out onto the pavement.

More gunfire cracked past as the other Blackhearts followed, pushing the National Army soldiers back until their angles of fire were cut off by the corner of the building.

They had to keep moving, keep pushing. The earlier caution had to be abandoned to some extent, now that they had made contact. The FPLCJ and the National Army might be blasting the shit out of each other at the moment, but that didn't mean any part of them wouldn't immediately engage a known threat that was closer than their other adversaries.

Gomez was already moving, even without Brannigan needing to say anything. Flanagan stayed right with him, watching down the line of warehouses at first before following his teammate around the corner as if they were going through a door, rifles leveled despite their length and weight.

The FAL was no M4, that was for sure.

They found the bodies of most of the National Army fireteam, but any survivors had fled. That wasn't ideal, since those survivors were going to bring more heat once they got to someone who could order reinforcements onto the flank.

If there had been more time, Flanagan would have bent to take some of the dead men's magazines. They were going to need all the ammunition they could get. But they were in the open and still vulnerable, so he followed Gomez as he quickly moved to the next corner, the two of them splitting and cross covering the next intersection.

The avenue between the building and the motor pool was mostly empty, except for a single National Army soldier who was running toward the parade ground. He was shouting, though the words were getting lost in the cacophony of gunfire and explosions that was still rocking the military base as the fight still raged on.

Flanagan shot the man and flung him onto his face. Yes, he was running away, but he still had his weapon, and he was still very much a threat.

Then they were moving again, Gomez turning to hold security toward the parade ground while Flanagan got moving across the avenue toward the corner of the motor pool, scanning the ground between the Blackhearts and the fence, pausing briefly to shoot the man in the guard tower who was leveling a rifle at Gomez before he reached the motor pool fence and kept going, moving around toward the back of the compound and toward their ultimate targets, where they thought they were safe behind a line of riflemen.

CHAPTER 40

Tackett jumped off the back of the truck as soon as it lurched to a stop. The crackle of gunfire was a constant roar not far ahead, and Wade wisely didn't want to drive right into the middle of that. Going the rest of the way on foot was the only good option.

The question Tackett had was, how far in were they going to go?

A quick scan of the street behind the truck revealed no guerrillas or soldiers. The local civilians all seemed to have hunkered down in the hope of just surviving the battle that was tearing the city apart.

Smoke drifted through the streets, even as several more explosions sounded from the direction of the base, though they were getting farther away. The guerrillas were pushing the National Army deeper in.

That didn't make any of this mission seem much more doable.

It had taken some doing to get back into the profession. He'd had to go along to rescue Price, Vernon, and Max. He hadn't realized what kind of a hold the action still had on him. Even when he'd insisted that he was only in for missions against the Humanity Front, the apocalyptic terrorist organization disguised as the world's foremost humanitarian NGO, he'd known, deep down, that he couldn't resist the siren song of battle anymore.

But now he was wondering if he shouldn't have stayed home, after all.

The Blackhearts were professionals and ferocious fighters. That much he wouldn't dispute. But they were vastly outnumbered and trying to break two factions at the same time, while those factions were locked in an all-out war.

He wasn't all that sure that any of them were going to live through the next few hours, and it worried him. Worried him in a way that could get dangerous.

He turned back toward the fight, as Wade led the way toward a small store on the corner, not far from the gate. It wasn't going to be the best cover, but it might be a decent vantage point for the blocking position Brannigan wanted.

The doubts and fears faded. That was what set the professionals apart from the amateurs and conscripts. The fight was here. He'd known he might die before he'd ever gotten on the plane to Colombia.

It was time to work.

Wade had barely slowed as he'd gotten out of the truck. Some of the guerrillas were visible even from where he'd parked, though they all seemed to be entirely focused on the gate and the base. The bombs they'd set off at the outset must have really diverted the National Army enough that they had a clear run on the gate without needing to worry about being flanked.

Or at least they seemed to think so, and so far, the locals hadn't proved them wrong, though there was enough gunfire stuttering elsewhere in the city to suggest that the guerrillas had set up some of their own blocking positions as well.

There was a body sprawled in the doorway, face down. It didn't look like either one of the soldiers or the guerrillas. The shopkeeper must not have gotten out of the way quickly enough, though he'd gotten the shutters down over his outdoor counter. Wade went in smooth, fast, and quiet, Bianco on his heels, while

Santelli and Tackett held security outside for a moment before following.

It impressed Tackett a little that Wade had foregone the easy targets. The guerrillas firing on the gate and moving toward the opening and the interior of the base had their backs turned and really weren't paying any attention to their rear security. It would have been easy, and with Wade's infamous temper and belligerence, it wouldn't have been that surprising if he'd decided to thin the herd.

The big man wasn't just aggressive and quick to anger, though. He was on mission, and the mission came first.

The inside of the shop was dark, the lights out to conceal anyone who might have taken shelter there. Wade and Bianco were already deep in the small building, checking every bit of dead space, but Tackett hadn't heard a raised voice or a gunshot since they'd made entry. That was good, but it was making him even more nervous, if that was possible. The strain of waiting for the shot that was going to give them away was awful, and he was already sweating just from the heat and humidity.

Suppressors would have been a very good thing, but the locals didn't use them, so there weren't any to be had.

Finally, Wade came back to the front, where Tackett and Santelli had already set in security on the door and the single unshuttered window facing the street, away from the base itself. Bianco had to be holding on the rear.

Wade took a knee next to Tackett by the door with a deep breath. "Now we get to wait."

He didn't sound happy about it. Tackett couldn't say he disagreed with Wade's dissatisfaction, either. They were stuck for the moment.

He just hoped that Brannigan's plan worked out. He didn't relish the idea of running for his life again, like he had in the South Pacific. The jungle was probably going to seem like a downright permissive environment compared to Santa Paz after this.

Watching the street, seeing a small slice of the gateway as the guerrillas started to move deeper into the base, pursuing their final victory over the junta.

He wondered where their target was in all of that.

***

Hank found himself right behind Flanagan, having pushed up past his father. He might have been an officer back in the day, but he'd listened to his NCOs, and he'd been a good enough officer that when he'd tried to lead from the front, as his father would have expected, he'd often had his own NCOs push him back, since his job was more to coordinate than to actually lead.

The elder Brannigan was in charge, and so in Hank's mind—he shied away from the knowledge that some of his fear was familial—he needed to be a few steps back, with the other Blackhearts taking more of the risks.

They'd made it past the cyclone fence around the motor pool, and now they were moving around the back of the mechanics' shops on the far side. There were barracks on the other side, but there didn't seem to be anyone in them at the moment. Every hand had been drawn to defend the headquarters building, and the fight was still raging out there, as smoke settled over the base, dimming the sun in the cloud of black and gray.

He was hoping that they'd have a chance to rally up before the final assault on the headquarters building, which was looming ahead of them, make one final, if quick, plan for the attack. But that was taken out of their hands a moment later.

They were nearly to the northernmost general's house, moving past the motorpool and bumping across the street between the motorpool and the much more opulent general's compound, which even through the smoke was obviously one of the fanciest structures in all of Costa de las Joyas. He and Flanagan reached the other side of the street just as a door opened in the headquarters building directly in front of them, and six of the National Army soldiers, armed and geared up, trotted out and headed straight for them.

270

Flanagan reacted first, while Hank was still moving toward the closest cover, which wasn't really cover at all, but one of the manicured bushes that surrounded the general's compound. He simply snapped his FAL into his shoulder and opened fire, still moving toward the oncoming soldiers.

Hank cursed, reversing course and following his teammate. He wasn't as good a shot on the move as Flanagan; he'd found that out during their little shooting package. But he still opened fire, even though too many of his shots went wide, low, or high.

The soldiers scattered, or at least they tried to. Flanagan had dropped the first two before they'd even realized what had happened, and as he continued to engage, three more crumpled, one of them screaming as a bullet pulverized his kneecap, just before a follow-up shot blew a hole through his collarbone and into his lungs.

Flanagan had moved to one side as he'd advanced, and after a second Hank realized what he was doing and followed suit, opening up the space between them. Bullets cracked through the air next to his ear, and two more of the National Army maneuver team went down. A few of them were still writhing on the ground in agony, but it was pretty plain that the entire crew was out of the fight.

When Flanagan sprinted toward the door, Hank had no choice but to follow. They were made. They had to push or die.

The bearded man reached the door first. The stone steps outside didn't present enough space to stack on the door, so he just went for it, and Hank had to rush to catch up, dropping his own muzzle level over Flanagan's shoulder as he went. They found themselves in a small entryway, with double doors leading deeper in and stairs leading up to Hank's right.

"Which way?" Hank had pivoted to cover the stairs while Flanagan stacked on the doors. There didn't appear to be a way down, which suggested that the junta didn't have a command center in the basement.

"Up. On you." Brannigan had come in right behind him, and so Hank started up the steps, his muzzle raised to cover the nearest gap where he might spot a target—or a defender could get a shot at him. "Keep this exit open." Hank couldn't see who his father was talking to, and he didn't try to look. He had his sector. He had his job. He needed to stick to it.

He continued to climb, heading for the top floor. That was *probably* where the generals would be, though if they weren't, it would still be easier to clear the building from the top down. He still covered the door on the second floor with his muzzle as he passed it, just long enough for his dad to take it before he shifted to the next landing up.

There were no windows in the stairwell, but he could still hear the thunder of gunfire outside. It sounded like the fight was dying down a little bit, as if the guerrillas were losing momentum. They'd certainly taken some horrific casualties already from what he'd seen.

As he neared the next landing, twisting around to keep his muzzle on the gap at the top of the steps, he paused. There was someone up there—he could hear movement and the faint rattle of metal on metal.

The junta was worried. They hadn't put *everyone* out on the parade ground to defend the base. They'd kept guards close to them. And one of them was at the top of the steps, probably sweating bullets, probably with his own weapon pointed down the stairs.

Hank gritted his teeth, even as the fear started to clench itself around his spine. He was entirely too conscious of what he was about to do. Every nerve screamed at him not to step out onto that landing and right into that National Army soldier's sights.

But he couldn't stop now. Couldn't just freeze in the stairwell. That would only get all of the rest killed.

Part of being in this profession was the understanding that your own fear had to be beaten down in favor of your brothers.

He threw himself across the landing, just as the soldier's rifle boomed, the flash seemingly almost blinding even as the bullet smacked fragments off the concrete behind him. He was shooting back, dumping rounds up the stairs, barely aware of his sight picture, just trying to get lead on target.

At that range, as he pumped half his magazine up the steps, he could hardly miss. At least two rounds smashed the defending soldier back against the door, his rifle falling from his grip with a clatter. Hank shot him one more time before it really registered that the man was out of the fight.

Eyes wide, blood pumping from at least three holes in his chest, the soldier slid to the floor, leaving a crimson stain on the door behind him.

Brannigan was on the landing next to him, so Hank advanced, though his father pushed ahead of him while he reloaded. If the generals really were on the top floor, they had to expect some serious resistance, so he needed to get that weapon in the best condition possible.

His father levered the body out of the doorway, staying away from the narrow window set in the door itself, his muzzle pointed at the ceiling. Then he moved to the door, pulling one of the precious grenades they'd gotten from Raul's cache out of his gear and pulling the pin. Hank stuffed his partial mag back into a cargo pocket, then stacked up behind his dad, reaching around to grasp the door handle.

Throwing the door open, he waited as the colonel threw the grenade inside, flinging it hard toward the ceiling, intending to bounce it around the hallway to keep any of the bad guys inside from scooping it up and throwing it back, then pulled the door shut again. The frag detonated seconds later, the concussion shaking the door and the fragmentation cracked the glass in the little window.

Hank threw the door open again, and he and Brannigan senior went through together, weapons leveled and already barking thunderously in the echoing hallway as they saw men still standing in the swirling smoke from the frag. Half a dozen men fell in as many seconds, the soldiers guarding the door in the

273

center of the hallway still rocked and disoriented by the grenade's concussion.

They kept advancing through the smoke, Hank's ears ringing from the deafening reports in the confined space. The smoke bit at the back of his throat, and the stink of blood and death joined the sharp chemical stench of explosives and burnt gunpowder.

The double doors that the men on the floor, most dead outright though a couple were still moaning and twitching, one trying to crawl away, trailing a flood of red on the tile that meant he didn't have long, were closed. Scarred by fragmentation, they were still solid.

Brannigan had been slightly ahead of Hank as father and son had advanced down the hallway, and now he set in on security down the long axis of the hallway, leaving Hank and whoever was behind him on the doors. Hank moved up, focusing his attention and his weapon on the junction between the two doors, remembering almost a moment too late to check the hinges. The doors opened inward.

He lifted his FAL's muzzle, tucking the stock under his arm to balance the heavy rifle, and reached for the doorknob. He felt a squeeze to his tricep. *With you.*

Flinging the door open, he went in fast, the other Blackhearts flooding the room behind him.

He registered the figures gathered behind the massive conference table as he entered the doorway, even before he'd crossed the threshold. At least two of them were pointing pistols at the doorway, and he fired as he moved, making one of them spin away, knocked halfway around by the .30 caliber bullet's impact, before he was through the threshold and pushing out of the fatal funnel, clearing his corner in a split second before pivoting back toward the conference table.

That first shot had thrown the men behind that table into disarray, and what followed was almost a firing squad. Blackheart weapons thundered deafeningly in the room, smashing men with pistols off their feet in a few seconds of violence.

274

Only after he'd dumped one last man who hadn't dropped his pistol did Hank realize that all of them had been in uniform. Uniforms with shoulder boards and a lot of gold braid.

The Blackhearts had spread out across the room, and now had the conference table in a sort of crescent, the doorway empty since by sheer force of habit, none of them wanted to stay in the fatal funnel.

"*No dispares! No dispares!*" A pair of hands in braid-encrusted sleeves rose from behind the bullet-scarred table. One of the generals had survived that punishing volley of fire.

Being on the end, he started to move around the end of the table, his FAL leveled, looking for any further threats below the table. At the other end, Burgess had taken a single step, but stopped as he saw Hank advancing on the dead space.

Seven bodies lay in attitudes of painful and violent death on the floor, pistols not far from flung out hands. They were all in uniform, most with bloody holes punched through chests and skulls. The nearest, a silver-haired man who looked almost old enough to be Hank's grandfather, lay staring at him with unseeing eyes, a puckered, bloody hole right alongside his nose.

The last man was on his knees, iron gray at his temple, splashed with his comrades' blood, looking over at Hank with his hands in the air. The man's rank was visible in the gold shoulder boards on his coat. There was no way to miss any of it.

They'd just killed all but one of the ruling junta.

Then more gunfire roared somewhere downstairs.

CHAPTER 41

Flanagan glanced over as Curtis joined him, covering the door they'd just entered, while the rest of the team went up the steps. It grated a little to be on rear security, but that was old, youthful exuberance talking, not the sort of common sense that got men through a combat situation. The part of him that hadn't really grown past the young, twenty-something infantryman wanted in on the kill.

He blinked. "Where did you get that?" Curtis was no longer carrying his FAL, but had an old, rust-speckled M60 in his hands, the belt looped over the receiver, a second worn over his neck.

"One of the dead guys outside had it. Seemed like a waste to just leave it on the ground."

Flanagan shook his head. "You know, accuracy by volume isn't always the end all and be all."

While he had turned his full attention back to the door leading into the lower floor of the headquarters building, Flanagan could still see Curtis shaking his head in disgust. "I don't even know you anymore, Joseph."

It was not exactly the time or the place for one of these arguments, though right at the moment they were in the middle of a pocket of calm in the chaos that was wracking the base. But that moment of calm had opened up the floodgates with Curtis.

"I mean, it's not like you haven't seen what I can do with one of these. Or that you have suddenly forgotten the use of fire support. I have to assume in some way that you've simply decided to be a contrarian all of a sudden."

Flanagan rolled his eyes, in no mood for the repartee, but then the building shook with a double thunderclap, one from above, the other seemingly from the front. As he looked in through the narrow window in the door, he saw smoke billowing through the entry foyer. "Looks like someone just breached the front doors."

The banter stopped dead. The switch had been flipped again. Curtis was situated where he could watch the entry door, but he could see the inner door out of the corner of his eye. "Hierro's people?"

"Who else?" Flanagan could see the figures of men with guns moving through the smoke inside, muzzle flashes spitting as they murdered the handful of surviving soldiers who were crawling away after having been flattened by the explosion that had blown the doors open.

He was reaching for the door when Curtis joined him, that M60 pointed at the opening. "Don't let me get shot in the back." His shorter companion looked up at him sideways, a faint grin creasing his ebony features. "Time for some accuracy by volume, I think."

Flanagan didn't even shake his head this time. He just took a step back, pulling the door open as he shifted to cover the outer door. This time, as much as he hated to admit it, Curtis had a point.

The short, muscular Blackheart took a knee at the doorway, barricading himself on the doorjamb itself and bracing the machinegun just before he opened fire.

The longest shot in that large foyer, which took up almost the entire front half of the lower floor of the building, was about twenty yards. There was no way he could miss.

With a chugging roar, the M60 spat a stream of high-velocity metal as he played it across the wide, high-ceilinged room. Bullets smashed moldings, wooden trim, desks, flesh, bone, and weapons. He punched bloody holes through knees and pelvises, sending guerrillas—and a few soldiers—falling into the long, ripping burst, where more rounds tore apart guts, lungs, hearts, and limbs.

He ran the belt dry, then rolled back out of the doorway, flipping up the M60's feed tray cover. "Not one jam!"

"Miracles will never cease." Flanagan shifted to where he could cover both doors for a moment while his friend reloaded. His ears were ringing from the nearness to the machinegun fire, but even with that, he could still hear that everything had just gone strangely quiet.

Looking out into the foyer as Curtis shifted back to covering the outside, he saw little more than smoke and bodies, except for a bit of movement that might have been someone fleeing back out through the front entrance.

They'd stopped the FPLCJ's offensive, from the looks of things. He just hoped that the team upstairs had taken control of the junta, or else they were still going to have one hell of a time getting out.

***

Wade watched the gate over his sights, the FAL now braced in the doorway. It exposed him a little bit, but the fighting outside the base had calmed down a little bit, even while the roar of gunfire and explosions from inside had intensified. Hierro's Communists were making headway, and as much as Wade despised the junta—mainly for what they'd done to Bianco—he really hated to see Commies make any headway for any reason.

He didn't see the eruption of violence at the headquarters building. He couldn't. He couldn't even hear it happen, not that he could distinguish it from the storm of gunfire and explosions that had been rocking the city for nearly an hour already. Even so, he could sense something had changed. He blinked, his alertness ratcheting up another notch, and shifted his stance a little, trying to get a better view of the base compound.

That was how he saw the first of the masked men with red armbands fleeing out the gate. He didn't know what had happened, but it looked like the FPLCJ had suddenly lost their momentum and were trying to run.

He didn't even hesitate, but lined up the first one and shot him through the body, dropping him spinning to the ground.

Switching targets, he dumped two more in a matter of seconds. None of the fleeing guerrillas seemed to realize what was going on, but they started to look for cover.

The man who came sprinting down the street, his bloodied arm hanging uselessly at his side, had lost his mask on the way. He turned toward the shop where the four Blackhearts were set up, his attention drawn by the gunfire.

Wade looked Ernesto Hierro right in the eye, just for a second.

His trigger broke a heartbeat later, sending a single round smashing through Hierro's cheekbone and blowing blood and brains out the back of his skull.

The leader of the People's Front for the Liberation of Costa de las Joyas collapsed to the dusty street like a sack of rocks.

The rest scattered, though Wade and Santelli managed to pick off a couple more. Neither man said anything about it. None of the fleeing Communists had surrendered. Letting them run would only let them kill more people later.

Then the gunfire had pretty much died away, as the smoke drifted across the city of Santa Paz, and a call in Spanish began to go out over the base's loudspeakers. Wade couldn't make it all out, but it sounded like a cease fire order.

It was over.

EPILOGUE

Brannigan stood over General Andres Mejia as the man spoke into the public address system, telling the National Army soldiers to hold their positions and fire only if fired upon. Brannigan wasn't sure if that was the greatest idea in the long run, as it wouldn't have been a bad thing to thin out the FPLCJ's ranks a little more, but he also didn't want any more Blackhearts getting hit.

Burgess was working on Puller. Their doc had taken a pistol round to the upper chest. It looked like it had missed anything vital, but he was in bad shape, and Burgess—who had himself gotten clipped with a bullet that had cut a furrow in his arm—was sealing up the hole for the moment. They'd need to get the doc to a hospital soon, and Brannigan wasn't that interested in trying to test the benevolence of the locals here in Santa Paz.

Or the quality of their medical care, for that matter.

Mejia turned to look at him. "Now what?" The general spoke English, though not well.

"Now, you send some of your men to get Raul Estevez." Brannigan didn't know whether their contact was going to be willing to step up, but he was kind of winging this at that point. The job hadn't been to overthrow the junta themselves, but when the alternative had been to put the country in the hands of a Communist guerrilla group, then choices had had to be made.

281

"You are going to replace us with him? What makes you think that our men will follow his orders?"

Brannigan stepped closer, looming over the man, who shrank back, his eyes flitting involuntarily to the line of covered bodies on the floor nearby. "I'm not necessarily putting him in charge, unless you force me to kill you. You had the smarts to surrender, so I figure I'll give you a chance. I get that this isn't the United States. You've got a hostile insurgency to deal with, being supported by your neighbors. We've removed a bit of that problem for you." Wade had radioed up that Hierro was confirmed dead, and he, Santelli, Bianco, and Tackett were on their way in, though they were still going to take their time and be very careful not to provoke the trigger-happy National Army soldiers. They'd come through this relatively unscathed, so far.

"So, here's the deal. You, General Mejia, stay in charge, though with Raul as an advisor. You cut off the pirates and leave shipping alone—American shipping especially. You do that, we'll leave you alone." He leaned in close, knowing that he smelled like sweat, dust, gunsmoke, and explosive residue.

"If I hear that you've started taking ships in the Caribbean again, well. Then I'll come back down here, and I don't care how long it takes. I'll burn your whole power structure down. Starting with you. Am I clear?"

Mejia looked again at the bodies on the floor. His eyes strayed to the window and the carnage outside. Sure, it had been possible because of the FPLCJ's attack, but this small team of Americans had gotten right into the heart of the National Army's power and eviscerated the command. These same men had gotten inside the most secure prison in the country and broken out their most dangerous prisoner.

He knew when he was beaten. He nodded.

"Just so we understand each other." Brannigan straightened. "Now, I'm going to need that yacht the pirates were using. Consider it payment for leaving you alive."

They needed to get out of this country, and not only to get Puller to treatment.

Someone had set them up here, and that someone was going to pay.

AUTHOR'S NOTE

Thank you for reading *Concrete Jungle*. This was a story idea that was kicking around as far back as the *American Praetorians* series, in which The Broker was going to be targeted by some of the underworld elements he'd dealt with in the course of helping the Praetorians. I thought it worked out better here, though adding the Front just made sense along the way. I hope you enjoyed it.

To keep up-to-date, I hope that you'll sign up for my newsletter—you get a free American Praetorians novella, *Drawing the Line*, when you do.

If you've enjoyed this novel, I hope that you'll go leave a review on Amazon or Goodreads. Reviews matter a lot to independent authors, so I appreciate the effort.

If you'd like to connect, I have a Facebook page at https://www.facebook.com/PeteNealenAuthor. I'm also on Twitter at https://twitter.com/AmericanPraeto2. You can also contact me, or just read my musings and occasional samples on the blog, at https://www.americanpraetorians.com. I look forward to hearing from you.

Also By Peter Nealen

Brave New Disorder (Pallas Group Solutions Thrillers)
Gray War
The Dragon and the Skull
Silver or Lead
Frontiers of Chaos
Non-State Actor

Galaxy's Edge – Order of the Centurion
Always Legion

The Brannigan's Blackhearts Universe
Kill Yuan
The Colonel Has A Plan (Online Short)
Fury in the Gulf
Burmese Crossfire
Enemy Unidentified
Frozen Conflict
High Desert Vengeance
Doctors of Death
Kill or Capture
Enemy of My Enemy
War to the Knife
Blood Debt
Marque and Reprisal
Concrete Jungle
Legacy of Terror

The Maelstrom Rising Series
Escalation
Holding Action
Crimson Star
Strategic Assets
Fortress Doctrine
Thunder Run

Area Denial
Power Vacuum
Option Zulu
SPOTREPS – A Maelstrom Rising Anthology

The Lost Series
Ice and Monsters
Shadows and Crows
Darkness and Stone
Swords Against the Night
The Alchemy of Treason
The Rock of Battle

The Unity Wars Series
The Fall of Valdek
The Defense of Provenia
The Alliance Rises

The American Praetorians Series
Drawing the Line: An American Praetorians Story (Novella)
Task Force Desperate
Hunting in the Shadows
Alone and Unafraid
The Devil You Don't Know
Lex Talionis

The Jed Horn Supernatural Thriller Series
Nightmares
A Silver Cross and a Winchester
The Walker on the Hills
The Canyon of the Lost (Novelette)
Older and Fouler Things

IF YOU ENJOYED THIS BOOK, YOU MIGHT LIKE

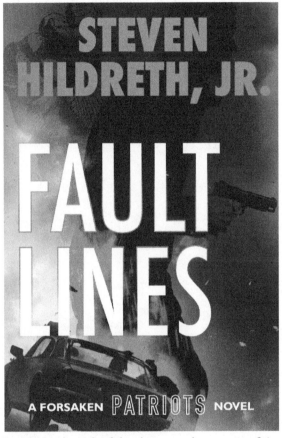

From the mountains of Afghanistan, to the streets of American cities...

From the Indonesian underworld, to the jungles of Central Africa...

They operate...without sanction...without backup...without mercy...

Forsaken Patriots.
New look.
Same kinetic action.

Available now!

Follow Steven Hildreth, Jr.:

FACEBOOK: http://www.facebook.com/stevenhildrethjr

WEBSITE: http://www.stevenhildreth.com

TWITTER: http://www.twitter.com/StevenHildreth

Made in the USA
Middletown, DE
18 May 2024

54536184R00177